Praise for

GIRL IN THE BLUE COAT

The 2017 Edgar® Award Winner for Best Young Adult Mystery
A New York Public Library Best Book for Teens of 2016
An *Entertainment Weekly* Best YA Book of 2016
A *Booklist* Best Young Adult Book of 2016

"*Girl in the Blue Coat* is **a powerful, compelling coming-of-age story** set against the dark and dangerous backdrop of World War II. It's an **important and page-turning** look at the choices all of us—including young adults—have to make in wartime. **A beautiful combination of heartbreak, loss, young love, and hope.**"
—Kristin Hannah, #1 *New York Times* bestselling author of *The Nightingale*

"A tapestry of guilt and acceptance, growing responsibility, and reluctant heroism, Hanneke's coming-of-age under heartbreaking circumstances is a jarring reminder of how war consumes and transforms the passions of ordinary life. Every **devastating** moment of this **beautiful** novel is both **poignant** and **powerful**, and **every word feels true.**" —Elizabeth Wein, *New York Times* bestselling author of *Black Dove, White Raven; Rose Under Fire;* and the Printz Honor–winning *Code Name Verity*

"In an occupied city, a young woman's daring transforms into true courage when she confronts a mystifying disappearance. From page one, **I couldn't turn the pages fast enough. Enthralling.**"
—Judy Blundell, *New York Times* bestselling author of *Strings Attached* and the National Book Award–winning *What I Saw and How I Lied*

"It's no small feat to **bring the past to life**, especially a history as dark and desperate as World War II. Monica Hesse does just this with Hanneke's story. Brace yourself, dear reader, to have your heart bruised—and possibly even broken—in the most meaningful of ways."
—Ryan Graudin, author of *The Walled City* and *Wolf by Wolf*

★ "[An] **affecting novel**.... Hesse's pacing infuses her story with **thriller suspense**, enriching the narrative with dramatic surprises both small and large." —*Booklist*, starred review

★ "**Riveting**.... Themes of guilt and betrayal, ingenuity and courage, and the divisive effect of the occupation on friendship and community weave through a **gripping historical mystery** in which people and places, including the title character, are often not what they appear."
—*Publishers Weekly*, starred review

★ "A **heartrending, moving** story." —*VOYA*, starred review

★ "*Girl in the Blue Coat*... is not only **an intriguing missing persons case**, it's a **poignant, wonderfully crafted** story of love and loss, courage and redemption." —*Shelf Awareness*, starred review

"Hesse crafts a **thought-provoking** and **gripping** historical novel. The themes of love, betrayal, heroism, social responsibility, and atonement are beautifully intertwined with well-developed characters and a compelling story line....A **must-read** for fans of historical fiction." —*School Library Journal*

"Hesse's **impeccable research** meshes almost seamlessly with Hanneke's present-tense narration, bringing the time and place to life. **Rich in content and emotion**, this is a **first-rate** companion to the historical tales of the onderduikers, the hidden Jews of Holland, and a **compelling read**." —*Kirkus Reviews*

"**Stirring, impressive**." —*Family Circle*

"**Intelligent**." —*Wall Street Journal*

"This **heartbreaking** story of terror and loss sweeps you into a time-is-running-out mystery that **delivers plot twists and a shocking final punch that'll haunt you for days**." —*Justine* magazine

"**Gripping**." —*Entertainment Weekly*

"The detail here is astonishing, as Hesse weaves an **utterly thrilling** story." —Paste.com

"**Refreshing**....**Powerful**....A **riveting** read from start to finish that **you won't want to put down**." —Hypable.com

"This is **a stunning literary work** as well as a **wonderful** addition to WWII and Holocaust collections." —*BookPage*

GIRL IN THE BLUE COAT

MONICA HESSE

LITTLE, BROWN AND COMPANY
New York · Boston

Copyright © 2016 by Monica Hesse
Discussion Guide copyright © 2016 by Little, Brown and Company
Excerpt from *The War Outside* copyright © 2018 by Monica Hesse
Excerpt from *They Went Left* copyright © 2019 by Monica Hesse

Front cover collage copyrights © Jarno Gonzalez Zarraonandia/Shutterstock.com; © InnervisionArt/Shutterstock.com; © Malgorzara Maj/Arcangel Images; © Collaboration JS/Arcangel Images; © akg-images. Cover design © KidEthic. Cover copyright © 2017 by Hachette Book Group, Inc.

Little, Brown and Company

Hachette Book Group
1290 Avenue of the Americas, New York, NY 10104
Visit us at LBYR.com

Originally published in hardcover and ebook by Little Brown and Company in April 2016
First Paperback Edition: April 2017

Little, Brown and Company is a division of Hachette Book Group, Inc.
The Little, Brown name and logo are trademarks of Hachette Book Group, Inc.

The publisher is not responsible for websites (or their content) that are not owned by the publisher.

The Library of Congress has cataloged the hardcover edition as follows:
Names: Hesse, Monica.
Title: Girl in the blue coat / Monica Hesse.
Description: First edition. | New York ; Boston : Little, Brown and Company, 2016. | Summary: "In 1943 Nazi-occupied Amsterdam, teenage Hanneke—a 'finder' of black market goods—is tasked with finding a Jewish girl a customer had been hiding, who has seemingly vanished into thin air, and is pulled into a web of resistance activities and secrets as she attempts to solve the mystery and save the missing girl"—Provided by publisher.
Identifiers: LCCN 2015020565 | ISBN 9780316260602 (hardback) |
ISBN 9780316260640 (ebook)
Subjects: LCSH: Netherlands—History—German occupation, 1940–1945—Juvenile fiction. | CYAC: Netherlands—History—German occupation, 1940–1945—Fiction. | World War, 1939–1945—Underground Movements—Netherlands—Fiction. | Holocaust, Jewish (1939–1945)—Netherlands—Amsterdam—Fiction. | Black market—Fiction. | Jews—Netherlands—Fiction. |
Missing children—Fiction. | Mystery and detective stories. | BISAC: JUVENILE FICTION / Historical / Europe. | JUVENILE FICTION / Historical / Holocaust. | JUVENILE FICTION / Mysteries & Detective Stories. | JUVENILE FICTION / Social Issues / Prejudice & Racism. | JUVENILE FICTION / Social Issues / Death & Dying. | JUVENILE FICTION / Social Issues / Friendship.
Classification: LCC PZ7.1.H52 Gi 2016 | DDC [Fic]—dc23
LC record available at http://lccn.loc.gov/2015020565

ISBNs: 978-0-316-26060-2 (hardcover), 978-0-316-26064-0 (ebook), 978-0-316-26063-3 (pbk.)

Printed in the United States of America

LSC-C

20 19 18 17 16 15 14

For my sister Paige,
and her sister Piper

A long time before Bas died, we had a pretend argument about whose fault it was that he'd fallen in love with me. *It's your fault,* he told me. *Because you're lovable.* I told him he was wrong. That it was lazy to blame his falling in love on me. Irresponsible, really.

I remember everything about this conversation. It was in his parents' sitting room, and we were listening to the family's new radio while I quizzed him for a geometry exam neither of us thought was important. The American singer Judy Garland was singing "You Made Me Love You." That was how the conversation began. Bas said I'd made him love me. I made fun of him because I didn't want him to know how fast my heart was pounding to hear him say the words *love* and *you* in the same sentence.

Then he said it was my fault, also, that he wanted to kiss me.

Then I said it was his fault if I let him. Then his older brother walked in the room and said it was both of our faults if he got sick to his stomach listening to us.

It was only later that day, when I was walking home—back when I could walk home without worrying about being stopped by soldiers or missing curfew or being arrested—that I realized I'd never said it back. The first time he said he loved me, and I forgot to say it back.

I should have. If I'd known what would happen and what I would find out about love and war, I would have made sure to say it then.

That's my fault.

JANUARY 1943

ONE

Tuesday

*H*allo, sweetheart. What do you have there? Something for me?"

I stop because the soldier's face is young and pretty, and because his voice has a wink in it, and because I bet he would make me laugh during an afternoon at the movies.

That's a lie.

I stop because the soldier might be a good contact, because he might be able to get the things that we can't get anymore, because his dresser drawers are probably filled with row after row of chocolate bars and socks that don't have holes in the toes.

That's also not really the truth.

But sometimes I ignore the whole truth, because it's easier to pretend I'm making decisions for rational reasons. It's easier to pretend I have a choice.

I stop because the soldier's uniform is green. That's the only reason I stop. Because his uniform is green, and that means I have no choice at all.

"That's a lot of packages for a pretty girl."

His Dutch is slightly accented, but I'm surprised he speaks it so well. Some Green Police don't speak it at all, and they're annoyed when we're not fluent in German, as if we should have been preparing our entire lives for the day when they invaded our country.

I park my bicycle but don't dismount. "It's exactly the right number of packages, I think."

"What have you got in them?" He leans over my handlebars, one hand grazing into the basket attached to the front.

"Wouldn't you like to see? Wouldn't you like to open *all* my packages?" I giggle, and then lower my eyelashes so he won't see how practiced this line is. With the way I'm standing, my dress has risen above my knee, and the soldier notices. It's navy, already tighter than it should be, frayed at the hem and several years old, from before the war. I shift my weight a little so the hemline rides even higher, now halfway up my goose-bumped thigh.

This interaction would feel worse if he were older, if he were wrinkled, if he had stained teeth or a sagging belly. It would be worse, but I would flirt the same anyway. I have a dozen times before.

He leans in closer. The Herengracht is murky and fish-stinking behind him, and I could push him into this canal and ride halfway home on my disgrace of a secondhand bicycle before he paddled himself out. It's a game I like to play with every Green Police who stops me. *How could I punish you, and how far would I get before you caught me?*

"This is a book I'm bringing home to my mother." I point to the first parcel wrapped in paper. "And these are the potatoes for our supper. And this is the sweater I've just picked up from mending."

"*Hoe heet je?*" he asks. He wants to know my name, and he's asked it in the informal, casual way, how a confident boy would ask a bucktoothed girl her name at a party, and this is good news because I'd much rather he be interested in me than the packages in my basket.

"Hanneke Bakker." I would lie, but there's no point now that we all carry mandatory identification papers. "What's *your* name, soldier?"

He puffs out his chest when I call him *soldier.* The young ones are still in love with their uniforms. When he moves, I see a flash of gold around his neck. "And what's in your locket?" I ask.

His grin falters as his hand flies to the pendant now dangling just below his collar. The locket is gold, shaped like a heart, probably containing a photograph of an apple-faced German girl who has promised to remain faithful back in Berlin. It was a gamble to ask about it, but one that always turns out well if I'm right.

"Is it a photograph of your mother? She must love you a *lot* to give you such a pretty necklace."

His face flushes pink as he tucks the chain back under his starched collar.

"Is it of your sister?" I press on. "Your little pet dog?" It's a difficult balance, to sound the right amount of naive. My words need to have enough innocence in them that he can't justify getting angry with me, but enough sharpness that he'd rather get rid of me than keep me here and interrogate me about what I'm carrying. "I haven't seen you before," I say. "Are you stationed on this street every day?"

"I don't have time for silly girls like you. Go home, Hanneke."

When I pedal away, my handlebars only barely shake. I was mostly telling him the truth about the packages. The first three do hold a book, a sweater, and a few potatoes. But underneath the potatoes are four coupons' worth of sausages, bought with a dead man's rations, and underneath those are lipsticks and lotions, bought with another dead man's rations, and underneath those are cigarettes and alcohol, bought with money that Mr. Kreuk, my boss, handed me this morning for just that purpose. None of it belongs to me.

Most people would say I trade in the black market, the illicit underground exchange of goods. I prefer to think of myself as a finder. I find things. I find extra potatoes, meat, and lard. In the beginning I could find sugar and chocolate, but those things have been harder recently, and I can only get them sometimes. I find tea. I find bacon. The wealthy people of Amsterdam stay plump because of me. I find the things we have been made to do without, unless you know where to look.

My last question to the soldier, about whether this street is his new post—I wish he'd answered that one. Because if he's stationed on the corner every day now, I'll have to either consider being friendly to him or change my route.

My first delivery this morning is Miss Akkerman, who lives with her grandparents in one of the old buildings down by the museums. Miss Akkerman is the lotions and lipstick. Last week it was perfume. She's one of the few women I've met who still care so much about these things, but she told me once that she's hoping her boyfriend will propose before her next birthday, and people have spent money for stranger reasons.

She answers the door with her wet hair in pins. She must have a date with Theo tonight.

"Hanneke! Come in while I get my purse." She always finds an excuse to invite me in. I think she gets bored here during the day, alone with her grandparents, who talk too loudly and smell like cabbage.

Inside the house is stuffy and dim. Miss Akkerman's grandfather sits at the breakfast table through the kitchen doorway. "Who's at the door?" he yells.

"It's a delivery, Grandpa," Miss Akkerman calls over her shoulder.

"It's who?"

"It's *for me*." She turns back to me and lowers her voice. "Hanneke, you have to help me. Theo is coming over tonight to ask my grandparents if I can move into his apartment. I need to figure out what to wear. Stay right here; I'll show you my options."

I can't think of any dress that would make her grandparents approve of her living with her boyfriend before marriage, though I know this wouldn't be the first time this war made a young couple reject tradition.

When Miss Akkerman comes back to the foyer, I pretend to consider the two dresses she's brought, but really I'm watching the wall clock. I don't have time for socializing. After telling her to wear the gray one, I motion for her to take the packages I've been holding since I arrived. "These are yours. Would you like to make sure everything's all right?"

"I'm sure they're fine. Stay for coffee?"

I don't bother to ask if it's real. The only way she would have real coffee is if I'd brought it to her, and I hadn't, so when she says she has coffee, she means she has ground acorns or twigs. Ersatz coffee.

The other reason I don't stay is the same reason why I don't accept Miss Akkerman's repeated offer to call her Irene. Because I don't want her to confuse this relationship with friendship. Because I don't want her to think that if one day she can't pay, it doesn't matter.

"I can't. I still have another delivery before lunch."

"Are you sure? You could have lunch here—I'm already going to make it—and then we could figure out just what to do with my hair for tonight."

It's a strange relationship I have with my clients. They think we're comrades. They think we're bound by the secret that we're doing something illegal together. "I always have lunch at home with my parents," I say.

"Of course, Hanneke." She's embarrassed for having pushed too far. "I'll see you later, then."

Outside, it's cloudy and overcast, Amsterdam winter, as I ride my bicycle down our narrow, haphazard streets. Amsterdam was built on canals. The country of Holland is low, lower even than the ocean, and the farmers who mucked it out centuries ago created an elaborate system of waterways, just to keep citizens from drowning in the North Sea. An old history teacher of mine used to accompany that piece of our past with a popular saying: "God made the world, but the Dutch made the Netherlands." He said it like a point of pride, but to me, the saying was also a warning: "Don't rely on anything coming to save us. We're all alone down here."

Seventy-five kilometers to the south, at the start of the occupation two and a half years ago, the German planes bombed Rotterdam, killing nine hundred civilians and much of the city's architecture. Two days later, the Germans arrived in Amsterdam by foot. We now have to put up with their presence, but we got to keep our buildings. It's a bad trade-off. It's all bad trade-offs these days, unless, like me, you know how to mostly end up on the profitable side of things.

My next customer, Mrs. Janssen, is just a short ride away in a large blue house where she used to live with her husband and three sons, until one son moved to London, one son moved to America, and one son, the baby of the family, moved to the Dutch front lines, where two thousand Dutch servicemen were killed when they tried but failed to protect our borders as the country fell in five days' time. We don't speak much of Jan anymore.

I wonder if he was near Bas, though, during the invasion.

I wonder this about everything now, trying to piece together the last minutes of the boy I loved. Was he with Bas, or did Bas die alone?

Mrs. Janssen's husband disappeared last month, just before she became a customer, and I've never asked any more about that. He could have been an illegal worker with the resistance, or he could have just been in the wrong place at a bad time, or he could be not dead after all and instead having high tea in England with his oldest son, but in any case it's none of my business. I've only delivered a few things to Mrs. Janssen. I knew her son Jan a little bit. He was a surprise baby, born two decades after his brothers, when the Janssens were already stooped and gray. Jan was a nice boy.

Here, today, I decide Jan might have been near Bas when the Germans stormed our country. Here, today, I'll believe that Bas didn't die alone. It's a more optimistic thought than I usually allow myself to have.

Mrs. Janssen is waiting at the door for me, which makes me irritated because if you were a German soldier assigned to look for suspicious things, what would you think of an old woman waiting for a strange girl on a bicycle?

"Good morning, Mrs. Janssen. You didn't have to stand out here for me. How are you?"

"I'm fine!" she shouts, like she's reading lines in a play, nervously touching the white curls escaping from her bun. Her hair is always in a bun, and her glasses are always slipping down her nose; her clothes always remind me of a curtain or a sofa. "Won't you come in?"

"I couldn't get as much sausage as you wanted, but I do have some," I tell her once I've parked my bicycle and the door is closed behind us. She moves slowly; she walks with a cane now and rarely leaves the house anymore. She told me she got the cane when Jan died. I don't know if there's something physically wrong with her or if grief just broke her and made her lame.

Inside, her front room looks more spacious than normal, and it takes me a moment to figure out why. Normally, between the china cabinet and the armchair, there is an opklapbed, a small bed that looks like a bookcase but can be folded out for sleeping when guests visit. I assume Mr. Janssen made it, like he made all the things in their house. Mama and I used to walk past his furniture store to admire the window displays, but we never could have afforded anything in it. I can't imagine where the opklapbed has gone. If Mrs. Janssen sold it so soon after her husband's disappearance, she must already be struggling with money, which I won't allow to be my concern unless it means she can't pay me.

"Coffee, Hanneke?" In front of me, Mrs. Janssen disappears into the kitchen, so I follow. I plan to decline her coffee offer, but she's laid out two cups and her good china, blue and white, the famous style from the city of Delft. The table is heavy and maple.

"I have the sausage here if you want to—"

"Later," she interrupts. "Later. First, we'll have coffee, and a stroopwafel, and we'll talk."

Next to her sits a dust-covered canister that smells like the earth. Real coffee beans. I wonder how long she's been saving them. The stroopwafels, too. People don't use their bakery rations for fancy pastries; they use them for bread. Then again, they don't use them to feed black market delivery girls, either, but here is Mrs. Janssen, pouring my coffee into a porcelain cup and placing a stroopwafel on top so that the waffle sandwich softens in the steam and the sugary syrup inside oozes around the edges.

"Sit, Hanneke."

"I'm not hungry," I say, even as my stomach betrays me with a growl.

I *am* hungry, but something makes me nervous with these stroopwafels, and with how eager Mrs. Janssen is to have me sit, and with the irregularity of the whole situation. Has she called the Green Police and promised to deliver them a black market worker? A woman desperate enough to sell her husband's opklapbed might do such a thing.

"Just for a minute?"

"I'm sorry, but I have a million other things to do today."

She stares down at her beautifully set table. "My youngest. Jan. These were his favorite. I used to have them waiting when he came home from school. You were his friend?" She smiles at me hopefully.

I sigh. She's not dangerous; she's just lonely. She misses her son, and she wants to feed one of his old classmates his after-school snack. This goes against all my rules, and the pleading in her voice makes me uncomfortable. But it's cold outside, and the coffee is real, and despite what I just told Mrs. Janssen about my millions of tasks, I actually have an hour before my parents expect me for lunch. So I set the parcel with sausage on the table, smooth down my hair, and try to remember how to be a polite guest on a social call. I knew how to do this once. Bas's mother used to pour me hot chocolate in her kitchen while Bas and I studied, and then she would find excuses to keep checking in to make sure we weren't kissing.

"I haven't had a stroopwafel in a while," I say finally, trying out my rusted conversational skills. "My favorites were always banketstaaf."

"With the almond paste?"

"Mmm-hmm."

Mrs. Janssen's coffee is scalding and strong, a soothing anesthetic. It burns my throat, so I keep drinking it and don't even realize how much I've had until the cup is back on its saucer and it's half empty. Mrs. Janssen immediately fills it to the top.

"The coffee's good," I tell her.

"I need your help."

Ah.

So the purpose of the coffee becomes clear. She's given me a present. Now she wants a favor. Too bad she didn't realize I don't need to be buttered up. I work for money, not kindness.

"I need your help finding something," she says.

"What do you need? More meat? Kerosene?"

"I need your help finding a person."

The cup freezes halfway to my lips, and for a second I can't remember whether I was picking it up or putting it down.

"I need your help finding a person," she says again, because I still haven't responded.

"I don't understand."

"Someone special to me." She looks over my shoulder, and I follow her line of vision to where her eyes are fixed on a portrait of her family, hanging next to the pantry door.

"Mrs. Janssen." I try to think of the right and polite way to respond. *Your husband is gone,* is what I should tell her. *Your son is dead. Your other sons are not coming back.* I cannot find ghosts. I don't have any ration coupons for a replacement dead child.

"Mrs. Janssen, I don't find people. I find things. Food. Clothing."

"I need you to find—"

"A person. You said. But if you want to find a person, you need to call the police. Those are the kinds of finders you want."

"*You.*" She leans over the table. "Not the police. I need *you.* I don't know who else to ask."

In the distance, the Westerkerk clock strikes; it's half past eleven. Now is when I should leave. "I have to go." I push my chair back from the table. "My mother will have cooked lunch. Did you want to pay now for the sausage, or have Mr. Kreuk add it to your account?"

She rises, too, but instead of seeing me to the door, she grabs my hand. "Just look, Hanneke. Please. Just look before you go."

Because even I am not hardened enough to wrench my hand away from an old woman, I follow her toward the pantry and pause dutifully to look at the picture of her sons on the wall. They're in a row, three abreast, matching big ears and knobby necks. But Mrs. Janssen doesn't stop in front of the photograph. Instead, she swings open the pantry door. "This way." She gestures for me to follow her.

Verdorie. Damn it, she's crazier than I thought. We're going to sit in the darkness now, together among her canned pickles, to commune with her dead son. She probably keeps his clothes in here, packed in mothballs.

Inside, it's like any other pantry: a shallow room with a wall of spices and preserved goods, not as full as it would have been before the war.

"I'm sorry, Mrs. Janssen, but I don't know—"

"Wait." She reaches to the edge of the spice shelf and unlatches a small hook I hadn't noticed.

"What are you doing?"

"Just a minute." She fiddles with the latch. Suddenly, the whole set of shelves swings out, revealing a dark space behind the pantry, long and narrow, big enough to walk into, too dark to see much.

"What is this?" I whisper.

"Hendrik built it for me," she says. "When the children were small. This closet was inefficient—deep and sloping—so I asked if he would close off part of it for a pantry and have the other part for storage."

My eyes adjust to the dimness. We're standing in the space under the stairs. The ceiling grows lower, until, in the back, it's no more than a few feet off the ground. Toward the front, there's a shelf at eye level containing a half-burned candle, a comb, and a film magazine whose title I recognize. Most of the tiny room is

17

taken up by Mrs. Janssen's missing opklapbed, unfolded as if waiting for a guest. A star-patterned quilt lies on top of it, and a single pillow. There are no windows. When the secret door is closed, only a slim crack of brightness would appear underneath.

"Do you see?" She takes my hand again. "This is why I cannot call the police. The police cannot find someone who is not supposed to exist."

"The missing person."

"The missing girl is Jewish," Mrs. Janssen says. "I need you to find her before the Nazis do."

TWO

Mrs. Janssen is still waiting for me to respond, standing in the dark space, where the air is stale and smells faintly of old potatoes.

"Hanneke?"

"You were hiding someone?" I can barely get the words out as she re-latches the secret shelf, closes the pantry door, and leads me back to the table. I don't know if I'm more shocked or scared. I know this happens, that some of the Jews who disappear are packed like winter linens in other people's basements rather than relocated to work camps. But it's too dangerous a thing to ever admit out loud.

Mrs. Janssen is nodding at my question. "I was."

"In here? You were hiding someone in *here*? For how long?"

"Where should I begin?" She picks up her napkin, twisting it between her hands.

I don't want her to begin at all. Ten minutes ago I was worried Mrs. Janssen might have called someone to arrest me; now I know she is the one who could be arrested. The punishment for hiding people is imprisonment, a cold, damp cell in Scheveningen, where I've heard of people disappearing for months without even getting hearings. The punishment for being a person in hiding—an onderduiker—is immediate deportation.

"Never mind," I say quickly. "Never mind. I don't need to hear anything. I'll just go."

"Why don't you sit down again?" she pleads. "I've been waiting all morning for you." She holds up the pitcher of coffee. "More? You can have as much as you like. Just sit. If you don't help me, I'll have to find someone else."

Now I'm conflicted, standing in the middle of the kitchen. I don't want her bribe of coffee. But I'm rooted to the spot. I shouldn't leave, not without knowing more of the story. If Mrs. Janssen tries to find someone else, she could be putting herself in danger, and me, too.

"Tell me what happened," I say finally.

"My husband's business partner," Mrs. Janssen begins, the words spilling out in a rush. "My husband's business partner was a good man. Mr. Roodveldt. David. He worked with Hendrik for ten years. He had a wife, Rose, and she was so *shy*—she had a lisp and it made her self-conscious—but she could knit the most beautiful things. They had two daughters. Lea, who had just turned twelve and was the family pet. And the older daughter. Fifteen, independent, always off with her friends. Mirjam." Her throat catches at the last name, and she swallows before continuing.

"The Roodveldts were Jewish. Not very observant, and in the beginning, it seemed that would make a difference. It didn't, of course. David told Hendrik they would be fine. They knew a woman in the country who was going to take them in. That fell through when the woman got too scared, though, and in July, after the big *razzia*, when so many Jews were taken, David came to Hendrik and said he and his family needed help going into hiding."

"And Hendrik brought them here?" I ask.

"No. He didn't want to put me in danger. He brought them to the furniture shop. He built the Roodveldts a secret room behind a false wall in the wood shop. I didn't know."

"You didn't *know*?" I can't imagine my own parents being able to keep such a secret from each other.

"I knew Hendrik was spending more time in the shop. I thought he was just working longer hours because David was no longer around to assist him. I thought the Roodveldts had gone to the safe house in the country. I didn't know that all of them were right there, in hiding."

"When did he tell you?"

"He never told me. Last month I was home alone when I heard knocking at my door. Frantic knocking; it was after curfew. I thought Hendrik had forgotten his key, but when I opened the door, there was this girl, this pale girl, wearing a blue coat. She'd grown so much. I hadn't seen her in a few years, and I wouldn't have recognized her if she hadn't introduced herself. She told me my husband had been hiding them, but now she needed a new safe space. She said everyone else was dead."

"Mirjam Roodveldt."

Mrs. Janssen nods. "She was *shaking*, she was so scared. She said the Nazis had come to the factory that night and gone straight to the wood shop. Someone betrayed Hendrik, an employee or customer. Hendrik wouldn't show them the hiding space. He pretended he had no idea what they were talking about. Because he wouldn't speak, the officers began threatening him. And David heard. And he tried to help. But the officers had guns."

She gulps in a breath. "When the shooting was done, Hendrik was dead, and David, and Rose, and Lea. Only Mirjam managed to escape."

It must have been complete chaos. I've heard of people imprisoned, taken away and never returned. But *four people*, including a woman and a child, shot dead in cold blood?

"How did Mirjam escape?" I ask. "They shot everyone else. How would one young girl manage to escape from Nazis with guns?"

"The bathroom. The shop has a restroom in the front. The Roodveldts could use it once the sales floor was closed. Mirjam had just gone in to get ready for bed when the Nazis came, and she ran out the front door when she heard the gunshots, to the closest safe place she could think of. My house. That was three weeks ago. I was hiding her until last night."

"What happened last night?"

Mrs. Janssen reaches into the pocket of her sweater and pulls out a folded slip of paper. "I wrote everything down so I would have the timeline exactly right for you."

She traces the first line with her index finger. "She was here yesterday at noon, because I went in to bring her some bread and a copy of *Het Parool*. She liked to read the news of the underground, over and over again, memorizing even the classified advertisements."

"Are you sure it was noon?"

"I'd just heard the Westerkerk strike, and people outside had left for their lunch hours." She looks back down at the paper to find her place again. "She was here at a quarter past four, because I went in to warn her that Christoffel, my errand boy, was going to drop something off, and so she would need to be still. She was here at five thirty, because I asked her if she wanted some dinner; she told me she had a headache and was going to lie down. Right after, my neighbor Mrs. Veenstra asked me to come over. Her son, Koos, hadn't been home, and she was scared for him. After I sat with her for an hour, Koos came up the street. His bicycle had lost a tire; he walked it twenty-five kilometers. I went home and called out to Mirjam to ask if she was feeling better. She didn't answer. I assumed she'd fallen asleep. A while later, I opened the door to see if I could bring her anything."

"She was gone?"

"Vanished. Her bed was empty. Her coat was gone. Her shoes were gone. She was gone."

"What time was it by then?"

"Around ten. After curfew. Sometime between five thirty,

when Mirjam said she was going to lie down, and ten, she disappeared, and there is no explanation."

Finished with her story, she refolds the paper and starts to put it back in her pocket before handing it to me instead. There are matches near the burners on Mrs. Janssen's stove. I fetch one now, strike it against the box, and let Mrs. Janssen's penciled sleuthing burn into sulfur and ash.

"What are you doing?" she asks.

"What are *you* doing, keeping written records of the girl you've been illegally hiding?"

She rubs her forehead. "I didn't think of that. I don't know these rules. It's why I need your help, Hanneke."

The Westerkerk chimes again in the background. Another quarter hour has passed. Before, I was using the time as an excuse to leave, but now it really is getting late. I fold my arms over my chest. "You were visiting with a neighbor for an hour. Couldn't Mirjam have walked out then?"

"Mrs. Veenstra lives right across the street. We sat on her steps and faced my house; it wasn't too cold yesterday. Mirjam couldn't have left through the front door without me seeing her."

"You have a back door?" I shouldn't be getting her hopes up by asking questions like this, when I'm not planning to help her. But the situation she's described is strange and unbelievable, and I keep feeling like she must be explaining it wrong.

"The rear door doesn't close properly—it hasn't for years. I used to get so mad at Hendrik; to think of a furniture maker not making the time to fix his own door. Finally last year I got fed up with asking and I installed a latch myself. When I noticed

Mirjam was gone, I checked it. It was still closed. She couldn't have left through the back entrance and closed a latch on the inside of the door."

"A window?" It sounds unlikely even as I'm saying it. This neighborhood is wealthy, the kind of place people would notice unusual things like girls climbing out windows.

"Not a window. Don't you see? She had no way to leave. And no reason to. This was the last safe place for her. But she can't have been discovered, either. If the Nazis had come to take her, they would have taken me, too."

There has to be a rational explanation. Mrs. Janssen must have turned away for a few minutes at Mrs. Veenstra's and not seen the girl leave. Or maybe she has the timing wrong, and the girl disappeared while Mrs. Janssen was taking an afternoon nap.

The explanation doesn't matter, really. I can't help her, no matter how sad her story is. It's too dangerous. Survival first. That's my war motto. After Bas, it might be my life motto. Survival first, survival only. I used to be a careless person, and look where it got me. Now I transport black market goods, but only because it feeds me and my family. I flirt with German soldiers, but only because it saves me. Finding a missing girl does nothing for me at all.

From outside the kitchen, I hear the front door squeak open, and then a young male voice call out, "Hallo?" Farther away, the sound of a dog barking. Who is here? The Gestapo? The NSB? We hate the Gestapo, and the Green Police, but we hate the Nationaal-Socialistische Beweging most of all. The Dutch Nazis, who have betrayed their own people.

Mrs. Janssen's eyes widen until she places the voice. "Christoffel, I'm in the kitchen," she calls out. "I forgot he was coming back today," she whispers to me.

"Pick up your coffee. Behave normally."

Christoffel the errand boy has curly blond hair and big blue eyes and the tender skin of someone who hasn't been shaving long.

"Mrs. Janssen?" He fumbles with his hat in his hands, uncomfortable to have interrupted us. "I'm here for the opklapbed? This is the time you said?"

"Yes, of course." She begins to rise, but Christoffel gestures for her to stay seated.

"I can manage on my own. I have a cart, and a friend waiting outside to help." He nods toward the window, where a tall, stout boy waves from the street.

When he disappears for his cart and his friend, Mrs. Janssen sees my alarmed face and reassures me. "Not *that* bed. Not Mirjam's. He's taking the one in Hendrik's office. I barely go in that room anymore. I asked Christoffel if he could find a buyer, and I was going to use the money to help support Mirjam."

"Now?"

"Now I'll use the money to pay you to help me." I'm shaking my head in protest, but she cuts me off. "You have to find her, Hanneke. My older sons—I may never see them again. My youngest son is dead, my husband died trying to protect Mirjam's family, and her family died trying to protect him. I have no one now, and neither does she. Mirjam and I must be each other's family. Don't let me lose her. Please."

I'm saved from having to respond by the squeaking wheels of

26

Christoffel's pushcart, to which he and his friend have lashed Mrs. Janssen's other opklapbed. It's more ornate than the one in the pantry, the wood smooth and varnished and still smelling faintly of lemon furniture oil. "Mrs. Janssen? I'm leaving now," he says.

"Wait," I tell him. "Mrs. Janssen, maybe you don't need to sell this bed now. Wait a day to think about it." It's my way of telling her I'm not going to be able to agree to this proposition.

"No. I'm selling it now," she says definitively. "I have to. Christoffel, how much do I owe you for your trouble in picking it up?"

"Nothing, Mrs. Janssen. I'm happy to do it."

"I insist." She reaches for her pocketbook on the table and begins to count out money from a small coin purse. "Oh dear. I thought I had—"

"It's not necessary," Christoffel insists. He is blushing again and looks to me, stricken, for help.

"Mrs. Janssen," I say softly. "Christoffel has other deliveries. Why don't we let him go?"

She stops searching through her pocketbook and folds it closed, embarrassed. Once Christoffel leaves, she sinks back to her chair. She looks tired and old. "Will you help me?" she asks.

I drain the rest of my cold coffee. What outcome does she think I can deliver? I wouldn't know where to start. Even if Mirjam managed to escape, how far could a fifteen-year-old girl with a yellow *Jodenster* on her clothing get? I don't need to take Mrs. Janssen's money to know what will happen to a girl like Mirjam, if it hasn't happened already: She'll be captured, and she'll be relocated to a labor camp in Germany or Poland, the type from which nobody has yet to return. But how did she get out in the first place?

There has to be a rational explanation, I tell myself again. People don't disappear into thin air.

But that's a lie, actually. People disappear into thin air every day during this occupation. Hundreds of people, taken from their homes.

How can she expect me to find just one?

THREE

Mama's lips are a thin, tight line when I get home. "You're late." She accosts me at the door; she must have been watching through the window.

"It's twelve fifteen."

"It's twelve nineteen."

"Four minutes, Mama?"

Our apartment smells like frying parsnips and sausages, which I brought home yesterday. It's a small space: just a front room, a kitchen, a toilet, and two tiny bedrooms, all on the second floor of a five-story building. Cozy.

Papa reads a book in his armchair, using the page holder he made to keep the book flat as he turns the pages with his good left arm. His shriveled right arm is tucked into his lap.

"Hannie." He calls me by my pet name as I lean over to kiss him.

The injury happened before I was born, during the Great War. He lived on the Flanders side of the Dodendraad electric fence that had been built to separate occupied Belgium from Holland. My mother lived on the Dutch side. He wanted to vault over to impress her. He'd done it once before. I didn't believe that part of the story when he first told it, but then he showed me a book: People had managed to cross the Wire of Death in all kinds of ingeniously idiotic ways, using tall ladders or padding their clothes with porcelain to deflect the shock. This time when he tried to cross, his shoe grazed the wire and he plummeted to the ground, and that was how my father immigrated to Holland.

The right half of his body, all the way down his leg and partway up his face, has been paralyzed ever since, so he has a twisted and slow way of speaking. It embarrassed me when I was a child, but now I barely notice.

Papa gently pulls me closer to whisper in my ear. "Your mother is anxious because they came looking for Mr. Bierman. Be nice to her."

Mr. Bierman runs the greengrocer across the street. Jews haven't been able to own businesses for months now, but his wife is a Christian and he transferred the papers to her name. They have no children, just a flirtatious white cat named Snow.

"Who came?" I ask. "The NSB filth?"

Papa puts one finger to his lips and then points to the ceiling. "Shhhh." Our neighbor upstairs is a member of the NSB. His wife used to braid my hair and make me spice cookies on Sinterklaas

Day. Behind me, Mama rattles the lunch tray, setting food down on our small table, so I kiss Papa's other cheek and take my place.

"Why were you late, Hannie?" Mama asks.

"To teach you not to panic when it's only *four minutes* after the time I usually get home."

"But you're never late."

I'm never asked to find missing girls, either, I think. Without meaning to, I'm picturing Mrs. Janssen again, worrying over an empty pantry.

Mama ladles me a spoonful of parsnips. We eat better than a lot of people. If Papa and Mama left the house more, they would probably start to question what exactly it is that I do to bring home so much food.

"It was nothing." The peppery sausage warms my mouth. "A German policeman stopped me." That's true, of course. I just don't mention that it happened early this morning, before I learned about Mirjam.

"I hope you didn't provoke him," Mama says sharply. I'm not the only one in the family who has been changed by the war. She used to teach music lessons from our apartment, and Chopin would stream out the windows. Nobody has the money for music anymore, or the translating work Papa used to do.

"He spoke Dutch," I say, as a way of responding without answering. "He sounded fluent."

Papa snorts. "We fattened him up after the last war so he could come back now and starve us during this one." Germany was so poor after the Great War that lots of families sent their children to Holland, to grow strong on Dutch cheeses and milk.

They would have died without us. Now some of the boys have grown up and returned here again.

"When do you need to go back to work?" my mother asks me.

"I have another twenty minutes."

Officially, I work as a receptionist for an undertaker. It wasn't my ideal position, but I didn't have many options. No one wanted to hire a young girl without work experience or typing skills. Mr. Kreuk wouldn't have, either, but I didn't give him a choice. I'd already been turned away from seven other shops when I saw the HELP WANTED sign in his window, and I refused to leave until he gave me a job.

Mr. Kreuk is a good man. He pays me fairly. He gave me my other, secret job, which pays even more.

In Holland, and probably everywhere else in Europe, the Germans have issued us monthly ration cards with coupons for food, clothing, kerosene, rubber. The newspapers tell you what you can purchase: five hundred grams of sugar, two liters of milk, two kilograms of potatoes. That's where Mr. Kreuk comes in. Mr. Kreuk uses the ration allowances of the dead to stock up on supplies, then resells them at higher prices. At least this is how I think it works. I don't ask questions. All I know for sure is that several months ago, Mr. Kreuk came to me with a stack of cards and asked if I would do some shopping.

It was terrifying the first time, but I was even more scared to lose my job, and after a while, I became good at it, and after a longer while, it began to feel noble, even. Because the Nazis were the ones who made us have rations to begin with, and if I flout their system, then I am also flouting them. High-priced ham: the only revenge I have been able to get on the people who killed Bas, but I'll cling to even that small satisfaction.

What we're doing is technically illegal. War-profiteering, it would be called. But Mr. Kreuk isn't wealthy, and I'm certainly not, either. It seems to me like what we're really doing is trying to reorganize a system that has come to make no sense in a country that has come to make no sense.

"*Hannie.*" Mama has obviously been trying to get my attention. "I asked what you said to the Green Police."

Is she still fixated on that? If only she realized how many soldiers I encounter every week. "I told him to get out of our country and never come back. I suggested he do rude things with tulip bulbs."

She covers her mouth in horror. "Hannie!"

I sigh. "I did what I always do, Mama. I got away, as quickly as I could."

But Mama's attention is no longer on me. "Johan." Her voice drops to a whisper and she clutches my father's good arm. "Johan, they're back. Listen."

I hear it, too. There's shouting across the street, and I run to the window to look from behind the curtain. "Hannie," Mama warns me, but when I don't come back, she gives up. Three NSB officers in their beetle-black uniforms pound on the Biermans' door, ordering Mr. Bierman to come out.

His wife answers, her hands shaking so intensely that it's obvious even from a distance.

"Your husband was supposed to present himself for deportation last week," the oldest-looking officer says. Our street is narrow, and he's not being quiet. I can hear almost everything he says.

"He—he's not here," Mrs. Bierman says. "I don't know where he is. I haven't seen him in days."

"Mrs. Bierman."

"I swear. I haven't seen him. I came home from shopping, and he was gone. I searched the whole house myself."

"Step aside," the officer instructs, and when she doesn't, he shoves past. Mama has come up beside me. She grabs my arm so tightly I can feel her fingernails through my sweater. *Please, let Mr. Bierman really be gone,* I beg. *Please let him have escaped while Mrs. Bierman was shopping.*

Mama is moving her lips, praying, I think, although we don't do that anymore. The soldiers reappear in the doorway, this time dragging another man. It's Mr. Bierman, bleeding from the nose, his right eye split and swollen.

"Good news, Mrs. Bierman," the soldier says. "We found your husband after all."

"Lotte!" Mr. Bierman calls as they force him toward a waiting truck.

"Pieter," she says.

"I should bring you, too, to keep him company," the soldier offers. "But I feel bad punishing a good Christian woman who is too stupid to know where her husband was." His back is mostly to me, so I can't see his face, but I can hear the taunt in his voice.

"Lotte, it's all right," Mr. Bierman calls from the truck. "I'll be home soon."

Still she doesn't cry. She doesn't do anything but watch and shake her head back and forth as if to say, *No. No, you won't be home soon.*

The truck drives away, and Mrs. Bierman still stands in her doorway. It's an intrusion to watch her, but I can't avert my eyes. Mrs. Bierman used to give me presents for Sinterklaas Day, too. And when I visited their shop, she would let me taste the strawberries, even if we weren't buying any.

Mama yanks me away from the window, grabbing my sweater and pulling me to the table. "Finish eating," she says stiffly. "It's not our business; there's nothing we can do."

I shake her hand loose, ready to protest, to remind her about the Biermans and their strawberries. But she's right. There is nothing I can do that will repair what just happened.

We finish eating mostly in silence. Mama makes a few attempts at conversation, but they crumble. The food doesn't taste like food. When I can't manage any more, I excuse myself, saying I have a few things to do before going back to work.

"Don't be late. It's a good job you have," Mama reminds me. She loves my job. She knows mine is the only steady paycheck in the house. "You don't want Mr. Kreuk to question whether he made the right decision in hiring you."

"He doesn't."

I just want a minute away from my parents, my work—a minute to close out the rest of the world. In my bedroom, I pull the window shades closed and open the bottom drawer of the bureau, feeling around in the back until I find it: a faded diary, from a birthday when I was nine. For a week I wrote faithfully, describing friends I liked and teachers who were mean to me. Then I abandoned it for five years and didn't pick it up again until I met Bas, when I transformed it into a scrapbook.

Here is the school photograph he gave me, casually asking for one of mine in return. Here is the note he slipped in my books, telling me that my green sweater matched my eyes. He signed it *B*, and that was the first time I realized he preferred *Bas* instead of *Sebastiaan*. A nickname from the middle of the name, like a lot of Dutch boys do, rather than the beginning.

Here is a ticket stub from the first film we ever saw together, the one where I begged my best friend, Elsbeth, to come along, too, in case I got tongue-tied around Bas. This memento is doubly painful, because I don't have Elsbeth anymore, either, because she is gone in a different way.

Here is a ticket stub from the second.

Here is the tissue that I used to blot my lipstick the night he first kissed me.

Here is the tissue I used to blot my tears the night he told me he would be volunteering for the military when he turned seventeen. Here is the lock of hair he gave me the day before he left, at his going-away party. I gave him something, too. It was a locket with my picture in it. That was how I could guess what German girls would do. I was so stupid then.

I close the book quickly, shoving it into the back of the drawer and covering it with clothes. I'm thinking of Bas. And without meaning to, I'm also thinking of Mirjam Roodveldt again. I'm annoyed with myself for it, for wasting time thinking about that missing girl from the pantry, who I know nothing about, who could only get me into trouble.

Except that I do know one thing about her: The film magazine on the shelf in the pantry—I'm almost positive that the photograph it was opened to was a scene from *The Wizard of Oz*, a movie about a girl who gets caught in a tornado and wakes up in a fairyland. I so desperately wanted to see it, but it hadn't yet come to Holland when the war broke out. So I never saw *The Wizard of Oz*, but now I'm thinking of Judy Garland singing in Bas's parlor while Bas told me he loved me on the sofa, and we laughed and laughed and memorized the words to her song.

Bas would have agreed to help Mrs. Janssen. I'm sure of that, without a doubt. Bas would have said that this was our chance to do something real and important. Bas would have said it like it was an adventure. Bas would have said, *Obviously you'll decide to help her, too; the girl I love would completely agree with everything I'm saying,* because Bas wouldn't know anything about the kind of girl I am now.

And what would I say in return? I would say, *You think I would agree with everything you're saying? You're awfully full of yourself.* Or I would say, *My parents depend on me to keep us all alive. Helping Mrs. Janssen means endangering my whole family.* Or I would say, *Things are different now, Bas. You don't understand.*

I would give so much to be able to say anything to him. Anything at all.

Finding this girl is not who I am anymore. That action is soft; I am practical. That action is hopeful; I am not. The world is crazy; I can't change it.

So why am I still thinking about Mirjam Roodveldt?

So why do I know that this afternoon, unless I manage to talk myself out of it, I'll go back to Mrs. Janssen's?

FOUR

Things that have changed about my country in the past two years: everything and nothing.

When I get on my bicycle after lunch, the Biermans' shop assistant is selling vegetables to a customer, as though the store's owner wasn't just put into a truck and carted away, as though Mrs. Bierman's world wasn't just turned upside down.

Back at work, Mr. Kreuk has actual work for me, the kind my official job entails. There's a funeral tomorrow, and I need to write a notice for the newspaper and arrange things with the florist. But at half past one, Mr. Kreuk comes to my desk and shows me the draft of the notice: I'd written the wrong address for the church.

"Are you feeling all right?" Mr. Kreuk is a round little man, with circular glasses that make him resemble a turtle. "You don't usually make mistakes." He blinks and stares at his shoes. We've known each other for almost a year, but he's so awkward. Sometimes I think he became an undertaker because it was easier for him to spend time with the dead than the living.

"I'm sorry. I guess I'm a little distracted."

He doesn't pry. "Why don't I handle the ad and the flowers? I have a few errands for you this afternoon: the butcher's and then to Mrs. de Vries's." He winces while saying her name, and now I see why he's given me a pass on the newspaper mistake. It's an exchange for dealing with Mrs. de Vries.

"Thank you," I tell him, and grab my coat before he can change his mind. I'll deal with Mrs. de Vries later. First I'll go to Mrs. Janssen.

Outside, something new: *Long Live the Führer* has been written on the building across the street in white paint, still wet, and now I'll see it every time I leave work. Did the shop owner do it as a show of Nazi support? Or did the Nazis do it as propaganda? It's always hard to tell.

There have been acts of protest since the start of the occupation—an organized worker strike that was squashed quickly and left dead bodies in the streets. Papa thinks there should be more. It's easy for him to say, when his leg keeps him from participating. Mama thinks Nazis are beasts, but she wouldn't care as much if they stayed in Germany. She just wants them out of her country. After the war, people will sit around and recall the brave ways they rebelled against the Nazis, and nobody will want to remember that their biggest "rebellion" was wearing a carnation in honor of our exiled royal family. Or maybe people will sit around and speak German, because the Germans will have won. There are those who would celebrate that, too. Who believe in the Nazis, or who've decided it's smarter to support the invaders. Like Elsbeth. Elsbeth, who—

Never mind.

I almost turn around twice on my way to Mrs. Janssen's. Once when I walk past a soldier interrogating a girl my age on the street, and once just before I ring the doorbell. When Mrs. Janssen sees me, her face breaks into such a relieved smile that I nearly turn around a third time, because I'm still not quite sure what I'm doing here.

"You decided to help me." She flings opens the door. "I knew you would. I knew I made the right decision to trust you. I could see in your face. Hendrik always said—"

"You haven't told anyone else, have you?" I interrupt. "Before or after me?"

"No. But if you hadn't come back, I don't know what I would have done. I've been sitting here worrying about it."

"Mrs. Janssen. Stop. Inside." I grab her elbow and guide her into her own sitting room, where we sit on her faded floral couch. "First, I haven't agreed to help," I tell her, because I want to be clear. "I'm here to talk to you about it. To consider it. For now we'll just talk about Mirjam, and I'll *consider* it. But I'm not a detective, and I'm not promising anything."

She nods. "I understand."

"All right. Then why don't you tell me more?"

"Anything. What would you like to know?"

What *would* I like to know? I have no idea what the police would ask. But usually when I'm finding black market objects for people, I begin with a physical description. If they need shoes, I ask what size, what color. "Assuming I decide to help you, it would be nice to know what Mirjam looks like," I say. "Do you have pictures? Did Mirjam bring any with her? Any family photographs?"

"She didn't have time to bring anything. Just the clothes on her back."

"What were those? What was she wearing when she disappeared?"

Mrs. Janssen closes her eyes and thinks. "A brown skirt. A cream-colored blouse. And her coat. The workroom in the furniture store got so drafty you had to wear a coat all the time back there. She was wearing that on top of her clothes. It was blue."

"Like this?" I point to the royal blue on Mrs. Janssen's Delft saucers in the china cupboard.

"More like the sky. On a sunny day. With two rows of silver buttons. I lent her other clothes while she was here, but when she disappeared, her original things were the only clothes missing."

I keep asking questions, about any physical detail I can think of, mentally drawing a girl in my head. Curly dark hair, falling to her shoulders. A slender nose. Bluish-gray eyes.

"The Roodveldts' neighbors might have a photograph," Mrs. Janssen offers. "After the Roodveldts disappeared, the neighbors might have tried to save some things from the apartment."

"Do you know anything about the neighbors?"

She shakes her head. That means I can't go to the apartment and ask questions. Not when the Roodveldts' unit is probably occupied by an NSB family already. Amsterdam is a crowded city, where even in normal times it's difficult to find housing.

Now, when a Jewish family disappears, a family of sympathizers reappears in its place, carrying on as if they'd always lived there. Besides, the war makes friends turn on each other. The neighbors might have been the ones to reveal the family's secret hiding place.

Where else could I find a photograph?

"Have you been to the hiding place in the furniture workshop?" I ask.

She nods. "The day after Hendrik was—the day after it happened. Completely ransacked. The Germans took almost everything, or maybe the Roodveldts didn't bring much to begin with. Hendrik's secretary might have tried to save something, but she left on her honeymoon the day after the raid. I can write to her, but I'm not sure when she gets back."

"Where did Mirjam go to school?"

"The Jewish Lyceum, since Jewish students were segregated. I don't know where it is."

I do. It's right along the Amstel River in a redbrick building with tall windows. I pass by it all the time and now add it to my mental file on Mirjam. I have a location in which I can place the girl I've created in my head.

"What happens next?" Mrs. Janssen asks. "Are you going to speak with your friends about this?"

"Friends?"

"Who are going to help you? Who know about these things?"

Now I'm beginning to understand why Mrs. Janssen came to me. Because she has no idea how illicit activities work. The resistance, the black market—she thinks we're all one network, sharing information, plotting against the Germans. But what I do for Mr. Kreuk works only because my link in the chain is so small. If I were to be caught and questioned about Mr. Kreuk's operation, I could say that I didn't know if he'd involved anyone else, and that would be telling the truth.

I don't have a resistance network. My profiteering shopkeepers will be useless for this task. I don't have anything, really, except an imaginary picture of a girl I've never seen, who I still haven't fully promised Mrs. Janssen I'll find.

"I need to see the hiding space again," I tell Mrs. Janssen.

She lets me in by unlatching the hidden hook, and then calls after me. "I already looked in here. Before you came, I went through everything yesterday."

I wait for my eyes to adjust. The space is maybe four feet wide. All but a few inches are taken up by the unfolded opklapbed. I pull back the quilt, examining the sheet below, doing the same for the mattress and pillow. On the narrow shelf, the magazine I'd noticed earlier, an old issue, from before the war. Mrs. Janssen probably had it among Jan's old things and gave it to Mirjam as something to read.

None of the magazine's pages have notes or markings on them, but tucked underneath is the latest issue of *Het Parool*, the paper Mrs. Janssen mentioned giving Mirjam yesterday. People read the resistance papers voraciously, then passed them along. Mrs. Janssen's neighbor or delivery boy must have given this one to her.

I fold up the opklapbed to look at the floor underneath, peeling back the thin rug.

Nothing. Nothing anywhere.

But what did I expect to find? A letter from Mirjam explaining where she went? A trapdoor, where a Nazi could have sneaked in and carried Mirjam away? When I emerge into the kitchen, rubbing my eyes against the brightness, Mrs. Janssen starts to set out coffee again.

"Is your neighbor across the street home?" I ask her. "Mrs. Veenstra? The one whose son got waylaid?"

"I don't think so." She frowns. "Did you want to interview her? She doesn't know about Mirjam."

I shake my head. "Stay at your door. And sometime in the next five minutes, open it and come out. Anytime in the next five minutes. Just don't give me warning when."

Wrapping my arms around my waist against the cold, I cross the street to the house belonging to Mrs. Veenstra and stand on the steps, my back facing Mrs. Janssen's home. After a minute it comes: an audible click, followed immediately by a yapping dog. When I turn around, Mrs. Janssen stares at me, confused.

"I don't understand," she says when we're back in the house. "What were you doing?"

"I noticed it earlier when Christoffel left with the opklapbed. Your door is so old and heavy; it can't be opened without making a sound. And as soon as that dog next door—"

"Fritzi," Mrs. Janssen supplies. "The neighbor boy's schnauzer."

"As soon as that dog hears the door, it starts barking. Even if you were looking in completely the other direction, you would have heard the dog and noticed Mirjam leaving through the front door."

"That's what I said." She's cross at my conclusion. "I already told you that. She couldn't have left through that door. And I already looked through Mirjam's hiding place. You're wasting time doing things I already did."

"Did you already find her?" My voice is sharper than it needs to be; I'm covering my inexperience with false confidence. "You keep telling me I'm doing things you already tried, but unless you already found her, I need to see everything with my own eyes. Now, take me to the back door."

She opens her mouth, probably to tell me again that Mirjam couldn't have escaped through there because of the inside latch, but then thinks better.

The rear door is a heavy oak, and it's immediately apparent what she meant by it not closing. Age and the settling of the house have warped the door completely, so that the top half of the door bulges away from the jamb. That's why Mrs. Janssen has added the latch. It's heavy, made of iron, and when engaged, it holds the door properly shut. When it's not engaged, a thin stream of air seeps in through the top.

She's right. I can't think of any way that a person could leave through this door and lock the latch behind herself.

Mrs. Janssen is staring at me. I haven't told her that I'll help, not officially. And yet I haven't walked away. It's so immensely dangerous, much more than anything I've allowed myself to do.

But Mrs. Janssen came to me, the way Mr. Kreuk had come to me, and I'm very good at finding things.

I can feel myself getting sucked into this mystery. Maybe because Bas would. Maybe because it's another way to flout the rules. But maybe because, in a country that has come to make no sense, in a world I cannot solve, this is a small piece that I can. I need to get to Mirjam's school, the place that might have a picture, the place that might explain who this girl is. Because assuming that Mrs. Janssen is correct in her timeline, assuming the dog always barks when someone leaves, assuming Mirjam couldn't have gone through the back door, assuming all that is true, it seems this girl is a ghost.

FIVE

'____ve been gone from my daily tasks for nearly an hour. If I don't get back to my deliveries, Mrs. de Vries will complain.

The line at the butcher's is almost out the door with tired housewives trading tips on where they've managed to locate which hard-to-find item. I don't wait in the line. I never do. As soon as the butcher sees me come in, he waves me toward the counter while he disappears into the back. It took me at least a dozen visits to build this relationship. The first time, I listened while he told another customer that his daughter loved to draw. The second time, I brought some colored pencils and told him they were old ones I'd found in the back of my closet. They were obviously brand-new, though, and I watched his reaction to this: Would he allow himself to believe a white lie, if it meant he got something he wanted? Later, I talked about a sick grandmother, and her sick, wealthy friends who were willing to pay extra money for extra meat.

When the butcher returns, he's carrying a white paper parcel.

"That's not fair," a woman behind me calls after she sees the exchange. She's right; it's not fair. The other customers never like me much. They might like me better if I were hungry like them, but I'd rather not starve.

"Her grandmother is sick," the butcher explains. "She's caring for a whole family at home."

"We're all caring for people at home," the woman presses on. She's tired. Everyone is tired of standing in so many lines for so many days. "It's just because she's a pretty girl. Would you let a *boy* skip the line?"

"Not a boy who looks like your son." The other people in line laugh, either because they think it's funny or they just want to remain in the good graces of the man who supplies their food. He turns to me and smiles, whispering that he's tucked a little something extra into my packet for me to take to my family.

It started to rain while I was in the butcher's shop, fat, slushy drops mixed with ice. The roads are dark and slick. I put the meat in my basket, covering the package with a newspaper, which soaks through in minutes. At the door of Mrs. de Vries's apartment, my teeth chatter and water slides off my skirt and pools into my shoes, which would matter more if my feet hadn't already gotten soaked in the rain. The soles of my shoes are worn through and growing useless in wet weather. I knock on the de Vrieses' door, and inside I hear the clinking of china. "Hallo?" I call. "Hallo?"

Finally, Mrs. de Vries answers, overdressed as usual in a blue silk dress and straight-seamed stockings. She's in her thirties, with regal features, two irritating twins, and a husband who publishes a ladies' magazine and spends so much time at work that I've met him only once.

"Hanneke, come in." Mrs. de Vries waves me vaguely into her apartment but doesn't bother to take her packages, or to thank me for coming out in a monsoon just to bring her some beef. "My neighbor and I were having tea. You don't have anywhere to be, do you? You can wait in the kitchen until we're finished." She nods toward the older woman sitting on the sofa but makes no introductions. It's clear she doesn't mean to interrupt their conversation to tend to me. Mrs. de Vries is one of those people who behave as if the war is a nuisance happening in the periphery around her. Today I ignore her suggestion to wait in the kitchen, even though she obviously considered it an order. I don't want to make it easy for her to forget that I'm here, so I set her packages on a table, stand in her foyer, and drip.

The neighbor in question, a gray-haired woman, arches one eyebrow at me and clears her throat before turning back to Mrs. de. Vries. "As I was saying. Gone. I heard about it only this morning."

"I don't believe it," Mrs. de Vries says. "Does anybody know where they went?"

"How would we? They stole off in the middle of the night."

"Hanneke, would you get us some more biscuits from the kitchen?" Mrs. de Vries calls, picking up a crumb-filled plate and holding it aloft until I walk over and get it.

In the kitchen, a half-empty tin of store-bought buttery cookies sits on the table. I cram two of them in my mouth as I refill the plate. A pair of solemn eyes stare at me from around the corner. One of the twins. I can never remember their names or tell them apart; they're equally spoiled. I could give him a cookie, but instead, I shove another one deliberately in my mouth and lick the crumbs off my lips.

"So you think they went into hiding, then?" Mrs. de Vries asks her neighbor. "They weren't rounded up?"

"Certainly not rounded up. I should know. I have friends in the NSB. I've told them before, several times, that there was a Jewish family living in my building. If they'd been taken, I would know. The Cohens sneaked away like thieves in the middle of the night."

I bring the cookies back into the sitting room, making as much rattling as I can to catch Mrs. de Vries's attention. She sips her coffee. "I can't believe nobody saw them! You're sure?"

"I was hoping to at least get a look in their apartment. My son and his wife have been looking for a larger place—she's expecting, you know—and it would be so nice to have them in the building."

The neighbor is vile. They both are, with their oily, refined support of the Nazis. But also rich. I don't think Mr. Kreuk considers morals when he chooses who to sell to. If they can pay, they can buy.

"Mrs. de Vries," I finally break in, gesturing toward the window, where outside the sky is cloudy but not raining. "I'm sorry, but I really should go soon. It was pouring earlier, but it looks like there's a break in the weather now. May I leave your things?"

If the nosy neighbor weren't here, Mrs. de Vries would insist on inspecting the contents of the parcel. As it is, she just raises one eyebrow. "I didn't realize your schedule was so important, Hanneke. Fetch my handbag from the hallway closet."

She hands me a few bills, and I don't even bother to count out her payment before putting it in my pocket and leaving, traipsing wet footprints over her parquet floors.

———

The Jewish Lyceum. Should I go there now? It's a little after 3:00 PM, on a day that began with me delivering lipstick to a woman at her grandparents' house and has become something very different, and all at once I am exhausted. I am exhausted by the enormity of the day. I am exhausted by the things I'm always exhausted by: the soldiers, the signs, the secrets and strategies and effort. I'm exhausted enough to know that I probably shouldn't go to the Lyceum right now, because being exhausted means I won't be thinking as quickly on my feet. I've learned that through working the black market.

On the other hand, now is the perfect time to sneak into a school. Classes will likely be dismissing for the day, with enough commotion that nobody would notice an out-of-place person walking the halls. The Lyceum is only a few blocks away; I'd practically have to ride past it on my way home. And when you're trying to find things, it's better to find them as quickly as possible, before someone else takes what you're looking for. I've learned that through the black market, too.

I roll my bicycle to a stop in front of the Lyceum. The school's architecture reminds me of the school I attended.

Three years ago: My friends and I would all have been sitting on the steps outside right now, arguing about where to go before our parents expected us home. Elsbeth would announce that she didn't have enough money to go anywhere, then sit back while two or three boys fought over who would get to pay for her coffee or pastries, and then she would wink at me to show she really did have enough money—she just liked the dramatics. A few others would try to protest that they couldn't come because they had to study. Finally, Bas would announce that we were *all* going to Koco's, and that he would personally fail the test to help the grading curve for the people who were so concerned with studying.

Now Elsbeth is gone, in the way I don't like to think about.

And Koco's had Jewish owners. Nine months after the invasion, a fight broke out in the shop, which led to the earliest major roundup and hundreds dead.

And Bas will never have to study again.

My whole life has been demolished, brick by brick. It happened two and a half years ago, but standing in front of this school makes me feel like it happened two weeks ago. Or like it's still happening, again and again, every day.

In the school, it's quiet. Eerily. No students in the halls, no sounds from the classrooms. At first I think I've misjudged the time and the day is already over, but when I peek into one classroom, there *are* students; they're just so few in number. Only five pupils are left in this room. The rest must be gone, taken by the Germans or in hiding or worse. A whole school, torn apart. This was Mirjam's world. Until she went into hiding, this was where she went every day, leaving traces of herself behind, I hope.

Two students, girls of twelve or thirteen, look up when I walk past their classroom. I wave to show them I mean no harm, but their faces fill with fear and they watch me until I pass.

In the next room, a thin man in spectacles lectures in front of a chalkboard while a girl in one corner studiously takes notes. That was where I used to sit, in the front right corner, and Bas would try to get my attention through the window when he passed, pressing his nose against the glass or mouthing *Booor-ring* as he pointed at the teacher. In the other corner, one of the boys catches my eye. And he winks at me. He winks and then laughs, and the instructor whirls around, barking at him to be quiet. The boy is dark and moon-faced and looks nothing like Bas, but the gesture is so much like him that immediately I step away from the window, trying to stop memories from flooding back.

It wasn't a good idea for me to come here. I don't know why I didn't listen to my instincts. It was unsafe and poorly planned. Anyone could see me, and I don't have a good story to tell if they do. I need to come back later for the photograph. I'll come with real coffee; I'll come with bribes.

Booor-ring, he used to say through the classroom windows.

This school feels like a maze. I can't remember the turns I took when I came in the building. There's an exit straight ahead of me, and even though it's not the one I entered through, I head toward it.

"Can I help you with something?"

A woman stands in the doorway of what I assume is the school office. She's taller than I am but looks only a few years older, with sharp, wary eyes and her hair piled in a knot on top of her head. She wears a cardigan with a yellow star sewn to it. *Jood.* "Are you lost?"

"I was just leaving."

She hurries to catch up with me, planting herself between me and the doorway. "But why were you *here*? You're not a student."

"I was . . ." But a lie won't come, not as easily as it usually does. "I was looking for a photograph."

"Of?"

"Just of students."

"Of students," she repeats. "Which students?"

"Never mind. I'll come back another time. I shouldn't have bothered you." I try to slide around her, but she shifts her position so the only way I could exit would be by literally pushing her aside. She's testing me, to see how desperate I am to get what I came for.

"Of whom?" she persists. "Why are you really here?" She grabs my arm. "Why are you really here?" she asks again, softly.

"Bas," I whisper, before I can stop myself. It just slipped out. The composure I had fifteen minutes ago is coming undone, thread by thread. Everything about this school makes me think of him—the chalkboard smell and the writing desks, and how it used to feel to have his schedule memorized and know precisely the minute when I might walk by him in the hall. He wasn't a dedicated student, but he passed anyway because everyone loved him, students and teachers both.

She jerks her head and her grip tightens. "We don't have any students named Bas. Who is Bas?"

But now I'm spilling the emotions I work so hard to keep bottled. "Bas died. I loved him."

Her face softens, but her eyes are still suspicious. "I'm sorry. But we don't have any pictures of him. Whoever Bas is. We don't have pictures at all. A fire damaged our records a few weeks ago."

"I'll go."

She hasn't let go of my arm. "I don't think you should. I think I should take you to the principal. You are trespassing."

My wits are slowly returning. I twist my arm so she's forced to drop it, and brush past her again. "I need to go."

"Stop. What's your name?"

But she won't report me. Who could she report me to? A Jewish woman wouldn't want to draw attention to herself for any reason, even to report a crime. She doesn't have any recourse.

"Stop," she says again, but it's halfhearted. I continue toward the exit, and she doesn't do anything. I can feel her eyes on me, though, watching as I walk out the doors of a building that reminds me too much of things that hurt to remember.

The cold wind slaps my face as I pedal home, brings me back to my senses, makes me furious with myself. All I had to do was find a picture, and I failed. I should have come with my bribery coffee and a well-practiced story. I could have said I was looking in on a girl I used to babysit for, or who used to live next door. I come up with stories every day. I should have done that, but I didn't, and now I've ruined one of the few leads I had. Stupid. Amateur. *Careless.*

I run a few more errands for Mama, and then when I try to get home, soldiers have blockaded the streets I would normally take.

They're having a march, another one, a chance for rows of them to peacock through the streets in their helmets and black boots. They sing, too. Today it's "Erika," a song about German girls and German flowers. It crawls like a maggot into my head and gets stuck, unwelcome lyrics and music playing on a loop.

By the time I finally get to my front door, I can barely stand. A velvety aroma hits me as I walk inside. Mama is making hot chocolate. Why? I've told her that the little we have left should be saved for a celebration. Mama isn't the type of person to think of errant celebrations, at least not anymore.

"Hot chocolate—did I forget someone's birthday?" I unwind my still-damp scarf and hang it on a hook near the door. If I were younger, I would curl up with the chocolate and tell Mama about my hard day. If I didn't have to keep this house together, I would tell my parents that I'd been asked to do a job that was too big for me and let my mother pet my hair.

"We have a visitor," Mama says. I can't tell if her smile is the real one or the false one she makes because her lips have forgotten how to smile naturally. It looks almost real.

Only then do I notice the figure in the chair seated across from my father—the hair, the freckles, the slightly crooked nose—and my heart jumps and falls at the same time.

Bas.

But of course it's not. I'm lonely enough to let myself believe that for one second, but I'm not hopeful enough to let myself believe it for any longer. It's not Bas. It's Ollie.

SIX

Ollie. Olivier. Laurence Olivier, when Bas was feeling silly, after the English film star. Bas's serious older brother, who looks almost like him, except his hair is not as red and his eyes are not as blue, and now that I'm seeing him sitting with my father, I'm realizing he doesn't look very much like Bas at all, actually; it was just a trick of the eyes and the heart.

Ollie was finishing his first year of university when Bas died; now he must be nearly through his studies. They were never close. Bas was quick to laugh, and Ollie took himself so seriously. At their house on Saturday evenings, Ollie would heave dramatic sighs every time he thought Bas and I were disrupting his work. I haven't seen him since the memorial service, the horrible, body-less memorial service, where Mrs. Van de Kamp clung to Ollie and cried, and I felt sick to my stomach because I wanted to cry, too, but didn't feel I deserved it. I tried stopping by the Van de Kamp house once, early on, but Mrs. Van de Kamp made it clear that she didn't want to see me, and honestly I couldn't blame her.

But here is Ollie Van de Kamp now, sitting in my front room, losing a game of chess to my father. "What brings you here?" I ask as he stands to greet me, kissing me formally on the cheek.

"My mother. She was just wondering about you, and I told her the next time I found myself in your neighborhood, I would stop in and see your family."

"And a wonderful surprise it is," my father says, "because Ollie is terrible at chess and he's agreed to play for money."

This is why I don't want to be around Ollie. Because it's not only his looks that are all wrong. Bas would beat the shirt off my father in a game of chess, gleefully teasing him while my father pretended to be upset. Ollie is losing methodically and gracefully. Ollie is like ersatz Bas.

"You made the chocolate." I return to a safe topic, both for something else to say and because the rude part of me wants to convey that I don't think Ollie's visit warrants it.

"She wasn't going to." My father playfully jabs the air at my mother. "I told her we should."

"I told her we shouldn't," Ollie offers. "I knew I couldn't stay long. There's no point in wasting it on me." He mustn't have exerted himself too much in protest. The cup next to him is almost empty.

"Will you stay for dinner, Olivier?" my mother asks. "It's just spinach and potatoes with the skin." Across the room, my father grimaces at the description of the food. The Bureau of

Nutrition Education has distributed endless flyers encouraging us to eat potato skins, drink skim milk, try cow brains. My mother religiously follows the recipes in these pamphlets as her main acknowledgment of the war. "I'm happy to set another plate. Though we're eating late tonight; you might not have time to get home before curfew."

Now I know her smile is forced. It's barely after six and curfew isn't until eight. Ollie would have plenty of time to get home. It's just that inviting Ollie for dinner, even if she likes him, is a step out of the ordinary, and that always makes her worry.

"Thank you, Mrs. Bakker. But I've already eaten. Actually, I was hoping Hanneke might come for a little walk with me." He rubs his neck exaggeratedly. "I've been hunched over books studying most of the day. It would be good to have a walk and catch up." Mama looks at the wall clock. "Just down the street," he assures her. "I'll have her back before curfew." He nods toward the coat I never had a chance to take off. "And look, you're already dressed for it. Unless you'd rather we just stay in and talk with your parents."

Something about the final suggestion makes me feel his invitation isn't one after all. He's suggesting that we go for a private walk, but if we don't, he'll say what he needs to in front of my family.

"I'll be back soon," I reassure my mother, and then look to Ollie. "Very soon."

———

Even though the rain has stopped, it's still damp, the kind of frigid humidity that makes you feel icicled and wet all the way through.

Ollie doesn't bother to offer me his arm. He just places his hands carefully in his pockets and begins to stroll, assuming I'll follow him, and because I don't have a choice, I do. "It's been a long time," he tells me. "Your hair is longer. You look older."

"Better than the alternative," I respond immediately with the joke my father always uses whenever someone tells him he's looking older. Ollie cocks his head.

"What's the alternative?" he asks.

And then I don't know what to say, because the only alternative to growing older is to be dead, and after Bas, Ollie and I don't make those kinds of jokes anymore.

"Where are we going?" I ask instead of answering.

He shrugs as if he hasn't really thought about it. "Het Rembrandtplein?"

It's one of my favorite squares in Amsterdam, with a statue of the painter in the middle and cafés around the border, where Mama used to take me for special treats. Coffee for her, hot anise milk for me. I haven't been able to stand the taste of anise milk for two and a half years. I was drinking it when I heard the radio broadcast that the Dutch had surrendered.

Ollie asks me about my job, and I ask him about his studies, and he says he's moved out of his parents' home to live with a roommate closer to the university. But I can tell both of us are only half listening, and by the time we reach the corner, I drop the pretense. "Why are you really here, Ollie? I don't think your mother just thought of me."

"I would bet that my mother thinks of you every day," he says, "since you're a connection to Bas."

I can't tell if he's meant that to be as painful as it is.

"But you're right," he continues. "That's not why I'm here." Ahead of us, another couple walks slowly, heads tilted toward each other the way people do when they're newly in love. Ollie stops, pretending to read a plaque on a wall, but I've used this trick myself enough to recognize he's creating distance so the other couple won't hear him. "What did you want at the Jewish Lyceum, Hanneke?"

"The what?"

He repeats his question.

I swallow. "Why would I go to the Jewish high school?"

"Do you think you have to lie to me?"

"I already graduated from school. Not with marks like yours, but they gave me a diploma and everything."

"Hanneke, stop playing dumb. I'm not the one whose mother is waiting for her at home, worried about curfew. I can have this conversation until dawn or we're arrested. Whichever you prefer."

He smiles tightly, and I give up. "If I *was* there, how would you have found out about it?"

"My friend Judith is the school secretary. She visited me just an hour ago because she wanted to tell me about a strange thing that happened."

Judith. That must be the Jewish girl with the sharp eyes and messy bun.

"Judith said a girl had come by and claimed to be looking for pictures of a boy named Bas, whom she loved and who was dead. It scared her. She thought it might be a Nazi scout, and she came to me because she was terrified."

The couple in front of us has stopped, too. The woman looks angry. So this isn't a first date, as I thought, but people who have known each other long enough to fight. "But how did you know it was me?" I ask.

"I asked Judith to describe the person who visited her, and she said it was a tall girl, about eighteen, with honey-colored hair and angry-looking green eyes. She said she was—let me make sure I get this right—'the girl Hitler is dreaming of to put on his Aryan posters.'" He pauses, giving me a chance to deny it. I don't bother. There are photographs of me in the Van de Kamps' home. He could easily show one to Judith, at which point she would confirm that it was me she had seen.

We've reached the statue, in the middle of the plaza. Ollie pulls on my sleeve, turning me to face him, and leans in close under the shadow of Rembrandt. "So what were you doing there?"

"I was looking for something. That's all."

"I know that. But it obviously wasn't a picture of Bas, who wasn't Jewish and didn't go to that school."

"I can't tell you."

He rolls his eyes, as if I'm being a difficult little girl. "You can't tell me? Do you think it would be too hard for me to understand?"

It's the voice I used with Mrs. Janssen, to chastise her for writing down Mirjam's story, and I'm irritated that Ollie is using it on me. What would he know about understanding? I might be three years younger, but he's the one who is tucked away in a university. He knows nothing of the real world.

"Unless—" he starts again, and his eyes flicker. "Hanneke,

you weren't there on behalf of the NSB, were you? I heard through a few people that you were involved in the black market, but is the NSB the side you're on?"

The smart answer would be to tell him yes. Because then he would leave me alone. He'd ask no more questions, and I'd never have to see him again. But my pride gets in the way of agreeing to such a grotesque lie. "Of *course* not."

"Then what? Tell me. I won't be angry. I promise."

I look into his not-quite-as-blue-as-Bas's eyes. The Jewish Lyceum is the only lead I've been able to think of. "Can you introduce me to Judith properly?" I ask. "Can you ask her to meet with me?"

"It's Judith you're interested in?"

"No. I'm just—I'm looking for someone, and I think Judith might be able to tell me more about them."

He's turned away from me now, toward the base of the Rembrandt statue, pretending to read the inscription but looking at it for much longer than he would need. When he finally speaks, it's very quiet. "Are you asking about *het verzet?*"

"No, Ollie, I'm not insane." I'm surprised Ollie would even bring up the resistance. He's never been a rule breaker. "It's something else."

"Hanneke, I'm not going to help you if you don't tell me why you want my help."

"It's nothing *bad*, Ollie. But I won't tell you, because it's too d—" I cut myself off. I almost said it was too *dangerous*, but that word would only make him less likely to help me. "Because it's dishonorable. I promised someone I wouldn't tell."

"Because it's too *dangerous?* Is that what you were going to say?"

I press my lips and look away.

"Hanneke." He's speaking so softly I can barely hear him. I'm watching his lips move more than listening. "Whatever you're doing, stop. Stop now."

"Please take me to Judith. Tell her I just need a few minutes. I won't get her in trouble."

"Time to go home, Hannie. Your mother will be worried about curfew."

He's businesslike again; I'm losing him. Finally, I make a calculated decision because I don't see any other options. Because Mirjam has been missing for almost twenty-four hours already. Because Ollie might be pedantic and boring, but he could never be a Nazi. "Ollie. I need to talk to Judith because I'm looking for a girl. Named Mirjam. She's just fifteen. Just Pia's age."

It was manipulative to bring up Pia, Ollie and Bas's little sister. The whole family loves Pia. I loved her, and the way she used to tell me she couldn't wait until I married her brother and became her sister for real. *He'll propose after he finishes university,* she assured me. *He's crazy in love with you.*

"You're bringing Pia into this?" His pale eyes are flashing. Let him be angry. I've said worse things to get what I want. I'll probably say worse things yet before this war is over. What I said worked, from the way he's clenching and unclenching his jaw.

"Ten minutes," I say. "I only need to talk to Judith for ten minutes. I can go back to the school to find her if I need to, but I don't think she wants that. It's a good thing I'm doing, Ollie. I promise."

He turns away and rakes his hand through his thick strawberry-blond hair. When he turns back and speaks again, his voice is a little louder, almost normal. "It's too bad you didn't come to university, Hanneke. You meet very nice people. I joined the student supper club. That's where I met Judith; we get together a couple of times a week."

"When?"

"The next meeting is tomorrow."

"Where?"

Before he can answer, a loud, throaty chuckle interrupts. German soldiers, two of them. I catch enough of the conversation to realize that, bizarrely, they're talking about Rembrandt. One of them is telling the others that his favorite painting is *The Night Watch*. Too bad for the soldier that when the war broke out, curators removed *The Night Watch* from Het Rijksmuseum, rolling up the canvas and trucking it to a castle in the country somewhere.

"Rembrandt." The art fan points at the statue and then at us. "A good painter," he continues in mangled Dutch. "Rembrandt."

This soldier is older. Around him, I should behave like a daughter, not a girlfriend. I'm preparing to compliment his taste, but Ollie answers before I need to. "Rembrandt! One of our best painters," he responds in German. He sounds calm, his accent is impeccable. "Do you know Van Gogh?"

The soldier holds his nose and waves away an imaginary smell, making it clear he doesn't think much of Van Gogh. His friend laughs, and Ollie laughs, too. "No Van Gogh!" he jokes.

It's nice to have someone else do the talking for once, to not have to summon the energy for another false conversation. After a few minutes, Ollie places his hand on the small of my back and steers me away from the statue. "Good night," he tells the soldiers, who wave back cheerfully.

Once we've left the square, he doesn't speak again the rest of the walk, and neither do I.

My life now is filled with guilt, often; anger, frequently; fear, usually. But it's not normally filled with self-doubt. I've constructed this new life carefully enough to feel that I'm protecting myself and my family as best I can. But in the past twelve hours, I've accepted a dangerous assignment. I've lost my composure in front of a stranger, and ripped open the sutures of my Bas-shaped wound, all over again, because they never seem to heal. And now I'm filled with nothing but doubt. Am I doing the right thing?

It's only after Ollie leaves me at home, after finishing the hot chocolate at Mama's insistence, that I realize he never told me where it was, this meeting of his student group. But that night, when I'm getting ready for bed, I find Ollie's hot chocolate napkin in my coat pocket, scrawled with an address near the campus of the Municipal University of Amsterdam.

The first time I met Bas:

He was fifteen, I was fourteen. I'd seen him at school and I liked his curious kitten eyes and the way one curl fell over his forehead no matter how many times he pushed it back. Elsbeth was a year older than me, so she was in the same class as him already. She knew his two friends, and one day we walked out of the building and his brown-haired friend called out to Elsbeth and asked her if she could settle something. "Which do girls prefer?" he asked. "Blonds or brunets?" Elsbeth laughed, and because she didn't want to give up her opportunity to flirt with either boy, she told them she liked both equally well.

"Ask my friend," she said, because she was always doing that, making sure I got equal attention, pushing me to the center in ways that made me annoyed and then grateful. "Ask Hanneke."

"What about you? Which do you prefer?" the blond friend asked me, and I still don't know how I was so bold, because I looked past both of them to where Bas was sitting on a ledge, and his auburn hair caught in the sunlight.

"I like redheads," I said, and then I blushed.

The first time I kissed Bas:

He was sixteen, I was fifteen. It was after our first trip to the cinema, our first real trip, when I didn't feel the need to make Elsbeth chaperone. I suggested a street early that we get off our bicycles and walk. I said it was because the weather was nice, but really I wanted to be alone with him before my parents could see us outside the window.

"You have something in your hair," he said, and I let him brush it out even though I knew there was nothing in my hair, and when he kissed me, he dropped his bicycle and it clattered to the ground, and we both laughed.

The last time I saw Bas:

He was seventeen, I was sixteen.

It was getting late. My parents had come to his going-away party, too, but they had already left. Mama said I could stay an extra hour, as long as Elsbeth and I walked home together. Bas and I kissed again and again in a dark corner of his dining room until my hour was up. I'll never forget his hand, pressed against the window as he watched me—

That's not what really happened.

I'm not ready to think about the last time I saw Bas.

SEVEN

Wednesday

just don't understand." Mrs. de Vries bows her head, as if she can't even look at me because she's so disappointed. "I asked for Amateurs."

I stare at the green-and-white cigarette pack in my hand, trying to arrange my face into an appropriate expression of understanding, when what I really want to do is slap her. I have found her two packs of cigarettes. In 1943, in this absurd country of ours, I have managed to find her two packs of cigarettes—not just cigarette paper and tobacco to roll, which are hard enough to get ahold of, but actual *cigarettes*—and she's upset because these don't have the right label on them?

"I couldn't get that brand, Mrs. de Vries. I'm sorry. I tried."

"Honestly, you would think I'd asked for the moon. I don't

understand what makes it so difficult. I wrote down for you exactly what I was looking for."

She did ask for the moon, very nearly. I had to try four different contacts; eventually I got these cigarettes from a woman who gets them from a German soldier. She says he's her boyfriend and he gives them to her; I think she might steal them. I also think he's not her boyfriend but someone paying her for what she does in the bedroom, but I don't ask questions. And I only go to her when I don't have any other options.

Now my temples are pounding. I don't know whether to yell or laugh at Mrs. de Vries. Her worries are so pedestrian, so soothing in an absurd way, like a holiday from all the things that real people have to care about. One of the twins tugs desperately on Mrs. de Vries's skirt while the other, the one who always looks naughty, like he has something to hide, tries to poke his head into my bag to see what else I may have brought.

"Stop that," Mrs. de Vries chastises the skirt-puller. "We'll have tea as soon as Hanneke leaves."

"Mrs. de Vries." I try a new approach to keep her on track. "If you don't want these, I won't have a problem finding someone else who does." The minute hand on her grandfather clock ticks another notch toward the top of the hour. I have somewhere to be.

"No!" She grabs the cigarettes, clutching them to her chest, only now realizing I don't have to give them to her, that she could be left with no cigarettes at all. "I'll take them. I just thought...if there were any others."

What does she think, that I'll slap my hand to my forehead

and say, "But of course! I forgot that I actually did have the brand you wanted. I've just been hiding them from you"?

"Mama, it's crowded in here," the naughty twin says, staring at me and poking his tongue between his lips. "I'm tired of it being so crowded."

"I'm leaving soon," I assure him. Horrid child.

———

The Municipal University of Amsterdam is where I might have gone, if the war hadn't started. I wouldn't have taken it seriously. It just would have been a way to pass time until Bas's mother thought he was old enough to inherit his grandmother's wedding ring. Bas would have gone here, too. What would he have studied? He never talked about his career dreams; he wasn't the type to look more than a few months in advance, and I can't picture an adult Bas. It both bothers and reassures me that, in my mind, he'll always be seventeen.

The university doesn't have a central location; its buildings are scattered through the city. But everyone knows the Agnietenkapel. It's one of the oldest buildings in Amsterdam, a convent from the fifteenth century, and the address Ollie gave me is on the same street.

I'd planned on changing clothes before I got here, clinging to some vague memory of the vanity I used to have when going to parties, but Mrs. de Vries has made me late and I don't have time. I'm in a mauve wool dress that I inherited from Elsbeth, which fits me well but is such a regretful color that she and I used to call it the Tonsil. Her grandmother had given it to her. Elsbeth was relieved when it was too small and she got to give it away to me. It used to feel like a joke between us, whenever I wore it. Now it feels like a practicality: It's hard to buy new clothes, so I wear all the ones that fit me, even the ugly ones, even the ones that remind me of better times.

This supper club will be a roomful of boys carrying chewed-up pencils in their pockets—they're probably studying architecture, like Ollie is—and girls citing philosophers I've never heard of. On the rare occasions I run into one of my old friends who did continue on to college, I feel both inferior and dismissive. None of them would survive on their feet if they had to. I'm defensive about everyone in Ollie's supper club before I even knock on the door.

Ollie peers through the window on the door, and I show him my jar of pickles when he opens it. I meant to bring something better but ran out of time to make anything. Instead I've brought the canned goods that a grocer gave me as a secret present this afternoon. Nobody in my family likes them anyway.

Ollie isn't wearing the jacket and tie I expected. His clothes are even more ragtag than mine are: rolled-up shirtsleeves smudged with graphite as if he's spent the day at a drafting table.

"Welcome," he says in a cautious voice that makes me wonder if I'm truly welcome at all.

He waves me into a small, bachelor's apartment. A sofa and a couple of chairs are clustered on one side of the room, opposite a kitchenette with mismatched cups drying on the countertop. There are only two other people in the room: a boy with full lips and heavy-lidded eyes, and another boy, handsome with wavy hair, who looks like the American film star William Holden. Both of them drink tea, or tea substitute, out of chipped cups.

"The famous supper club," I say. "And I was concerned I wouldn't be able to find you in the crowd."

Ollie is not amused. He holds out both hands for my coat, hanging it on the prong of a swaying coatrack. I don't know why I'm being tart. He's doing me a favor. I'm nervous, I think. If he were a new contact I had to impress, I'd be able to wear a better mask, but I can't un-remind myself of the fact that this is Ollie, who I've known for years. "Judith isn't here," I notice out loud. "She's coming, isn't she?"

"She's coming." He has tired eyes, up-all-night-studying eyes. "But you can't accost her right when she gets through the door. Sit through the regular meeting first. She wasn't excited about talking with you. The least you can do is show a little restraint and prove you aren't a complete lunatic."

"Half a lunatic?"

"Do you promise?"

"I promise," I say.

"I went out on a limb for you and I don't want you to embarrass me."

"Ollie, are you going to introduce me to the other people in the room, or should I sit mutely in the corner and try to refrain from breathing?"

He grimaces, then relents, turning toward the other two boys.

"And Ollie?" I say.

"Yes?"

"Thank you. For inviting me."

Ollie nods an acknowledgment before leading me the rest of the way to the coffee table. "This is Leo." He gestures to the one with the full lips first. "He lives here—we're in his apartment." Now he turns to the one who looks like William Holden. "And this is Willem, my roommate." One name I won't forget, at least. *Willem* is the Dutch version of *William*, just like his American movie star doppelgänger.

Leo drops his cup into the saucer with a clatter, wiping his hand on his pants and banging against the coffee table as he moves to greet me. Willem smoothly kisses both of my cheeks and offers me his place on the sofa, moving to a less comfortable-looking chair. He has a friendly, open face. I bet everyone who meets him thinks they must have met him before.

"You were Bas's girlfriend, right?" he asks, once I've settled in and smoothed my dress over my knees. "I only met him once, but he made me laugh. Ollie says he made everyone laugh."

"He did make everyone laugh." Usually I'd be put off by a friend of Ollie's presuming to know anything about Bas, but Willem's face is too earnest not to like. "My mother used to say he could charm the hands off a clock."

"I'm glad to meet you. We're just expecting two more. Tea?"

I shake my head, declining. "This club is smaller than I thought it would be. Cozy."

"There are more of us. We try to meet in smaller groups instead of having everyone at once," Willem explains. "If there's a raid, we don't want them to have a way of catching us all. The only time we've all ever been in a room together was for our friend

Piet's wedding. Otherwise, it's small groups. Smaller is better for the work that we do."

"Work?"

"We do lots of things," Leo interjects, opening the jar of pickles I set down and fishing one out. "Right now, what we're trying to figure out—"

"Let's wait." Ollie cuts him off from across the room, still posted by the window on the door. "Until Judith and Sanne arrive."

"I'm sorry I didn't bring something more to eat," I tell Willem and Leo. "I came straight from work."

Leo snorts, spearing another pickle. "You don't see any of us carrying cakes, do you?"

"So are the others bringing the food? Or do you take turns, or ..."

A thin dribble of vinegar trickles down Leo's chin; he catches it before it hits the table. "What, now?"

"The food. Does one person host, and bring everything, or do you take turns?" His stare is blank. He has no idea what I'm talking about. I whip my head over to Ollie by the door. His shoulders are hunched up around his ears so his strawberry hair disappears into his collar, and the infinitesimal tilt of his head tells me he's been listening to everything we've said. Leo is still waiting for me to explain my question.

"I'm sorry," I say stiffly. "I got confused. Would you excuse me? I forgot to ask Ollie something."

He doesn't turn to face me, even though he'd have to be deaf not to hear me stomp up behind him. When I'm standing so close our sleeves are touching, I whisper quietly enough that Willem and Leo won't overhear.

"Ollie. Where did you bring me?"

"What do you mean?" He raises his eyebrows.

"You know what I mean. What kind of meeting is this? Judith's not even coming, is she?" My heart has started to thud. "Who are you really watching for?"

Was I a complete fool to trust Ollie after all? I thought he was safe, but it's not like you can tell a Nazi informant just by looking. I move toward the coatrack, but before I can take my coat, Ollie nods toward the door. On the other side, two figures approach, one of them clearly Judith.

"What is this meeting?" I ask again.

"It's about to start," he says, raising his eyebrows again. "If you're going to leave, be careful on your way out. The door closes fast."

So he won't stop me if I try to leave, but if I do choose to go, I'll also be missing out on my chance to ask Judith about Mirjam. My only lead, my only clue, and a decision to make in less than a second. How much do I want to find this missing girl?

"It's us," a sharp voice whispers. "It's Judith and Sanne."

Ollie opens the door, and I don't leave through it.

Judith really is stunning, with her pale parchment skin, molasses-colored hair, and a gaze that could cut glass. Sanne, the other girl, is friendly-looking, plump, and pretty, with white-blond hair that floats with static electricity when she takes off her hat. "Sorry we're late; roads blocked," Sanne explains, lightly patting Ollie's shoulder and moving to greet Leo and Willem.

Before I have a chance to say anything to Judith, she brushes past me, too—either preoccupied or deliberately ignoring me—and takes a seat on the sofa.

"Judith," I begin, but Ollie interrupts me by clearing his throat. *Later,* he mouths to me. *After the meeting. You promised.*

He sits on the edge of the sofa, and Sanne takes one of the chairs. It's a fluid movement, one that says she's done it a million times, that in this meeting everybody knows their place.

"Hanneke?" Ollie looks up at me. I'm the only one left standing, halfway between the door and the sofa. "Hanneke, are you sitting?"

One seat remains, a squat velveteen footstool. I move toward it slowly and sit down.

"Everyone, this is Hanneke," Ollie says. He doesn't introduce me further, so they must have been expecting me. There must have been a vote, or a discussion at least, about my presence. "As I told you all before, I vouch for her."

He says this last part seriously, and with it, he puts me in a terrible position. Because I can't say now that he shouldn't vouch for me. How will Judith ever talk to me about Mirjam if I say I can't be trusted? But still... what has he just implied that I can be trusted with? What is he bringing me into?

"Now," Ollie continues, "the first order of business is to discuss the ration-card bottleneck. The Germans are getting more and more strict with—"

"Wrong," Willem interjects. "The first order of business is for us to agree what it is that we're celebrating. It's been my birthday twice already this month."

"And Leo and I have already been engaged several times," adds Sanne.

Willem turns to me and explains, "We can't tell people what we're really doing, so we always have a pretend celebration in mind, that we'll all use as our excuse if we're stopped."

"We used to say it was Bible study," Sanne says. "But once I was stopped and the soldier asked me which book we'd been reading. I told him Genesis, because it was the only one I could remember, and then we decided none of us knew the Bible well enough to have that be our cover."

"It can be my birthday," Leo says. "It really is next week, so it's plausible."

"As I was saying," Ollie breaks in again. "The ration-card bottleneck. The forged ones aren't being produced quickly enough. We're taking care of sixteen more people, just since last month. It's too time-consuming for one person to produce all those cards. We need to find another forger or come up with another solution." I don't like the way his eyes land on me when he says that last part.

"In Utrecht, they've got someone on the inside of the ration-card office," Willem says. "They arranged a fake theft. The worker reported that the office had been broken into. Really, he'd stolen them himself and passed them on to resistance groups."

The conversation moves around me while I try to keep up. Ration-card fraud. I'm a solo criminal who has walked into a den of them. But instead of using the ration cards to sell goods for profit, like I do, they pass the cards to the resistance. For what? Food and goods for resistance workers? People in hiding?

"Judith, do you think your uncle might know anybody?" Ollie asks. "With his Council connections?"

. The Jewish Council. Judith's willingness to be out at night and her boldness at the school make more sense knowing that her uncle is on the Council. As the Jewish leadership appointed to be liaisons with the Nazis, they communicate German orders and have a little more freedom than other Jews.

Judith shakes her head. "Even if he does, you know I can't ask him. He'd disembowel me if he knew I came to these meetings."

"I can see if Utrecht has any ideas," Willem says. "Maybe their contact in the ration office knows somebody in our ration office."

So these five in Amsterdam are part of a larger network, spread into the suburbs and maybe through the whole country. In spite of my fear at being here, I can't help but feel professional curiosity. Their operation must be huge. How do they find enough merchants to work with them? How good is their forger? Are the soldiers stationed in Utrecht more or less lax than the ones here in Amsterdam?

My mind only snaps back to attention when I hear the end of one of Judith's sentences: "...and then bring the cards to the Schouwburg."

"To the theater?" I interrupt, wondering what I've missed of the conversation. "Why would the cards go there?"

"You don't know about the Hollandsche Schouwburg?" It's the first time Ollie has addressed me in the meeting, and he seems disappointed.

Of course I do. I've been there with him, even if he doesn't remember it. The winter I was fifteen, the Van de Kamps invited me to go see the Christmas premiere with them at the Schouwburg, an old playhouse that Mama let me wear her pearls to visit. Their whole family went. I sat next to Ollie, actually, holding hands with Bas on the other side. Ollie had only just started university; he was wearing new spectacles, serious and important.

"It's a theater," I say. "Or was. It's closed now, isn't it?"

Ollie nods. "It was a theater. They've renamed it the Jewish Theater, and now it's a deportation center. Jews are rounded up around the city and brought to the Schouwburg, kept for several days, and then transported—to Westerbork mostly, but sometimes other transit camps."

The dignified theater with velvet curtains is now a massive holding cell for German prisoners. I have clients who live right in that neighborhood. It's disgusting, the way the Germans take our lovely things and poison them.

"I didn't know," I say.

"Where did you *think* Jewish people were sent?" Judith asks.

"To work camps, or to be resettled in another country. I'm not ignorant," I say. Work camps is what we've always been told. I just never thought about how, exactly, the Jewish prisoners would get to them.

"'Work camps'?" Judith scoffs at my description. "You make it sound as if Jews are just going to a job. You have no idea, the sadistic things we've heard about those camps."

Before I can ask her to explain more, Sanne jumps in, peacemaking. "It makes sense that you wouldn't know more," she tells me. "The Nazis try to hide everything they're doing. At the

Schouwburg, they make everyone stay inside until it's time for their transport. The Council arranges food and blankets, and that's about all they can do. Judith volunteers there a few times a week, and her cousin works in the *crèche*."

"There's a nursery?"

Judith makes a face. "Because the Nazis thought it would be too disorderly, to have the children in the theater with their parents. The toddlers and smaller children wait in the *crèche* until it's time for their families to depart."

I don't know what to say to that, and I don't have to. Ollie clears his throat again, to regain control of his meeting. "So Willem will talk to Utrecht," Ollie says. "When do you think you can talk to them, Willem?"

"Wait," I say.

"And then, after Willem and Judith consult with—" Leo begins.

"*Wait.*" Everyone stops talking then and looks at me. "The Schouwburg. Is that where everybody goes, or only the people who were asked to report?"

Leo looks confused. "What do you mean?"

"If someone wasn't actually scheduled for deportation, and they were just found on the street, but they had Jewish papers, would they be brought to the theater, or to another prison somewhere?"

Ollie's voice is neutral as he answers my question. "There are a few smaller deportation centers in other parts of the city. But for the most part, yes. There's a good chance that a Jewish person who wasn't where she was supposed to be would be brought to the Schouwburg."

I notice his use of *she*, acknowledging that I'm not merely curious about procedure in general but about one person in particular. This discussion about taking ration cards to the theater has inadvertently led back to my reason for being here tonight. "Mirjam could be there?" I ask. "Right now?"

Judith and Ollie look at each other. "Theoretically," Ollie says carefully.

"How do I find out if she is?"

"It's difficult."

"How difficult?"

Ollie sighs. "The Jewish man who was assigned to run the Schouwburg, we rely on him for a lot of things. I can't approach him with a personal favor. We have to use our resources strategically. We have to think about what actions will be best for the largest group of people, for the movement as a whole."

"But maybe if I could just get a message to her. That would be possible, wouldn't it?"

He rubs his hands over his eyes. "Can we finish the business on our agenda? And then talk about this at the end of the night?"

"Your *agenda?*"

If I were an outsider watching this conversation, I would tell myself to stop pushing, that no one wants to help someone behaving childishly. But in this moment, I can't help it. Ollie brought me here under a false pretense, and I've finally learned a piece of information that could be useful, but he's told me help is impossible without really explaining why.

The others resume talking, about the ration-card bottleneck and fake identification papers. None of this helps me with Mirjam.

She's fifteen. How would she know to find a fake ID through the resistance? How would she know how to do anything? She's probably alone and afraid, and she's been missing for forty-eight hours now. Could a fifteen-year-old girl manage to elude capture on the streets for forty-eight hours?

As the official business winds down, I glue my eyes to Judith and pull her aside the minute she's not talking to anyone else.

"Judith?"

"Yes?"

"Can I talk to you for a minute?"

"We're talking," she says stiffly, but every syllable really says, *I don't know why Ollie let you come.*

"I wanted to first apologize. For sneaking into the school like that, and for scaring you."

"You didn't scare me," she says archly. "It takes so much more than that to scare me at this point."

"Surprised you, then," I compromise. "I'm sorry I walked into the school and didn't tell you what I was really looking for."

"You could have gotten me in trouble."

"I was desperate."

"We're all desperate."

If Judith was a soldier, now is when I would lower my eyes and talk softly about how she was right and I couldn't possibly understand any of it. But Judith's not a soldier. She probably deplores sycophants. "I've apologized," I say. "And I meant it. And I can do it again if you want. But I came tonight because I wanted help, regarding a girl who was also one of the students at your school." I stare at the bridge of her nose, which is easier than staring at her eyes, willing her to speak first. I'm stubborn enough to remain silent.

"Mirjam Roodveldt," Judith says. The air between us parts. "She went to the Lyceum until a few months ago."

"You knew her. Were you lying? I mean, when you said the photos were destroyed in a fire, is that the truth?"

"I wasn't lying. The photos were destroyed in a fire. I lit it myself." She juts out her chin, as if daring me to question this act. "I didn't want the Germans to have one more list of all the students who were left. Not that it matters. They find everyone anyway."

Something clicks in my brain. When the war first started and Germans burned down buildings, we hated them for it. But recently I've heard of public records buildings burning down, and I wonder if some of them are resistance jobs meant as acts of protection.

"You did know her, though? Dark hair? Petite? She might have worn a bright blue coat?"

Judith bites her lip. "I remember when she got that coat. She tripped and caught her old one on a rusty piece of fence and ripped a big chunk out of it. Ripped a chunk out of her knee, too. I remember thinking she was going to have a scar for life. She came back a few days later with stitches and the new coat. It was raining that morning and she asked me if she could come inside before the doors opened so it wouldn't get too wet."

"What else do you remember about her?" I can barely get out the words. Somewhere in the back of my mind, I didn't expect to find anyone else who knew her. Some twisted part of me maybe believed that Mirjam Roodveldt was a specter created by Mrs. Janssen. But she is real.

"Why do you care so much about her?" Judith looks at me shrewdly. "Is she a friend?"

"No. I'm—I'm being paid to find her." It's technically the truth, and right now it seems easier than explaining everything else, about me, and Bas, about how finding Mirjam feels like a task that will put order to the world. I'm still embarrassed by how vulnerable I was in front of Judith when I met her at the school.

"Just her?" Judith looks skeptical. "You're here because you're looking for just one person?"

"Please, do you remember anything else?"

Judith sighs. "Not a lot. She was beautiful; I think she had a lot of admirers."

"Anyone she was particularly close with? Was there anyone she might have gone to, or told where she was going into hiding?"

"I'm just a secretary. I only talked to the students if they came in late and needed a pass or something else like that. I'm sorry."

"You don't know *anything* else?"

"I did bring some things for you, though I doubt they'll be of any help." She leans over to her handbag and pulls out a rectangular white envelope, unaddressed and unsealed. "Just some old school assignments from her desk. Sometimes students disappear without having a chance to clean out their books or papers. I always think, just in case some of them came back... In any case, I went through my collection, and this is what we had of Mirjam's."

She hands me the envelope, and I quickly thumb through the contents. The top three pages are all math assignments, and the next two are biology quizzes. No photographs, nothing that looks immediately useful. I try to hide my disappointment; it was kind of Judith to bring this for me, and I don't want to seem more petulant than I already did earlier in the meeting.

"Ollie says you have connections," Judith says.

"It depends on what you mean by connections."

"Ollie says you can find things. We need more vendors we can trust, and we need people who can introduce us to them."

"That's not why I came here," I say.

"I see." She's staring at me evenly. It takes work for me not to return her gaze, to instead focus on Mirjam's schoolwork in my lap. Before I can look more closely at the other papers, Ollie puts his hand on my shoulder, and I look up in relief.

"It's almost curfew. I'll walk you home; Judith and Willem and Sanne will follow in a few minutes."

Judith stands to put on her scarf.

"Thank you," I say formally. "For trying to help me."

She pauses. "My cousin might have known Mirjam better. She doesn't come to these meetings, because she's just a kid, but she helps us sometimes. She's still a pupil at the school. I could arrange a meeting with her. Possibly."

"Please," I say greedily. "Should I come to the school tomorrow morning?" I'm sure I can find an errand for Mr. Kreuk that will require me to be in that neighborhood.

"Come to the Schouwburg in the afternoon. We'll both be volunteering there. Meet me outside. You can see what we're all about."

I don't want to see what they're all about, and Judith knows that. It's why she suggested the Schouwburg to begin with. Judith might have offered to help me further, but it came with a price.

"Ready?" Ollie asks me.

I tuck Judith's envelope into the waistband of my skirt so I won't have to carry it visibly down the street.

"Be careful," Ollie calls out to Judith and Willem.

Willem calls back, "Be safe."

EIGHT

"You had no right."

"No right to what?" Ollie scans both sides of the street before pulling me to the left, closing the door behind him.

"You're in the resistance." I don't bother to phrase it as a question. Ollie walks steadily ahead, but his shoulders tense at my statement. It's a sullen, vindictive cold outside, colder than it's been in months, and my breath vaporizes as we hurry along the canal.

"We don't have to talk about this now."

"You're in the *resistance*. You said you were inviting me to a supper club."

He halts. "It *was* a supper club. It used to be. We'd talk about books and politics. I joined with Willem and Judith. When Judith had to leave school because she was Jewish, some of us decided that we couldn't have a group to just eat dinner. We had to try to fix what was going wrong."

He starts walking again and I chase after. He's so smug with his half explanations, and so cavalier about the fact that he's dragged me into this. "I can't *believe* you, Ollie." Everything I've felt in the past two days, every emotion, every fear, every bitter word I didn't say to Mrs. de Vries, every doubting thought I had about finding Mirjam Roodveldt—all of it comes spilling out now, on the street, at Ollie. "How could you do this? Why didn't you tell me that's where you were taking me?"

"Because what if someone had stopped you on the way?" he says. "I wanted you to be able to truthfully say you were on your way to see a friend. I didn't know how well you could lie."

I can lie so very well, better than he thinks. Ollie has never seen me, flirting with soldiers while vomit rises in the back of my throat, or convincing my parents that my job is all flower-ordering and consoling sad families. Ollie has never seen the way I make everyone believe that I am a whole person after Bas's death. Ollie is the one who shouldn't be able to lie. "*You*, in the resistance," I say finally. "You're such a rule-follower."

He cackles, an explosive, mirthless noise. "Don't you think rule-followers are the best people to organize against the Nazis? It's not all daring rescues and explosions. It's a lot of tedious paperwork."

"Ollie, why did you *bring* me?" I demand as he walks ahead. "I didn't ask for it. I didn't want to be involved in any of this. You could have just arranged for Judith to meet me at a café. Why are you trusting me at all? I could tell the police everything that I saw."

He whirls around and his eyes are cold. "Are you going to? Are you going to go to the police? Do you think what we're doing is wrong?"

"You know I don't think it's wrong." Not morally. But in this world, you can be right, or you can be safe, and the type of danger Ollie is dabbling in makes my own work look like nothing. It's not finite and contained, like dealing in black market goods or finding Mirjam. It's huge and sprawling, an endless hole of needs that would swallow me whole. The Nazis might imprison a black market worker. They might imprison people who hide Jews, or send them to labor camps. But resistance workers caught in the act of stealing ration cards, working to overthrow the German regime? Those workers could be shot. The lucky ones, at least. The unlucky ones would be tortured first. How many more ways can my careful world be upended?

"I just don't want to *join*," I say. "I'm an Aryan poster girl, remember, Ollie? I don't help the resistance. I find black market cheese."

"We need black market cheese! We need food for the onderduikers in hiding. We need false identification papers. We need girls who are pretty so the soldiers don't notice that they're also smart and brave and working against them."

"Judith already made me feel guilty. She made it clear how altruistic the rest of you are. I'm not."

He grabs my shoulders, a sudden movement that throws me off balance. "Did you ever think that maybe you're better than you believe you are, Hanneke?" We smell like wet wool, both of us do, and his fingers are cold even through the layers of my coat. I start to push his arms away, but he tightens his grip. "Did you ever think that maybe that's why I brought you?"

"What are you talking about, Ollie?"

"I'm talking about *that's* why. That's why I brought you. Because despite your insistence that you don't want to get involved, you know that what's happening in this country is wrong, and you're already in a position to help us."

"None of that means I'm ready to risk my *life*. I already take care of my parents, and they would starve if something happened to me. I'm already looking for a missing girl. That's how I'm resisting. I keep people fed, and I'm going to find a girl I was asked to find. Isn't that enough, for one person to save one life? What you want from me is too much. I'm not ready to do more, and it's not fair for you to ask."

Ollie's voice softens and so do his eyes, quiet and blue. "I think you *are* willing to risk your life. You've felt this is wrong for a very long time. You were fourteen and you were already talking about how evil Adolf Hitler was. Remember the dinner?"

I can't look away from him. I know what he's referring to. A dinner conversation from four years ago, at the Van de Kamps'. I was talking and talking about Hitler, while Mrs. Van de Kamp tried to distract me by passing the peas and then the rolls, and then finally she came out and told me that polite people didn't discuss politics at the table. Bas hadn't even been paying attention. Ollie was listening, though. I think he was even nodding along. But that was years ago. That was a lifetime ago. Ollie knows nothing about me now, certainly not enough to make these grand, sweeping speeches. He doesn't know that Bas is dead because of—

Ollie gives my shoulders a final shake, and then releases them, raking his fingers through his hair. "We're losing, Hanneke," he says softly. "People are disappearing faster and faster, and being sent into God only knows what hell. One of the earlier transports? The families of deported men received postcards from their sons and brothers saying they were being treated well. Then the families received notices from the Gestapo, saying the men had all died of disease. Does that make any sense to you? Healthy young men—first they send postcards saying they're fine, and then suddenly they're dead? And now nobody sends back any postcards at all."

"Do you think all the Jews are being *killed?*" I ask.

"I'm saying we don't know what to think, or what's true. All we know is that farms and attics are busting at the seams with onderduikers. The country is running out of places to hide people who desperately need to be hidden. We need help, more help, quickly, from people in strategic positions like you."

"You don't know me," I whisper. "There are things about me where if you knew them, you wouldn't—"

"Shhh." He cuts me off.

I start to protest, but he presses a finger to his lips. His whole body has gone stiff, and his ear is cocked as he listens to something. We're both frozen now that I hear it, too: German shouting, in the distance but growing closer. Muffled crying, and unorganized feet on cobblestones. These days, the sounds only mean one thing.

Ollie realizes it at the same time. "A roundup."

The sounds are getting closer. My eyes meet Ollie's, our argument immediately forgotten. He raises his wrist and frantically peels back his coat sleeve. I don't understand what he's doing, until he taps his watch and shows me the time. We spent so long arguing in the street that now we're about to miss curfew. Both of us are on foot today, and we're still a mile from my house.

We can't be found, not in the middle of a roundup, when soldiers are already dangerously engorged with power.

"*This way!*" a soldier barks. His voice echoes off the cobblestones. "*Move!*" The voice is just around the corner. The soldier and prisoners will be on our street any minute.

"We need to—" Ollie starts.

"Follow me." I reflexively grab his hand, pulling him toward a small side street. We walk quickly down that one, and then turn onto another side street, and then another. For once, I am grateful for Amsterdam's winding street plan.

Beside me, Ollie's gait is relaxed, but his upper body looks tense, and we speak to each other in gestures while ignoring the shouting I can still hear from a few blocks over. Both of our palms are sweating. I don't want to have to see the people the soldiers are taking away. It's cowardly, but I don't want to be reminded that because I have blond hair and the right last name, they're not taking me.

The street we're on now is barely more than an alley, so narrow that I could nearly touch the buildings on either side with my outstretched arms. It's safer than a main road because there's less chance of being seen; it's more dangerous than a main road because if someone does see you, there's no way to run. I'm clutching Ollie's hand so hard we'll both have bruises tomorrow.

Our surroundings are beginning to look familiar. We pass a

bookstore, closed for the night, whose owner I find coffee for sometimes, and an optometrist, and a cobbler who is willing to trade shoes for beer. I know where this street ends: near a dancing studio where Elsbeth and I were forced to take horrible waltzing lessons.

From there, it's only a short walk home. If Ollie and I needed to, we could knock on a neighbor's door, pretending to borrow an egg, and one of them would probably let us in. We're almost safe. In the distance, I can still hear the cries from the raid. I quicken my pace to put more space between myself and that fear. Suddenly Ollie squeezes my hand even harder.

Two silhouettes wait at the end of the street, with long shadows that I know are guns.

We have to keep walking. There's no alternative. There never is. I know their uniforms are green, and so we have to keep walking. We have to pass them; it would look suspicious to turn and walk in the opposite direction. I wish Ollie weren't with me. Nazis don't like it when you wink at them while with another boy. It probably reminds them of what could be happening at home.

Their guns are pointed down. They're talking with each other in German too fast for me to fully understand. One of them slaps the other on the shoulder and laughs. It doesn't even look like they've come from the raid. They were just out on their regular patrol, and it was our misfortune that we chose the same street.

I fold myself in close to Ollie's body, making sure there's more than enough space for the soldiers to pass.

"Good evening," Ollie says in German as we quietly squeeze through. I nod and smile.

We brush by, and my body begins to un-tense. We'll be at the end of this alley in just a few seconds. Next to me, Ollie is doing the same things I am: keeping a measured pace, making it look like we're in no hurry to be anywhere.

"Wait!"

We have no choice, so we stop and face them. Several meters behind us, one of the Green Police has turned around, starting in our direction. I glance briefly back to the end of the alley, but Ollie firmly tugs on my hand. *Don't try running*, he's saying. Not while they have guns.

"Wait," he calls out again, closing the gap between us. "Wait, don't I know you?" He leans in, inches from my face.

Does he? It's hard to tell in this light. Where could he know me from? Is he one of the soldiers I've flirted with? Someone Mr. Kreuk has sent me to sell to, laughing at his bad jokes until the transaction is done? Or has he seen me more recently, going into the Jewish Lyceum?

A curtain flutters in a nearby house. Inhabitants all along this street are crouched in their living rooms, silently watching us.

"I do know you," he guffaws.

"I don't think so," I murmur, keeping my voice friendly. "I'm sure I'd remember *you*."

"Yes," he says. "You're the couple. The romantic couple!"

"We are!" It's Ollie, next to me, who answers the soldier. He's responding in German, talking more loudly than I've ever heard him. His accent is still impeccable, but he's slurring his words like he, too, has been out for a night of drinking. "Rembrandt!"

"Rembrandt!" the German agrees, and now I recognize him: the one from the square last night.

Ollie slings one arm around me. "How is our good friend, the fellow art lover? My fiancée and I love Rembrandt, don't we, darling?" He looks at me pointedly, and even though my heart is beating out of my chest, I reach up to Ollie's hand and give it an affectionate squeeze.

"Our favorite," I manage.

"If you come to Germany one day, we have magnificent art."

"We will," I promise, with what I hope is a friendly smile. "After it's all over."

His eyes narrow. "After what's all over?"

After the war, is what I meant. After we all get to return to normal. I don't think what I just said is offensive, but the soldier obviously didn't like it. "After," I say again, beginning to improvise an explanation.

"After our wedding!" Ollie exclaims. "After all the wedding madness!"

Bless you, Ollie, Laurence Olivier. I'm not used to other people being as fast on their feet as I am when it comes to dealing with Nazis.

"So nice to see a couple in love." The soldier pinches my cheek with cold fingers. "It reminds me of my wife, back home, when we were young."

"To your wife!" Ollie raises an imaginary glass in the air.

"To my wife!"

Ollie winks at me meaningfully, lasciviously. "Maybe we should get home, my soon-to-be wife."

"To your wife!" the Green Police yells.

"To my wife!" says Ollie.

"Kiss her!" he says, and so Ollie does.

There, in the street, for the benefit of the German Green Police and the people who are cowering in their houses but peeking out from their curtains, Ollie cups my face in his hands and kisses me. His mouth is soft and full, his eyelashes brush against my cheek, and only he and I know that our lips are shivering in fear.

Things that have changed about me in the last two days: everything and nothing.

I'm still lying to my parents, they're still worried about me, I still ride around a changed city on a used bicycle with a stubborn tire and feelings of perpetual numbness and fear warring in the pit of my belly.

But the things that I'm lying about are much bigger, the things I'm doing much more dangerous. I'm an accidental member of the resistance, and if I am caught, instead of slapping my wrist for black market beer, the Germans could kill me.

I also kissed my dead boyfriend's brother.

The last time I saw Bas:

I did go to the sad, stupid going-away party his parents held for him, the one in which his mother spent most of the time crying and his father stood in the corner so tight-lipped and still that people kept bumping into him and then saying, "I'm sorry; I didn't see you standing there." I did give Bas a locket with my picture in it; he did give me a lock of his hair.

I did kiss him in the dining room.

But when I left, he came running after and said he had something else for me. It was a letter. It was a letter in case he died. I was supposed to open it if the navy contacted his family, and inside it would talk about how much he loved and missed all of us, and how happy we had made him.

At least that's what I imagine letters like this usually say. I wouldn't know. I never opened Bas's. When he gave me that envelope on the street, I told him the letter could only court bad luck. I told him that in order to prove how unnecessary it was, I was going to destroy it as soon as I got home.

And I did. I ripped it to pieces and threw it out with the trash.

So I'll never know what Bas's final, final words for me were. Sometimes I think they were to tell me he loved me. Sometimes I dream that I open the letter and inside it says, "I never forgave you for what you made me do."

NINE

Thursday

t's nice to see you socializing again, Hannie," Papa says. My mother is gone this afternoon, a rare excursion into the outside world to visit her sister in the country. Because of the curfew, she'll probably stay overnight, so it's just Papa and me, alone. I came home from work to make him lunch, and now he's reading in his chair while I'm sitting with Mirjam's packet of school things, biding time until one afternoon delivery, and then I will go meet Judith and her cousin at the theater. Mr. Kreuk is running a funeral later; I'm hoping that he won't notice if I don't come back to my desk.

"Socializing?" I repeat after Papa, distracted.

"Out with friends, like last night. I can't remember the last time you did that."

He's right. It's been years. There used to be a group of us. Bas the ringleader. Elsbeth the brazen. Me, part of the inner circle but not quite as audacious, not as sparkling. Happy to bask in the glow. Other friends, moving like small moons around me and Bas and Elsbeth, the two other people I loved the best. Last night, all I could think about was how strange it was to be pulled into a resistance meeting. I didn't think about how strange it was to be pulled again into a group of friends.

"Ollie's not really a friend, Papa. He's just—" I realize, belatedly, that any way I qualify the statement will only bring suspicion. "I suppose he is a friend. It's nice to have someone to talk to."

"You're young. It would be nice to have someone to more than *talk* to." He winks, and I toss a cushion at his head. "Now you abuse an invalid?"

I toss another one. "What would Mama think if she heard you encouraging me to stay out late with boys?"

"She never minded when you stayed out late with Bas. Though we always thought the two of you would—"

Papa realizes what he's about to say and breaks off in midsentence. I should say something to end the silence, but I can't find the words. Instead I stare into my lap and look at Mirjam's paper at the top of the stack. "What are you reading?" Papa asks.

"Old letters and schoolwork," I say, which is true, I just don't mention that they're not *my* old letters and schoolwork. "Should we turn on the radio?"

He nods eagerly; I knew the suggestion would distract him from more questions. Information and communication with the outside world—it's so valuable. The Nazis already turned off most of the private telephone lines. We don't have ours anymore, though people in some wealthier neighborhoods where sympathizers live still do. There's a rumor that the Germans are going to demand we hand in our radios, too. Papa and I already pulled an old, broken one from a closet to turn in instead of our nice one.

As it is, we're supposed to listen only to approved propaganda. It's illicit to tune in to the BBC, which, along with underground newspapers, is our only source of real news now that the Dutch papers have been taken over. The Dutch government in exile broadcasts through that channel sometimes; we call it Radio Orange. Mama forbids the BBC entirely, terrified of getting caught, but Papa and I don't mind it at a low volume, with all the windows closed and towels stuffed under the doors to keep sound from escaping. Papa listens to the words that the British newscasters say. My English isn't as good as his, so I muddle through and he helps me later with anything I've missed.

The radio tuned to a droning hum, I go back to Mirjam's belongings in my lap. The dates on the pages are all from the late summer or early fall, just weeks before she would have gone into hiding. Her papers all have high marks on them, and she kept a running tally of her grades compared to everyone else's. She was a good student. Much better than I ever was. In addition to the schoolwork, she's kept a few torn-out magazine pictures of fashionable dresses and grand houses.

The quiet hum of the radio has been overtaken by a rhythmic sawing sound. Papa is snoring in his chair. As I sort through the papers, another flutters out. This one is smaller than the others, and folded intricately into a star pattern. The folding is familiar—I once spent two days learning to fold my notes just this way, instead of paying attention in math. It was a popular way girls in my school passed notes; Elsbeth learned first and then taught the rest of us.

It takes me a minute to remember how to open it, but once I find the right corner to start with, the rest comes back easily. It's the only paper written in casual printing rather than the formal cursive of a school assignment, and the handwriting is tiny. It looks like the sort of note Elsbeth and I used to pass, composed in secret behind our textbooks and handed off as we passed in the hallway.

Dear Elizabeth,

I'm sitting in math, and the teacher has this loose sole on his shoe, and every time he takes a step it makes the rudest noise you ever heard. It's practically indecent, and everyone is laughing at it. I wish you were in this class. I think T noticed me today, a proper noticing, not just accidentally stepping on my foot, or handing me my pencil after I drop it next to his desk, or saying "Excuse me" when I run into him in the hallway. (Have I mentioned I've tried all these things, Elizabeth? Have I mentioned I have become so pathetic that I have resorted to standing near doors when I know he's going to walk through them? Yes, darling, it is true. I am literally throwing myself in harm's way so he will talk to me. I can't believe that when we were little, he used to come and eat toast at my house after school and now I can't even say two words to him.) But! Today was different. Today in literature class I stood up to give my presentation and I made a little joke, and 'T laughed, a genuine chuckle, and afterward he told me it was a funny joke. A funny joke! So I'm not as pathetic as I feared. (Or am I?)

I miss you, dearest duckie, and write back soon, sooner, soonest!

Love and Adoration,
Margaret

I read the letter again, and then once more, the familiar rhythms of friendship sparking out from the page.

Didn't I tell Elsbeth about the first time I made Bas laugh in a note just like this one? How many notes did I once write, full of secrets and stories and folded into a perfect star? How many did I receive? Elsbeth gave me a box for them once, for the dozens of folded star-letters. It was an old cigar box that had been pasted over with colorful papers, and then shellacked with varnish: a just-because present. I asked her if she made it herself, and she laughed. "God, no. I'm not going to get my hands dirty like that. I just saw it and thought you'd like it, silly. To put notes in." That was Elsbeth. Generous and careless, giving presents that never made you feel indebted for receiving them, because they were done so casually. "You should tell Bas that another boy gave it to you," she said. "Make him jealous."

Do I still have that box somewhere? Would I still recognize myself in those letters?

Here is the thing about my grief: It's like a very messy room in a house where the electricity has gone out. My grief over Bas is the darkness. It's the thing that's most immediately wrong in the house. It's the thing that you notice straight off. It covers everything else up. But if you could turn the lights back on, you would see there are lots of other things still wrong in the room. The dishes are dirty. There is mold in the sink. The rug is askew.

Elsbeth is my askew rug. Elsbeth is my messy room. Elsbeth is the grief I would allow myself to feel, if my emotions weren't so covered in darkness.

Because Elsbeth isn't dead. Elsbeth is living twenty minutes away, with a German soldier. She says she loves him. She probably does. I met him once. Rolf. He was handsome and tall; he had a friendly smile. He even said the right things, like how he knew all the boys wanted Elsbeth and he felt lucky to have her, how he worked for someone high up in the Gestapo and if I ever needed anything, I should let him know because a friend of Elsbeth's was a friend of his. I shook his hand and wanted to throw up.

So right now, when I'm looking at these schoolgirl notes, it's like the light in my messy room has been flicked on, just for a moment. I'm not distracted by Bas. I can see Elsbeth again.

This note is such an optimistic one, exactly like the ones we would have written long before the war, as we puzzled through who might love us and who didn't, who ignored us and who didn't.

Who are Elizabeth and Margaret? Did another student's papers somehow get mixed in with Mirjam's? The girls sound like good friends, placed in different homerooms, maybe in different grades like me and Elsbeth. I add it to the mental list of things I need to ask Mrs. Janssen and Judith's cousin. What more have I learned about Mirjam since I first drew the imaginary picture of her almost forty-eight hours ago at Mrs. Janssen's? She was popular with boys. She was a good student, a little hard on herself, competitive enough with her classmates to bother keeping track of their grades. She was spoiled, maybe? After all, her parents gave her a new blue coat when her old one ripped, and lots of families now would insist the old coat just be repaired, even if they were able to find such a nice new one. She is ... dead? She's alive?

She left a house that could not be left, where the back exit was sealed and the front door was monitored.

Mirjam. *Where did you go?*

TEN

It's lucky, for Judith and her cousin to have an uncle who could help them get a place at the Schouwburg. Jews are hardly allowed to work anywhere anymore. Positions at the theater must be prized like the jobs at the Jewish hospital. I heard that those come with a special stamp on identification cards that allows Jews to be out past curfew, to not be deported. *Lucky* has become such a relative term, when the standards to meet it involve only not being treated like a criminal in your own home city.

The theater is white, with tall columns. When I was here last, with Bas's family, a colorful banner hung from its face, advertising the holiday pantomime. Now when I bicycle up to it, the front of the theater is naked. Posted outside are two guards who halt me at the door and ask for my identification card. I don't know if telling them that I'm here to meet Judith will get her into trouble, so instead I tell one that I've brought medicine for my neighbor, who was taken in last night's roundup. I hold up my own bag as if there's something important inside.

"I'll only be a minute. My mother said you'd *never* let me in," I improvise, "because she thinks it's not in your power, and you'd have to ask your boss."

They exchange glances with each other; one of them is about to refuse me—I can see it in his body language—so I lean in conspiratorially and lower my voice. "It's just that her rash was *really* disgusting. I saw it myself." I can only hope these two particular guards subscribe to the antigerm fanaticism that the Nazis are well known for. I put my hand to my stomach, as if even thinking about the rash makes me queasy. Finally one of the soldiers stands aside. "Thank you *so* much," I tell him.

"Be quick," he says, and I do my best to look purposeful while stifling my pride over talking my way past them. I'd never used that tactic before, and I'll have to remember it.

The smell hits me first.

It's sweat and urine and excrement and some other undefinable odor. It feels like a wall, extending to either side of me and over my head, and there's no way to climb over it.

What has happened to this theater? The seats have been wrenched from the floor and they're piled in stacks. The stage has no curtains, but the ropes that used to open them still hang from their pulleys, swaying and ghostlike in the middle of the stage. It's dark, except for the emergency bulbs that glow like red eyes along the border of the theater. And people. Old women on thin straw mattresses that line the walls, which they must sleep on, because

I don't see anything else that could be used. Young women huddling next to suitcases. It's unbearably hot.

On the other side of the door, just a few feet away, the door guards are talking about nothing in particular in cool, clean air while my stomach clenches and heaves as I struggle not to vomit right here in what used to be the lobby. Is this what my neighbors have been brought into? Where Mr. Bierman was taken, and everyone else who has disappeared?

"Please."

I turn to face the older man speaking in a soft voice behind me. "Please," he says again. "We're not allowed to talk to the guards, but I saw you just come in, and—do you know, can I be sent to Westerbork? My wife and children were sent there yesterday. They say I'm supposed to be sent to Vught, but—I'll do anything, I'll give anything, if I can be sent to Westerbork instead."

Before I can answer, another hand tugs on my sleeve, a woman who has overheard the conversation.

"Can you get a letter out?" she asks. "I need to send a note to my sister. I came with our mother, and she died in the room they're using for sick people, and I just want my sister to know. Just a letter, please."

"I can't," I begin, but I feel more people pressing in, more voices asking for help; it's confusing and disorienting and everyone's faces are dark and shadowed. "I can't," I start to say again, when another arm grabs me, this one roughly, and pulls me backward.

"What are you doing in here?" a voice hisses. Someone is holding my coat; I try to wrench myself away, but the hands don't let go.

"Stop," I start to scream. Before I can finish the word, a palm clamps over my mouth. "Hel—" I try again, when the hand slips.

"Shut up, Hanneke! It's me."

Judith. It's just Judith. My brain registers the voice before my body does; my arms keep flailing, and it takes a moment before they stop. She half drags me back toward the door, flashing her identification card to the guards and depositing me outside in front of the theater. While she stands with her arms folded across her middle, I gag in the street, trying to rid my lungs of the stench inside, and my brain from the memory of all those people. A white square of cloth appears in front of me.

"Here." Judith hands me her handkerchief. "Don't vomit on the street."

Already behind her, the two guards who let me in are peering around Judith to see what's happened to the girl with the medicine. The handkerchief scratches against my lips. I wipe my mouth, forcing myself to stand. "I'm sorry."

"What's wrong?"

"I didn't expect it to be like that," I say finally.

"What did you expect it to be like? A hotel? A teahouse? Hordes of people are kept in there for days with almost no working toilets. Did you think some actors would come on the stage and do a pantomime?"

I don't bother to answer. Anything I say will make me sound naive. I *was* naive. I knew it was a deportation center, but those words were abstract until I saw what they meant. All I can think about now is the sea of faces swimming in front of me, waiting and waiting in what used to be a beautiful theater.

I can believe all the rumors Ollie told me, about what might happen to the people who are taken from that place and never returned. I can believe there are postcards written by prisoners at work camps, who think they will be fine until they are dead. I can picture Mirjam Roodveldt's girlish handwriting, being forced to compose one of those postcards.

"Hanneke?" Judith's voice has lost a little of its harshness. "Are you okay?"

"I was only going in to find you and your cousin." I cough out the words, choking on my disgust. "You told me to meet you here."

"I told you to meet us *outside* the theater." Judith jerks her head toward the ornate stone building across the street. "The theater's nursery is on the other side of the road. Can you walk now?"

My senses are still swimming as I follow her across the street into the building. I try to banish everything I've just seen from my mind; it's the only thing that will let me focus on the task at hand. My brain gobbles up the new information around me, as if each new thing it sees will help me forget an old thing in the theater.

No guards are posted in front of this building. It looks like a regular nursery. Indoors, too: When we walk into the foyer, a young girl in a white nurse's cap paces back and forth with a sobbing toddler, trying to calm him. She gives me a funny glance; I don't know if they're used to getting strangers in here, and I must still be pale and sick-looking. But she smiles in recognition when she sees Judith behind me.

"Are you working here today? I didn't think it was your shift."

"I'm just visiting Mina. My friend is, too."

Judith leads us to a room that looks like a traditional hospital nursery, bassinets filled with sleeping or fussing babies. One girl with her back to us is bent over a crib, but she stands when Judith calls her name. Mina is short and compact to Judith's willowy height, but they have the same teeth and the same brilliant eyes. "Cousin." She greets Judith with a kiss on the cheek. "I was just wondering where you were. Did you get—"

"Permission. Yes. They only ask for a name and address, for after."

"We always do. But they have to understand that names might change, and we can't promise to keep track."

Judith nods, obviously understanding this code, which I assume is related to the fake ration cards they're creating for Jewish families. She touches me on the shoulder. "I have things to do," she says. "I'll leave you with Mina and be back for you in an hour? If I can, I'll see if my uncle can look at the records, to tell you if Mirjam has been brought through."

Once she's gone, Mina smiles. "I have work, too. I have to take baby Regina out for some fresh air. If you don't mind coming with me, then I can answer questions while we walk. It would be nice to have some company. I *never* get company anymore, and I love the babies, but sometimes it would be nice to talk to people who can speak in syllables. Judith says you want to know about Mirjam?"

Mina has a way of talking so that sentences come out in a ripple, without pausing to take breaths. I have to adjust myself to get used to her bubbliness. How can she manage it, working across from the building she does?

"I knew Mirjam a little," Mina continues. "I had a few classes with her. Here, could you get me one of those for Regina?" She nods toward a pile of washed blankets and gestures for me to help her wrap one of the sleeping babies in a pink flannel.

Eventually I manage to parcel Regina into a lumpy bundle, while Mina picks up a bag, presumably filled with diapers and supplies. "Would you carry this?" she asks. The strap digs into my shoulder. Who would have thought babies require so many accessories?

"There we go." Mina tucks Regina into a baby carriage. "Nice and cozy, aren't we?" She looks up at me and rolls her eyes. "I have *three* brothers. All younger. I was changing diapers when I was still *in* diapers. Should we walk?"

Mina leads me through the back exit, which leads to a small courtyard, and then through a gate belonging to a neighboring building. "Shortcut." Mina winks, and finally we're on a cobblestoned street.

A pair of older women smile when they see the baby carriage, and Mina smiles back. "Can we peek?" one woman asks, and Mina stops so they can coo at the sleeping baby. As soon as the woman tries to reach into the carriage, though, Mina swiftly starts walking again.

"I need to keep her moving," she calls over her shoulder. "She didn't sleep at all last night; she'll wake up again unless I keep walking."

"So," she says to me after we've reached the end of the block, "tell me about yourself. How do you know Judith? Are you in university? What are you studying? Do you have a boyfriend?"

I pick through her questions and decide to start by answering the middle one. "I'm not in university. I have a job."

Her face lights up at this news. "I want to have a job! I want to be a photographer and travel all over the world. I've already taken classes."

She's so . . . I search for the right word. *Exuberant.* Earnest and exuberant, like the world is full of possibilities.

"Can we talk about—" I cut myself off while Mina stops to adjust Regina's blankets, and start talking again once we're moving. "Can we talk about Mirjam?"

"What do you already know about her?"

I hesitate. "That she was smart. Top of the class. Maybe a little competitive."

"Now, *that's* an understatement. She was *completely* preoccupied with grades. I think it was her parents, though. They gave her rewards for good grades. On her own, I didn't get the impression she would have cared."

I suppress a smile. It shifts the perspective I have of the studious missing girl, but it sounds like me—like Mama and Papa telling me that if I only applied myself, they knew I was smarter than the middling grades I brought home. Somehow, the Roodveldts actually managed to get Mirjam to perform, though, while my parents eventually gave up.

"What did she care about?" I ask.

Mina purses her lips. "Domestic things, I guess? She would actually talk about things like china patterns, or about how many children she wanted to have, or how she would dress them. Things like that."

She says this incredulously, like there's something strange

about domestic ambitions, but the description only makes me ache for Mirjam. I know what it's like, to have modest, simple wishes, and then have even those taken away from you.

"Were you friends?"

Mina pauses. "The school wasn't big, so you knew everyone in it. I invited her to my birthday last year because my parents made me invite all the girls. I can't even remember if she came. I don't think I'd say we were really friends. She was more popular than me."

"Are there pictures from your party?"

"My camera was broken then. I got a brand-new one for my birthday, but the film I asked for was special and it hadn't arrived yet. Ursie knew Mirjam better. Ursie and Zef, those were her better friends at school."

"Where can I find Ursie and Zef?"

Mina looks at me curiously. "Gone. Ursie left school right before Mirjam, and Zef right after. I saw Ursie here at the Schouwburg, before her family's transport."

Mirjam's entire class, disappeared one by one, all of them in hiding or taken through that theater. This is all completely insane, and every new piece of information only compounds the insanity. I'm trying to find a girl who vanished from a closed house. Who cannot be reported missing, because if the police found her, it would be worse for her than if they'd never gone looking at all. In which the last people to see her before she appeared at Mrs. Janssen's are all dead. And in which her friends, the only living people who might be able to guess where she might have been likely to go, are now gone themselves.

"Was there a girl in your class named Elizabeth? Or Margaret? Even not in your year, but anywhere in the school?"

Mina frowns. "No, I don't think so."

"It's just—" I shift aside the heavy bag Mina has given me, pulling the paper from my pocket. "In Mirjam's things, I found this. It's a letter to an Elizabeth from a Margaret. I'm trying to figure out who it belongs to or how it got there."

Mina leans over, scans the letter, and laughs.

"What?"

"It's Amalia," she says.

"Who is?"

"Mirjam's best friend. Mirjam knew her from her other school, before all the Jews were forced to come to the Lyceum. She was always writing her notes in class. A few times she got in trouble and had to read them out loud."

"But her name was Amalia? Not Elizabeth?"

"Mirjam said they liked to joke that they were like sisters. And royalty. To be honest—and I feel badly saying this—she was a little irritating about it."

"Margaret and Elizabeth. The English princesses." The letter makes sense now. Mirjam must have written it to Amalia in class one day, but was forced into hiding before she could send it.

"Do you know where Amalia lives? Or her last name? Do you know how I can find her?"

Mina bends over to adjust the baby's blankets again. "I don't know her last name," Mina says. "And I don't think she lives in Amsterdam anymore. She wasn't Jewish. Mirjam said Amalia's parents were going to send her out of the city."

"Where?" I ask.

Mina shrugs. "Somewhere near Den Haag? Not Scheveningen, where the prison is, but what's the littler beach?"

"Kijkduin?" I guess.

"That's right. Mirjam showed us a postcard once of Amalia's aunt's hotel—some sea-green monstrosity she owned in Kijkduin. Let me see the letter again."

She strains her neck to read the tiny writing as we bump along the sidewalk. "Hmm. *T* might be—" She breaks off, bending over to dislodge a pebble from the wheel.

"You know who T is? A boy Mirjam might have liked?"

"It might be Tobias?"

Tobias. Tobias. "Was he Mirjam's boyfriend?"

"Tobias Rosen was everyone's boyfriend, in our dreams. The handsomest boy in school. Last week he smiled at me, and I'm still half blind from the glow."

"Last week?" My ears prick up. "He's still around, then?"

"Or was until a few days ago, at least. He's been out, but I heard he was just sick. His father is a dentist; that's about all I know about him personally. He was also too popular."

"Do you think he liked Mirjam back?"

"Someone did send Mirjam flowers on her birthday. The florist brought them to the school yard before class, and Mirjam had to carry them into the building. She was the *deepest* shade of pink. The flowers didn't have a card on them, but all of us were teasing her about them except for Tobias. He was staring straight at his desk. If he comes back to school, do you want me to ask him for you?"

"Ask him if he'll meet with me. That would be even better."

"All right. Maybe I could talk to other classmates, too. It would be nice if you could come back and visit sometime. I don't have very many friends left." She peers at me through dark lashes. "Do you think you could? Oh wait!"

She stops the carriage so abruptly I nearly trip over it.

"We're here," she says. I haven't been paying attention to our route, but we've walked a good distance, and now we're near Amsterdam Centraal, the main train station.

"We're here?" I repeat. "What are we here for? I thought we were just going for a walk."

"My delivery."

Oh. *Damn.* I should have paid more attention to her conversation with Judith. Mina has brought me along to one of her own exchanges. That's why the bag she gave me is so heavy. The blankets must be covering what she's really transporting: documents, ration cards, maybe even a pile of money to pay off an inside man. I must be carrying a modest fortune in illegal papers. I force myself to stay calm.

"Well, not quite here." Mina cranes her head to the sky, orienting herself. "We're supposed to meet by the weather vane." There are two clock towers on Amsterdam Centraal. One of them is a real clock; the other looks like a clock but is really a weather vane, and the hands swing in the wind. Mina pushes the baby carriage to the vane, scanning the crowd. "There she is." She raises her hand to someone halfway across the plaza.

The woman approaching is well dressed, neat blond hair and an expensive-looking suit. Mina's contact. She reminds me a little of Mrs. de Vries. "Am I late?" she asks.

"No, no," Mina tells her. "You're right on time."

"I didn't bring anything. Was I supposed to bring something? I think someone told me—"

"You didn't need to bring anything. I was happy to help you out. Are you ready?"

The woman nods and then holds out her arms. I scan the surrounding crowd to make sure no one is watching, then unsling the bag and begin to pass it to Mina to remove whatever she needs for the lady. Mina ignores my outstretched arm, bending over the baby carriage and scooping up Regina in one practiced, fluid motion.

"Her name is Regina," Mina says. And instead of taking the bag from me, Mina kisses Regina on her forehead, whispers something I can't hear, and hands the blond woman the baby.

"Oh!" The woman pulls back the blanket, touching the tip of Regina's nose. "Such a pretty name. Do I keep it? My husband always said if we had a daughter, he wanted to name her after his mother."

Mina swallows. "You have a daughter now," she says finally. "So you'll take care of her the best way you see fit. Do you have a car waiting?"

"Around the corner."

"So you're all set."

The woman looks like she wants to ask more questions, but instead she walks back into the milling crowd. Mina watches until she disappears.

ELEVEN

That was the delivery?" I whisper. "That was the delivery you
had to make?" Mina nods, and starts to walk away, back in
the direction we've come. "Wait. That was—Mina, what just
happened?"

She stops, looking uncertain as she takes the bag from my
shoulder and sets it in the carriage. "We never do it unless we have
permission from the parents. Some of them refuse to be separated.
We only hide the ones whose families believe they'll be safer away.
I thought you knew."

That was the dialogue I overheard earlier, between Judith
and Mina. It wasn't a code, and had nothing to do with people
receiving false papers containing names different from the ones
they were born with. Mina was warning Judith that parents who

gave up their children might not be able to find them again, after the war.

"How many?" Mina is only fifteen, and her head barely reaches my shoulder. The idea that she does this regularly, in broad daylight... "How many children have you placed?"

"Just me? More than a hundred. Judith works on the inside of the Schouwburg, tracking down families and getting permission. It's easier to hide a baby than an adult, since people don't need papers until they're fourteen. We have an inside person in the theater who alters the records to make it look like the children never arrived at the *crèche*."

Baby Regina wasn't a foil, hiding the illicit delivery. Baby Regina *was* the illicit delivery.

Mina has done this more than a *hundred* times. A hundred shootable offenses, and then she gets up the next day and does it again, and still she talks about school and boyfriends and what she wants to do after the war. One time, out of that hundred, I helped her.

Mina gives me a sidelong glance. "I thought you knew," she says again. "Judith didn't tell you?"

"Judith didn't tell me."

"Are you mad?"

I don't know what I am. This delivery is just one in the long line of involvements I didn't mean to have. But that theater was so dark, and Regina was so young, and we can do so little, all of us. What am I supposed to say? That I wish we had left Regina in the nursery to be deported? What am I supposed to believe—that Mirjam alone is worth taking risks to save, just because she was the one I was asked to find? That now that I've seen what I've seen in the deportation center, I'll be able to forget it?

"I don't know what I feel," I begin. "I feel—"

"Let me see the baby!"

The voice belongs to a man, speaking in giddy Dutch with a heavy German accent.

"Good afternoon, young ladies! It's a beautiful day in a beautiful city!"

I know this soldier. Not him in particular, but this type. This is the type of soldier who tries to learn Dutch and gives children pieces of candy. Who is kind, which is the most dangerous trait of all. The kind ones recognize, somewhere deep inside their starched uniforms, that there is something perverse about what they're doing. First they try befriending us. Then the guilt creeps up on them, and they work twice as hard to convince themselves that we're scum.

"Keep walking," I mutter to Mina. He doesn't know for sure that we've seen him; he might not even be talking to us.

"*Ladies!*" he calls out again. "Let me see the baby! I just learned that my wife had our daughter! Let me see what I'm getting myself into!"

He walks excitedly toward us. He can't be allowed to see that there's no baby in the carriage. He'll ask to see our papers. He'll take us both away. Mina will lead back to baby Regina. The whole *crèche* will be investigated. I usually have to worry only about myself, but when you work in a system, you are responsible for everyone's safety.

Over to my left, Mina smoothly adjusts her scarf. It looks like she's simply tightening it against the chill, but I can see she's really shifting it so it covers the Star of David on her coat. I mentally piece together a story: The baby is sick, and the soldier mustn't get too close or he'll catch the illness. That's what I'll say. Something repugnant, something with vomit.

Beside me, Mina is, improbably, smiling. "Congratulations!" she calls in German as he approaches. She has to realize how disastrous it would be, to call attention to workers from the *crèche* pushing around empty baby carriages. But when the soldier approaches, she reaches in the carriage and begins to open the bag. What does she have in there? A gun? False papers? Why haven't I run yet?

Instead, the bag is full of—I look twice to make sure I'm not imagining things—wood. Stubby tree branches, splintery scrap boards, even pieces of wadded-up paper that look like garbage.

"Unfortunately, we don't have a baby for you to hold," Mina apologizes. "Only kindling. We didn't have enough in rations; we've just come from scavenging. But congratulations."

"Too bad." He looks genuinely disappointed.

We both watch the soldier walk away, hearing the congratulations of other passersby who overheard the exchange. I don't speak until I'm sure he's out of earshot.

"I carried that bag the entire time," I say to Mina.

"You did."

"Do you know how heavy it was?"

"I've carried it myself, a dozen times. I've been carrying around the same kindling for months. But it works. If I'm ever stopped, I just look like any other Dutch citizen, collecting firewood. It's not illegal to scavenge for wood scraps."

"Why?"

"Why do we do it? So I have an excuse to be pushing around an empty buggy with no baby in it."

"But then why bring the carriage at all?" I ask. "Why not just carry the baby to the station?"

"Because."

"Because?"

Mina's eyes flit down to the carriage and then immediately back up again, like she didn't want me to notice the movement. "It doesn't matter. Let's get back," she says.

"Mina, is something else in that carriage?" I ask.

"No. Why would you think that?"

I don't believe her. I keep thinking of how many times she stopped to adjust Regina's blanket on the walk here. How much could the blanket have moved? Is that really what she was doing?

Before she can stop me, I lean into the carriage, feeling under the firewood bag with my hands. At the front, nestled along one of the sides, I feel something hard and rectangular beneath a patch of fabric. The patch seems to be some kind of pocket, but I can't immediately figure out how to open it. I start to pull.

"Don't!" Mina begs me. Her cheerfulness has finally disappeared.

"What is it?"

"Please don't. I'll tell you everything, but if you take it out here, you could get us killed."

I stop. Get us killed? This, coming from a girl who just smuggled a Jewish baby through the occupied streets of Amsterdam? "What is 'everything'? Tell me now. What's inside the carriage? Weapons? Explosives?"

She looks miserable. "A camera."

"A *camera?*"

Mina lowers her voice. "I read about some photographers in an underground paper. They take pictures of the occupation. They document it, so when the war is over, the Germans can't lie about what they did here."

"It's a group? And you're part of it?"

Mina blushes. "No, they're all professionals. But a lot of the photographers are women. They can hide cameras in their handbags or grocery bags and take pictures without anyone realizing what they're doing. That's what gave me the idea."

"Instead of a handbag, you used a baby carriage," I say. "The lens?"

"I cut a tiny hole for the lens in the front. You can't see it unless you're really looking. Now every time I take a baby for a walk, I can take secret photos. I have the whole war on my camera, and on rolls of film."

"What kinds of secret pictures?"

"*Razzias.* Soldiers. People being herded into the theater. People being taken from their homes while their neighbors do nothing to help them.

"But I have good things, too," she continues. "Photographs of the resistance, so people will know that some of us fought back. Photographs of crawl spaces where onderduikers are hiding. And every child from the theater—I take photographs of them, to help them reunite with their families after the war."

"How many photographs do you have?" This is a whole section of the resistance that I'd never even heard of. The Nazis have forbidden us from photographing them, and even if most of us wanted to, film is hard to come by. It's one of the harder things for me to track down on the black market.

"Hundreds," Mina says. "Camera film is all I've wanted for every birthday since I was eight. I had a lot saved up."

"What does Judith think of what you're doing?"

Mina's face darkens. "She doesn't know. And don't tell her, please. She and Ollie and everyone, they wouldn't understand. Because it's taking risks without actively saving as many lives as possible. But I still think it's important. Even if it doesn't make sense. It just feels like it's the way I'm supposed to be helping."

I don't respond. I understand something being important to you even when it doesn't fully make sense, even when others would think you were crazy. That's been every moment for me since I agreed to help Mrs. Janssen. Even though I understand what she's feeling, is a collection of photographs the same as what I'm doing? Those photographs would threaten everyone's safety. "I'll think about it," I say finally. "I won't tell her yet."

I wouldn't even know what to say. I watched a whole afternoon unfold under my nose, and I misread everything that was happening, from start to finish. All the clues were in front of me, but I still didn't see them.

Judith is waiting for us back at the *crèche*.

"Did everything go all right?"

"It was fine," Mina assures her. "The host family are good people."

"Good enough, at least." Judith sighs. She rolls her head and rubs the back of her neck with one hand. She must be exhausted, working at the school from the early morning and then coming here when she's finished. She looks at me.

"I have news for you." She waits until Mina has gone back in the nursery and checks to make sure the other attendants are not within hearing distance. "I talked to my contact. He went through the records for the past three days. According to the files, nobody named Mirjam Roodveldt has passed through the theater."

"Is your contact sure?"

She grimaces. "Nazis insist on excellent records. Everybody who comes through has papers."

"Thank you. Thank you for checking."

"You don't have to thank me. And, Hanneke, I said she hadn't come through *yet*. But it's only a matter of time."

TWELVE

When I get home, Ollie is waiting on the doorstep of my building. We haven't spoken since last night, the night with the drunk soldiers. This is what I'm going to call it in my mind. "The night with the drunk soldiers" is a much easier way to remember it than as "the night with the desperate kiss."

After the kiss, the soldier laughed, clapping both of us on the back in congratulations before moving along with his friend. Ollie and I remained trembling in place, watching their backs until they turned out of the alley. Then both of us, following the same, silent cue, started walking again, more cautiously this time, in case something else came around the corner.

We didn't discuss any of it. It's just something that happened, like things happen now, like things will probably happen again. When we reached the front stoop, the black curtains above us fluttered, meaning my parents were watching out our window, waiting to see if I got home.

Now Ollie rises from my steps to greet me. "I brought back your mother's bicycle," he says. She'd lent it to him last night so he could make it back to his apartment as quickly as possible; he swore he knew a route that soldiers didn't often patrol. "And I saw Judith while you were out with Mina. I didn't know they were going to take you along. I wish they hadn't. It's too soon, to involve you in a drop-off without your consent."

I raise my eyebrows. "I forgot. You're the only one who's allowed to involve me in resistance activities without my consent?"

Pink spreads from his cheeks to his ears. "I've been thinking about that. How maybe I should have warned you. I'm sorry."

I'm sorry. That was one thing Bas was never very good at. It wasn't even that he hated to apologize. It was more that he hated to stop fighting. There was nothing he loved more than a debate, dragging me into silly arguments, pushing me to passionately defend positions I didn't really care about.

"What did you think about all of it?" he asks.

"I'm still thinking about all of it." For a minute I consider telling him more, but I don't think I have the words yet, for everything going through my brain.

"I see," Ollie says.

"Judith and Mina are very brave."

"You could be brave, too. Just think about it. Come to our next meeting."

I look away. "Did you only come by to return the bicycle, or did you want to come inside?"

He folds his arms in front of his chest and shifts his feet. I wonder if he feels as embarrassed about what happened last night as I do. "All right," he agrees, surprising me. "I won't stay long, though. It's my turn to make dinner; I can't leave Willem hungry."

Upstairs he leaves his coat on until I gesture for him to take it off and hang it in the coat closet. He's wearing his architect's uniform of rolled-up shirtsleeves, smudged around the cuffs. My father has left a note on the table telling me that some neighbors took pity on him with Mama out of town, and invited him for dinner. I wish I'd known the house was empty before I asked Ollie up.

"Tea?" I quickly add, "It's not real."

"No, thank you."

I was already heading to the kitchen when he declined, and now I pause, unsure, in the middle of the room. If he's refusing tea, then what are we supposed to make forced conversation over?

Ollie paces around the apartment, looking at my father's books, craning closer to see the titles but not removing any of them from the shelves. "I used to have this one." He points to a collection of essays, mine, out of place among Papa's foreign dictionaries. "I don't know where my copy went."

"I think that probably *is* your copy. Bas gave it to me."

"Probably to impress you. I don't think he read it himself."

"I heard the German army isn't doing well in Stalingrad," I say, quietly so the neighbors won't hear, my contribution to this awkward dialogue. "On the BBC."

"You speak English?"

"Some. Papa's teaching me."

And then we've run out of conversation again, and it's so strange the way an ill-timed kiss can make someone feel like a stranger. "Ollie. About last night." He doesn't say anything, and so I keep talking, as if I think he doesn't remember when we kissed for the amusement of drunken soldiers in the street. "With the soldiers. What we did. When we..."

"When we were lucky," he fills in quickly. "Lucky to think so quickly on our feet."

"You did a good job with the soldiers. You hide from them better than I do."

He shrugs. "It's a skill with practical applications."

"Do you get tired of the acting and pretending?" I ask.

"Not if it keeps me alive."

I'm relieved by the matter-of-fact way he dismisses the incident, but also annoyed. It makes me feel like I'm a girl who made too much of a kiss that meant nothing.

"Did Mina help you with Mirjam?" Ollie asks, changing the subject like a gentleman.

"I need to find a boy named Tobias. His father is a dentist. I'm going to start visiting practices tomorrow." Ollie nods but doesn't say anything. "I feel like I'm racing against an alarm clock, but I don't even know when it's set for," I confess. "For everything I figure out, there's another problem to solve. I feel like I'm running out of time."

"We all are," Ollie says. "For us, for our little group, for the whole resistance—this war is a race against how many people we can save, and whether we can do it faster than the Nazis can take them."

"If Mirjam ends up in the Hollandsche Schouwburg, she'll never get out. I just know it. It smells like—" I start to say *uitwerpselen*, but realize that *excrement* is not a strong-enough word.

"Like what?"

"Never mind."

Ollie pauses in front of a family photograph tucked on one of the shelves: the three of us on vacation in the country, Mama and I on either side of Papa, each with a hand on his shoulder. You can't see from the photograph how red my nose got that day from the sun, but I remember it. It burned, and the skin peeled for days afterward. "That dress looks so familiar," he says, pointing to the photograph. "Why would I remember that dress?"

The dress is gingham with buttons at the collar. I look at it and feel my face turn red. I know exactly why he remembers it. "I don't know," I lie. He picks up the photograph to look more closely, and when he does, the little wrinkle on his forehead is so familiar it takes my breath away. "You look like him," I blurt out. "You look like Bas."

He winces, almost imperceptibly, before answering. "Not really."

"In this light you do," I insist. "In the light of my apartment you look like him."

"Maybe your family should trade apartments with mine. My parents would probably pay a lot of money for that light." His voice is somewhat bitter, but mostly sad. "They just miss him so much. We all do. That was why—" He breaks off.

"Why what?"

He sighs. "When I came here the first night, I was hoping I

could get you to join the resistance. And I was making sure you weren't working for the NSB, putting Judith in danger. But I was also just worried about you. When Judith told me what you said about Bas, I just felt so sorry for you. I thought you might be really ... damaged."

"Damaged," I repeat, and it doesn't hurt to hear him say that. It's almost a relief, to have someone else speculate over the things I think privately.

"But it's normal to miss him," Ollie says. "Pia and I talk about him all the time. Him and his obnoxious jokes, his laugh, what he would have become."

The apartment seems very still all of a sudden; I lean forward to hear every word coming out of Ollie's mouth. "What would he become?" I whisper.

"An attorney. And then a politician. City-level. He'd only want to hold offices where he could meet all his constituents. He'd sponsor socials and dances. He'd love his family." Ollie's eyes are wet, and he's looking at me. My throat is tight. It would be so easy for us to grieve together.

"The dress is from that day," I whisper. "That's why you remember it. I was wearing it that day."

That day. I don't need to say any more than that. Ollie puts his hand to his stomach, like I've punched him there. The dress is from the day we found out about Bas. Pia came to tell me. I ran to the Van de Kamps' home, and Mrs. Van de Kamp slapped me, hard, across the face, and Ollie stood there in the middle of their sitting room like if he moved the world would collapse. I went home, and tears poured down my face for hours and hours while Mama stroked my back, until they finally stopped coming because I was all dried up inside, and that was the last time that I cried.

"Oh," Ollie says. "I didn't remember."

"I'm going to make tea," I say. "You don't have to have any if you don't want."

Ollie follows me into the kitchen. He stands behind me—I can feel his eyes follow my movements. My hands are shaking when I reach for the kettle, and he steadies it for me, helping me place it on the burner.

"The Hollandsche Schouwburg," he says finally.

"What about it?"

"It smells like death." Ollie finishes the sentence I started earlier but couldn't complete. "That's what it smells like in there. Death and fear."

Fear. That's right. That was the odor I couldn't place before. That's the smell of my beautiful, breaking country.

I've been leaving something out, shielding myself. Before, all those times, when I remembered the tissue with my tears on it after Bas told me he was joining the military.

I don't like to remember that they were tears of pride.

The Netherlands tried to remain neutral. We wanted to be like Sweden, allowed to be left alone. Hitler said he

would. Up until the day he invaded our country, he said
he would leave us alone.

I was the one who said that joining the military would
be a symbolic stand, anyway, against the Nazis.

I was the one, all along, who had been saying how the
Germans shouldn't be allowed to just do whatever they
wanted, to conquer country after country.

I was the one who accompanied Bas to the navy office,
and watched while he enlisted. The officer there kept asking if he was sure. The draft didn't begin until men were
eighteen, the officer said. In the army, they didn't even
accept volunteers younger than that. Why didn't Bas go
home, the officer suggested, and wait a year in case he
changed his mind.

I was the one who told the officer that Bas had come
to the navy so he didn't have to wait in order to be brave. I
talked that officer into signing him up.

Bas wouldn't have joined if he didn't think it would
make me happy.

And it did make me happy. Until it made me sad.

I thought I knew so much then. I thought the world
was so black-and-white. Hitler was bad, and so we should
stand up to him. The Nazis were immoral, and so they
would eventually lose. If I had truly paid attention, I
might have realized that our tiny country had absolutely
no hope of defending itself, not when bigger countries
like Poland had already fallen. I should have guessed that
when Hitler told our country in a radio address that he

had no plans to invade and we had nothing to fear that it meant his soldiers were already packing their parachutes and we had everything to fear. Joining the military wasn't a symbolic statement. It was a fool's errand.

So that's why I hadn't talked to Ollie in more than two years. That's why I dream of Bas coming to me, angry that I never read his letter. That's how I learned that being brave is sometimes the most dangerous thing to be, that it's a trait to be used sparingly. That's why, if I'm being honest with myself, I've become obsessed with finding Mirjam. Because it seems like a fair and right exchange: saving one life after destroying another.

I'm to blame for Bas's death. Bas was stupid to love me. I only got him killed. It was my fault.

THIRTEEN

Fifty-two hours. I learned of Mirjam Roodveldt's disappearance fifty-two hours ago. Two sleepless nights. Three encounters with German soldiers. One rescued baby. One still-missing girl. I haven't seen Mrs. Janssen since I first agreed to help, so I bicycle to her house as soon as Ollie leaves, in the twilight before curfew, to tell her everything that has happened. She installs me at the kitchen table immediately, producing more real coffee and a plate of small croissants. When I bite into one, my mouth fills with almond paste. Banketstaaf, my favorite. Mrs. Janssen remembered from last time and had them waiting.

"I thought of a few more things also," she says after I sketch out what I've learned so far. "About Mirjam. I'm sure they're not helpful; they're just things I keep thinking about." She produces a piece of paper, squinting. "Number one: You said it would be dangerous to go to the neighbors, but Mirjam once mentioned a nice mainte-nance man in her building. Maybe you could talk to him? Number two: She liked the cinema a lot. She knew all the stars. Are there movie houses open still? You could try seeing if anyone had seen her there. Number three: She was a quiet girl, Hanneke. She didn't like talking about her family; it made her too sad. She wasn't afraid to ask about my family, though. Even Jan. Some people are afraid to ask about him, but Mirjam asked me lots of questions. I would come in to bring her a cup of tea, and we would talk and talk until it was late. And she was polite. She hated beets, but she never com-plained about eating them, not once. She never complained at all."

Mrs. Janssen looks up at me. "Should I go on?"

"No. No, that was very helpful."

So much happened today: the hidden camera, and Ollie, and the horrible red glow of the barren stage at the theater. I almost haven't had time to work through how it all made me feel. And when I do think about it now, I feel ashamed.

Because when I first told Mrs. Janssen that I would find Mir-jam, I had been viewing her as a discrete puzzle that I could try to solve. A way that I could put order back in my corner of the world. A way that I could take revenge on the Nazi system—a missing girl, like a missing pack of cigarettes. A way of finding the person I used to be. But in that horrible theater, and now in Mrs. Janssen's kitchen listening to her talk about Mirjam uncomplainingly eating beets, I am finally thinking of her as what I know she has been all along: a life, a scared girl, one of many.

"Should I burn this paper now?" Mrs. Janssen asks, holding up the notes she just read from.

I hesitate and then nod. "Yes, probably."

"All right."

She searches for the matches near the stove but doesn't seem to see them, even though they're less than a foot from her hand.

"Mrs. Janssen, where are your glasses?"

Her fingers fly up to her nose, where two deep marks are still indented on the bridge. "Oh. I dropped them. Behind the armoire."

"When?"

"The morning after you left."

"That was a couple of days ago."

"I know where everything is in this house, for the most part."

I feel nauseated with this thought of her, bumping around the house with her cane, half blind, ordering almond pastries on the chance that I'll come over to eat them, wishing that she still had someone to ask about her son. She's so alone now.

I brush the crumbs off my fingers. "Take me to the armoire. I'll get your glasses."

She leads me through the house to her bedroom, talking. "I'm just getting used to living alone. The boys or Hendrik would have helped me with my glasses. And then Mirjam, she would have. There's just always been someone around to help me. You know, I used to be a career girl, like you. Forty years ago, when almost no women worked, I met Hendrik because he hired me to be his shop assistant. I thought I was so independent, but then my life became about caring for other people, and now I don't want to be alone. I never would have thought."

Mrs. Janssen's armoire looks clunky and heavy, made of oak.

I won't be able to move it on my own. Underneath, I can see Mrs. Janssen's glasses, but the space is too slim for my arm to squeeze through.

"I was going to ask Christoffel, the next time he came," she offers. "It should be tomorrow."

"We don't need Christoffel. Do you have a long rod?" I ask. "Something very thin, maybe for closing the drapes?"

After several minutes of us both searching for something, Mrs. Janssen finally disappears into her back garden and returns with a flat wooden stake, slightly dirty at the bottom, and a seed packet affixed to the top depicting beets. "Will this work?"

I use the rod to push Mrs. Janssen's glasses out the other side. She thanks me profusely while dusting them off, and then adjusts them across her nose, and a minute later we're sitting back at the table.

"It could be that all this means nothing," I tell her, "but I do have a few names. People who might have known Mirjam well. It's all far-fetched, but did Mirjam ever talk about her friend Amalia?"

She purses her lips. "I don't think so."

"Ursie? Zef?"

"Ursie, maybe? But I could be confusing her with my seamstress. Her name is Ursie, too."

I've saved the most promising for last. "Tobias? He might have been her boyfriend?"

"She did talk about a boy she liked, but I don't remember.... Let me think."

It seems strange, to think of Mirjam talking about a boy while she was in hiding, mourning her family and fearing for her life.

But I suppose love doesn't stop, even in wars. There's only so much time a day that you can spend being terrified of something before your instinct to feel natural human emotions would kick in.

"Oh!" A light has gone on in Mrs. Janssen's eyes. She reaches for her cane, scooting her chair back from the table. "I've just remembered something."

"What? What is it?"

She stands and goes to the pantry. I hear rustling and the sounds of jars clanking, and when she returns, she's carrying several jars of food.

"I'm not hungry," I say, confused, but Mrs. Janssen shakes her head; she's brought the jars over for a different reason.

"The day before Mirjam disappeared, I asked her if she would help me by wiping down the dusty jars in the pantry," Mrs. Janssen explains. "I had to let go the woman who used to clean for me because I worried she'd hear Mirjam. Anyway, Mirjam had gotten most of the way done when my neighbor stopped by, so Mirjam stopped dusting and went to hide. This is what the ones she finished look like." Mrs. Janssen pushes forward a jar that is wiped down and smooth. "Now look at these."

At first, they appear the same as the ones Mirjam finished dusting. But when the light in the room shifts, something looks different. Someone has drawn a design in the dust, with an index finger probably—it reminds me of the designs I used to make on the windows before I cleaned them.

Mrs. Janssen rotates two of the jars, so I can see them right side up. The dust drawing on the first jar is an M. The second one is a T.

"I noticed them yesterday and thought they were just doodles," Mrs. Janssen says. "But they're not. They're *M* and *T*."

"Mirjam and Tobias," I say.

"Do you think it means something?"

Do I think it means something? Something like Mirjam running away from a safe place to try to find a boy she liked? Something like Mirjam risking her life for a relationship whose only evidence so far is a cryptic note, a dusty trail on jar lids, and some flowers Mina says Mirjam once received at school? It would seem crazy to rational people. But isn't this something like I would have done? Even if I hadn't seen Bas in months, wouldn't I still be thinking of him every day, mentally tracing his name on everything I saw? Isn't that what I'm doing now still?

Isn't love the opposite of rational?

Mrs. Janssen polishes her eyeglasses again while she waits for me to answer, rubbing off dust particles they picked up on the floor, murmuring something about the garden stake.

"Hmm?" I ask her absentmindedly.

"I was thinking I should keep the garden stake nearby in the house. The one you used to get my glasses? It could be useful for when I need to reach in small spaces."

I sit up, a lightning bolt down my spine.

"What did you say?"

"I'm sorry. You were trying to concentrate."

"No, no. You're helping," I tell her. "This stake was in your back garden?"

"Yes. I have a little plot of vegetables. Not now, obviously; it's winter. But in the summer. Why?"

"I need to see the back door again."

"*Why?*"

I brush past her, down the dim, narrow hallway to the back door. It's just as I remembered from last time: When it's not latched properly, there's a large, gaping crack of air, and the door blows open. The latch is heavy and black and looks to be made of iron. What I'm thinking could work—I'm sure of it. Theoretically, at least. Experimentally, I lift the latch up and let go. It falls back down, missing the eye and failing to lock. The same thing happens the next time. This is why she thought it would be impossible to lock the door behind you. The latch wouldn't naturally fall into place.

Mrs. Janssen is getting impatient behind me. "I don't understand," she says finally.

"Shhh." I lift the lock again.

I'm about to decide I must have been wrong. Then, on the fourth try of letting go, the latch naturally closes with a satisfying click.

I whirl around to see if Mrs. Janssen noticed. "See? Did you see that?"

"But it doesn't matter if you get it to close on its own," she protests. "You're standing right in front of it. Mirjam couldn't do that from the other side of a locked door."

"Hand me the garden stake. I'm going outside for a minute." Mrs. Janssen's vegetable plot is just a small square of frozen dirt. In the dead of winter, nothing is growing, but stakes with seed packets affixed to them stick out of the ground, labeling herbs and vegetables. There's a small hole missing where the beet stake should go. "Mrs. Janssen?" I call through the closed door. "Watch out, all right? I'm going to poke this through the door."

Jabbing upward, I use the vegetable stake to poke around until I feel it—the iron latch inside the door—and I try to use the stake to swing the latch up into place. The first time, it swings back down with a thud. But on the fifth try, I manage to swing the latch up at exactly the right angle, so that when it comes down again, it clicks into place with a heavy noise.

I've locked an unlockable door from the outside.

Mrs. Janssen opens the door, staring at me as I stand in her back garden with her dirty garden stake, the one I've just used to do what she thought was impossible. "How did you think to do that?"

"Girls in love will do desperate and creative things."

Today has been a very long day, but I have solved two things. First, I have learned the identity of the T in Mirjam's letter. Second: I still don't know where Mirjam is, but at least I know she didn't walk through walls to get there.

FOURTEEN

Friday

Tobias still hasn't been in school. That's what Mina tells me, when I visit her at the *crèche* the next afternoon.

"Sick?" I ask. "Or gone? Does anyone know?"

She doesn't know anything, just that he hasn't been in school, which could mean he has a cough, or it could mean he's gone into hiding, or it could mean he's dead. *It could mean Mirjam is already dead, too.* After yesterday afternoon at Mrs. Janssen's, I was feeling so optimistic. But now I've spent the morning visiting dentist after dentist, looking for Tobias or his father with no luck. How long do I keep looking for Mirjam? She's been gone for four days. As more time passes, any trail leading to her will only run colder. At what point does it grow so cold that I accept that Mirjam has either been killed or slipped so deep into the cracks of the underground that we will never see her again? Not yet. I'm not to that

144

point yet. But when? Will I be able to tell that I'm there? Will I be able to walk away?

She's not dead, I tell myself.

After I've been at the *crèche* only a few minutes, Judith calls to discuss business with Mina.

"I've saved up two pounds of ersatz coffee," Mina tells her on the telephone. "I was thinking of having a little party, if you know of any friends who are free this evening."

"Everyone I know is in the mood for tea these days," I hear Judith say on the other end of the line. "Nobody wants coffee."

Mina explained the telephone code to me already. *Tea* is light-complexioned children, who look more ethnically Dutch, and *coffee* is those with darker features. Families want blond toddlers, whose presence can easily be explained away.

I should go, I mouth finally. *I have time to visit one more dentist.*

Mina cups her hand over the phone receiver. "Judith is telling me there's a gathering at Leo's tonight. She wants me to invite you."

"I'll think about it," I say. And I will. I have been. I know they need my help, but I need to find Mirjam first.

"I wish *I* could go. I would if I were older," Mina says.

"Maybe."

"She says maybe," Mina tells Judith. "I know, I know, but that's all she'll say." I can imagine what Judith is thinking on the other end of the line: that she and Mina are Jewish, with Jewish names and Stars of David sewn onto their clothes, and they still risk their lives every day. I am blond-haired and green-eyed with pristine papers, and I still haven't agreed to help them. She'll think that, and it's true, because everyone is running out of time. I'm just not ready yet. Not quite.

Mina hangs up the receiver and looks slightly embarrassed. "Judith implied that if you don't go tonight, she's not going to use her contacts in the theater to ask about Mirjam again. She says the group has too much important work to spend time helping people who don't offer anything in return."

"I'll go."

———

Earlier this morning I told Mr. Kreuk I needed to miss work to go to the dentist. And then I went to six of them. One after the other, pretending to have an aching tooth, asking at each one for Dr. Rosen. I started with the two nearest the Jewish neighborhoods, then spiraled farther out. This afternoon I'd already arranged to meet with a prospective contact, a baker in North Amsterdam, so I cross the river by ferry and, after meeting the baker, go to a dental office in a tidy residential neighborhood. Inside, the receptionist is already wearing her coat. "The doctor was about to leave," she says. "It's nearly five."

"My tooth really hurts. Doesn't Dr. Rosen have just a few minutes?" I wait for her to tell me that there is no Dr. Rosen, which is what has happened at every office so far.

She sighs. "Dr. Rosen is out sick. You would have to see his partner instead, Dr. Zimmer."

"His—what?"

"Dr. Rosen is sick. But I'll get Dr. Zimmer for you. If you're sure it's an emergency?"

As soon as she disappears from view, I slink behind her desk. A large appointment book lies open on top. Off to one side, a wire mail holder, filled with bills. I flip through them quickly, hoping to find one with Dr. Rosen's home address, as I listen with one ear to the receptionist in the next room. No home addresses. Everything is addressed to the clinic. My eyes move up to the walls behind the desk, scanning diplomas and certificates. One corner has photographs: a dark-haired couple, who I assume are the Rosens, standing with—I step closer to make sure I'm seeing correctly. The boy with the round face who winked at me at the Lyceum. The cheeky, nervy boy who reminded me of Bas. *Tobias.*

"What are you doing?" The receptionist glares at me from the doorway.

"Do you have a spare handkerchief? I'm a receptionist, too. Sometimes I keep them in my desk."

She frowns and plucks me one from her pocket. "Dr. Zimmer can't see you today. He has a personal engagement after work. He told me to make you an appointment for tomorrow afternoon. He doesn't usually do Saturday appointments, but you can come in at one."

"What about—" I'm inventing as I go. "Maybe Dr. Rosen could see me at his house. Do you have the address?"

I've gone too far; she looks really suspicious now. I put my hand to my heart. "Goodness, I don't know what came over me, asking for Dr. Rosen's home address. I guess people will do any-thing when they have a sore tooth. Tomorrow, one o'clock."

A ferry is just arriving as I bicycle up to the port. The dis-embarking passengers are mostly businessmen coming home from work, but also young couples and mothers with small children. A crowd of young people waits near me to board the ferry, joking and jostling each other about school and movies and some farmer they must have passed on their outing. Maybe I should have stayed at Dr. Rosen's office. Maybe I should have been honest with Dr. Zimmer's secretary, or pretended to be concerned about the ailing Rosen family and asked where I could deliver a pot of soup.

Wait. I recognize one of the voices from the crowd of young people. I scan the group until I pick out the familiar blond head. It's Mrs. Janssen's errand boy, the one who sold her opklapbed on the day she asked me to find Mirjam.

"Christoffel!"

He turns and his face flushes red when he recognizes me. "Hanneke, right?"

The students surrounding him, the boys especially, have gone silent, jabbing one another with their elbows as they try to figure out who I am and how Christoffel knows me.

"Right. From Mrs. Janssen's," I say, trying to ignore the gawk-ing crowd.

"*Mr. Tof*—Mr. Cool—aren't you going to introduce me to your friend?" a wiry, donkey-nosed boy shouts from behind him.

Christoffel flushes at the nickname. He is a handsome boy who doesn't quite realize it yet. I bet the girls have started to. He seems young for his age, but in a year or two he'll grow out of his awkwardness and have willing girlfriends lining up around the corner. "I'm seeing Mrs. Janssen later tonight," he says. "My father had a little present for her from Den Haag—he goes back and forth for work—so I said I'd take it to her."

Den Haag, back and forth on the train? That's impressive. It must be an important job. Finding a ticket is difficult for most people now that the trains have been taken over by the German army for their own transportation. Dutch men mostly avoid them because soldiers prowl our public transportation looking for workers to send to their war-effort factories. So either Christoffel's father is a powerful businessman, or he's a member of the Red Cross, which has an office in Den Haag. Or he is a member of the NSB.

"Are you here on a school outing today?" I ask. "Did you have fun?"

"It was fine. I don't know. I don't really like big group outings. I don't really even like bicycling, but I don't know if I'm allowed to say that."

"Not and stay Dutch, you can't."

"What about you?" Christoffel asks. "What were you doing in North Amsterdam?"

"Nothing. The dentist."

"I hope it went all right. I used to cry and cry when I had to go to the dentist."

"It's scary for little kids," I say.

"Little kids? That was last year." His blush deepens even more when I laugh at his joke, and he smiles for having thought of it. Sweet, fumbling kid. "Well. I should go back to the group," he says finally. "They're already teasing me because I can't stay out with them tonight. Papa leaves early to go back to Den Haag for work tomorrow."

"It was nice to see you," I say.

He turns to walk away, but something else about his last statement paws at my brain. His second mention of Den Haag. Why was I just thinking of that city? Something to do with Mirjam. Something Mina knew.

"Wait, Christoffel. I have a favor to ask," I say. He turns back. "Do you think your father could make a small side trip? To a hotel in Kijkduin? I need to get a letter to someone there, and in the mail it would take forever. But if your father is already going there..."

"What kind of letter?" he asks.

I'm already taking out a pencil, using my knees as a table as I scrawl out a note. It will be harder for him to refuse if I hand him something already finished. "Nothing special," I say. "It's just that the postal system is so unreliable these days, and I'm trying to track down an old friend through a mutual acquaintance. I want to make sure it actually gets there."

Whatever I write now must be beyond reproach. Unlike Ollie, who I've known for years, I know virtually nothing about Christoffel. Whether his father is or isn't NSB, Christoffel could be a sympathizer. He's only sixteen, but I've seen members of the Nationale Jeugdstorm, the Dutch version of the Hitler Youth, far younger than Christoffel marching around public squares, performing drills.

Dear Amalia,

We've never met, but I understand that we have a pair of mutual acquaintances—Mirjam and Tobias. I wonder if you may have heard from them recently. I live in Amsterdam now and was hoping to introduce them to some other friends who are visiting. Please respond as soon as possible; I only have a short amount of time.

I add my name to the bottom of the message and mention that any response can be returned via the same man who delivered the letter. Then I read over the short note again, weighing whether to put in any more details. My pencil hovers just over the page. Finally, I decide to add just one more line.

I am a friend.

Behind Christoffel, the other students call for him to hurry up. I start to fold the paper in thirds, the way I would a normal letter, but instead decide to crease the paper into the complicated star pattern that Mirjam's letter to Amalia was folded into. I do it so Amalia will believe that I can be trusted, that I'm a girl just like her. I also do it because Christoffel won't dare unfold this letter to read it—he'd never be able to refold it into this shape. Across the face I write, in block letters, *AMALIA. C/O PROPRIETOR. GREEN HOTEL, KIJKDUIN.* I hope there's not more than one green hotel.

"Thank you," I say. The ferry has almost crossed the river. Passengers are beginning to line up their bicycles to get off quickly.

"Christoffel! Let's go! Come on, Mr. Cool!"

He blushes again at the nickname, which must be a private joke of some kind. I don't wait for him to leave before elbowing my own way to the front of the line for disembarkation. I don't want him to think he still has the option to give me back the paper, or that he has any other choice but to do me this favor.

FIFTEEN

Everyone but Judith has arrived at Leo's when I get there. I sit down on the stool I sat on last time, next to Sanne, who is obviously delighted that I've shown up and who promptly tells me to close my eyes and hold out my hands. When I do, she gives me a tiny glass filled with juniper-scented liquid.

"Jenever?" I can't remember the last time I had good alcohol.

"I got a little bottle for my birthday five months ago and hid it. So well, apparently, that I couldn't find it until this morning. Everyone gets two thimbles." I tip my head back to down the gin in one swallow. It burns and makes my eyes water.

"You're here." Ollie has come over to squat beside me. His eyes look tired but surprised and happy to see me.

"Judith told Mina I had to come."

"I'm glad." He reaches over and brushes his knuckles quickly over my cheek, an affectionate gesture, a gesture that comes from the Van de Kamp family. Mr. Van de Kamp used to do it to the children. Bas used to do it to me. It sends heat through my skin, and I immediately push the gesture from my mind.

When Judith doesn't show up at the appointed time, Willem jokes that she has forfeited the right to one of her thimbles, and he should get to drink it instead. When she hasn't shown up ten minutes later, Leo says that he wants Judith's other one.

But when she hasn't shown up ten minutes after that, the joking has stopped and we all eye one another silently. "Probably she's held up at the school or theater," Willem says. "Or there were more road closures."

"I bet she's coming down the street right now," Sanne says, forcing a wide, unnatural smile as she goes to the window to check. "She's always mad at me for making her late when we go places. This time I'll get to show her that it's not always my fault. Sometimes she's late on her own!" She stares outside for a few hopeful minutes before returning to her seat. The clock gets louder and the silence gets heavier.

We hear footsteps outside the door, and all of us relax, but as soon as they approach, they disappear. Just a passerby hurrying home.

It's Ollie who speaks next, in a pinched voice he struggles to keep neutral. "Does anyone here know where Judith's uncle lives? I wonder if it might be time for us to—"

Before he can finish, the door bangs open and Judith tumbles in, carrying a valise and brushing new-fallen snow off her coat. My chest lets out a breath I didn't know I was holding, and Sanne squeals in relief, jumping up to first embrace, then shake Judith. "We were *worried*," Sanne chastises.

"I'm sorry." Judith returns Sanne's hug, but her smile looks forced.

"Oh, you're all *sweaty*," Sanne says. The drops running down Judith's face—I'd assumed they were melted snow, but they're perspiration.

"I ran to get here. I knew I was late." She looks wan and shaky. Willem notices, too; he pours her a double serving of Jenever without first asking if she wants one. She accepts it but doesn't drink, holding the glass in both hands.

"Take my seat?" he offers, and makes sure she sits down.

The color has returned to Ollie's face. He clears his throat to get everyone's attention. "Let's socialize after the meeting. We need to get started," he says, all business again. "Leo says we're having trouble getting enough food for the onderduikers. Meat, especially. I'm glad Hanneke came again today. I was hoping she might know—"

"Wait," Judith interrupts. "We didn't decide yet. We didn't decide what our pretend gathering is about today. What we'll tell people about why we've come here."

"It's not important, Judith," Ollie says. "We're running late. It doesn't matter right now."

"It does matter." Her eyes look oddly bright and shiny.

"It's fine. You—"

"It *does* matter. I have an idea. For what to celebrate. It should be my going-away party."

"Your what?" Sanne's voice is strained. "What are you talking about, Judith?"

Judith wipes away tears with the back of her hand. "They've started to round up the family members of the Jewish Council," she says. "My uncle can't protect me anymore. I got my notification late this afternoon to report to the Schouwburg for transport." Her face completely dissolves.

Ollie is the first to react, wrapping his arms around Judith, the most tender I've ever seen him be. Sanne reaches for Judith's hand, and Willem and Leo simultaneously produce handkerchiefs from their pockets. I don't know what to do. I haven't even known Judith a week. I don't deserve to be as upset by this news as everyone else; I don't deserve to be upset at all. She asked me to help and I wouldn't. She asked again, and I wouldn't. I wouldn't, even though I had connections, even though it was less dangerous for me than for her and Mina. I came tonight only because she told me I had to. It doesn't matter if I would have gotten there eventually on my own. I didn't get there in time.

"I bet that was the Nazi plan all along," Sanne says viciously. "Recruit important Jews for the Council. Make them think that they have real influence and that joining will let them help their families. And then, when the Nazis get everything they need from them, deport the Council, too. The Council was supposed to be *safe*."

"It's despicable," Willem says quietly.

"It's worse than despicable," Sanne says. "It's evil."

"All right." Ollie tries to control the room again. "We knew this might happen." He looks at Judith. "Do you have everything you need?"

Judith takes a wavering breath before answering. "The essentials, at least. One bag of things, and I'm wearing most of my clothes." No wonder she's sweating. I should have noticed Judith looked heavier than usual. Her coat buttons are strained and at least two other skirts peek out from beneath the one she's wearing on top. "Do you have my place ready?"

Ollie nods. "It's too close to curfew to take you tonight. You'll stay with Willem and me tonight, and you and I will go tomorrow or the next day, whichever is safer."

"Where?" Sanne asks. "Where are you taking her?"

"He can't tell you," Judith says, at the same time that Ollie shakes his head. "Not until I'm safely there. The fewer people who know, the better. You know the rules."

"Judith, what about Mina?" It's the first time I've spoken in this conversation. It's a horrible question: Is your cousin, the one with the bubbly laugh and the dimples in her elbows who takes secret photographs of German atrocities—is she now a prisoner of the same theater she worked so hard to rescue people from?

"Mina is safe. She got her notice today, too. It was waiting for her when she got home. I took her to her hiding place just before I came here; Ollie already had it set up. Her parents and brothers will go to theirs tomorrow. It's been planned for weeks. Just in case."

"I'm sorry," I say. I'm apologizing for so many things with that sentence, but she doesn't look at me again.

In no time at all, it's almost curfew. We need to start leaving now, in groups of two. Sanne and Leo gather around Judith, embracing her and whispering things in her ear. When she's said her good-byes, Ollie takes her tapestry valise and puts his hand on the doorknob. "Are you ready?" he asks quietly.

"I'm ready," she says, and then he takes her out into the night.

SIXTEEN

Saturday

When I wake up the next morning, my jaw aches like I spent
the night clenching it, grinding my teeth together. I know
I dreamed of Judith and Mirjam Roodveldt. "Why weren't you a
better friend?" Judith asked me, but when I tried to answer her,
she was really Elsbeth. "Why don't you come and find me?" Mirjam asked, but when I told her I was looking for her, she was really
Bas. I woke up again and again in the night, never sure of where I
was, or when it was, or who was alive and who was dead.

When I stumble out of my bedroom, still in my nightclothes,
a whacking sound alerts me that Mama is on a cleaning tear. It
happens a few times a year. This morning, Mama stands on our
balcony, beating the rug with a broom. Papa sits at the table with
a rag, polishing all of our silver, which lies in neat piles around

him. "She's denying me food until I finish," he whispers. "Me—an invalid. I need to go into hiding."

I try not to let my face register as I pick up a rag and sit beside him. Hiding. *Judith.* My father is smiling, and the air is filled with the tangy smell of silver, and Judith and Mina have been folded into the Amsterdam underground. Gone.

Papa waits for me to respond. I try to remember what I would usually say to him, but our normal banter doesn't come easily to me. "Cruel woman," I manage finally, rubbing one of the candlesticks. "Mistreating you that way."

It's nine o'clock in the morning. Later than I'm usually allowed to sleep on Saturdays. Still more than three hours to waste before I have to leave for my appointment with Dr. Zimmer. And who knows how many hours to waste before I can find out whether Judith made it to her hiding spot. It's going to be a long, horrible morning.

I've finished only two candlesticks when Mama lugs the rug back inside and sees what I'm doing. "Good, Hannie, you're awake. I have another job for you."

I pause, the rag in my hand. "I don't have to clean?"

"Your closet," Mama says. "So many papers, you can't still need them all. Sort through them to figure out which can be used for kindling."

It's an odd relief to be in my bedroom, sorting papers, while my parents do chores in the next room. It's familiar and mundane, and requires just enough concentration to distract me from what happened last night. After a few minutes, Mama knocks on the door, bringing bread and jam. "See? I'm not *such* a cruel woman." She pretends to be stern, but her eyes aren't angry.

Mama kneels next to me and picks up the item I've just set aside, a birthday card from when I turned sixteen. "Do you remember this birthday? We all went ice-skating. Elsbeth wore that short skating skirt, and Bas challenged me to a race because he thought it would be funny, him against your forty-year-old mama—"

"But then you beat him. He wouldn't stop claiming you tripped him when no one was looking."

She reads the card again, and for a minute there are no sounds but the fluttering of papers as I sort them in stacks. "You must think I'm truly cruel sometimes now," she says quietly. "I must drive you crazy with my worrying."

"What are you talking about?"

"You know what I'm talking about. The ways I frustrate you. The way you look to your father for reassurance when you can't stand my questions."

She's right; I think these things at least three times a day. I say them to her at least once a day. But not now, while her face looks so lost and vulnerable.

"It's just that I've seen wars, Hanneke," she continues. "I know what can happen in them. I know what can happen to young girls in them. I try to protect you so you can grow up and not have to worry as much as I do. There is nothing in the world I care about more than you. Do you understand?"

I nod, flustered, but before I can figure out how to respond,

Mama puts the birthday card down again, rising to her feet and brushing the dust off her skirt. She kisses the top of my head, perfunctorily. "Enough of a break. Back to the rugs." Moments later, the whacking on the balcony starts up again.

Mama's right that this closet had become a mess; some of these papers are years old. Papa and I are both packrats: he because of sentimentality and me because I never want to throw away anything that could be worth something. These days we find uses for things two or three times again. Mama will keep some of these papers to light fires; others will be used to wash windows or line our shoes.

"Mama, where are your sewing scissors?" I call into the hallway, thinking of the way my feet got so cold when I was trapped in the rain the other day. "I was going to make some liners."

Once I have the scissors, I place my shoes on top of a sheet of newspaper. Before making the first tracing, though, I see the newspaper I'm about to ruin is from Mama's birthday. Papa won't want me to use that one; he saves the newspapers from our birthdays every year. The one underneath is an issue of *Het Parool,* one that I vaguely remember being given by a customer several weeks ago, one that I should have destroyed long before now rather than store in my house. I'll use it to make liners. I like the idea of that small rebellion, carrying a paper piece of the resistance in my shoes.

Mama's shears have been freshly sharpened, and they cut through newsprint like nothing. I'm halfway through cutting the second liner. The scissors slip through my hands to the ground.

I can't believe what I'm seeing.

I bring the shredded newspaper closer. *Am I imagining things?* But no: There it is, inadvertently circled by the tracing I'd made. I read the newsprint again, the words swimming in front of me.

"Hannie, what was that noise?"

Mama's voice comes like I'm hearing it from underwater, far away and muted. "What?" I ask finally, unable to drag my eyes away from the paper.

"What happened to my floor?" She sighs, coming into the room. I look down dully. The shears are sticking out of the floor, gouging a hole in Mama's maple. "Oh, Hannie. I'll get the floor polish; we'll see if we can—"

"I need to go." I scramble to my feet, riffling through my closet for a clean skirt and pulling off my nightgown without even asking for the privacy I usually demand while changing.

"You need to go? Where?"

My blouse and skirt hideously clash; I've put on the first clothing my hands touched. "You're wearing that?" Mama frowns. "Why are you getting dressed now?"

"I have to go."

"But we've barely started the chores! Hanneke, that blouse really doesn't match."

I brush past her and collect my coat from the closet. "I'll be back as soon as I can."

"Hannie!" Mama is still calling after me as I run downstairs, take my bicycle, and start down the street.

I pedal furiously through my neighborhood, taking the potholed roads I usually avoid because I know today they'll be faster.

Is it just a coincidence? What I saw in the paper, was it just a coincidence? It wasn't, though. I know it wasn't.

Across the street, an old classmate of mine is shopping at Mrs. Bierman's store. She waves her hand in greeting, but I don't stop. I don't stop, either, for the customer of Mr. Kreuk's who calls out my name, wanting to place an order for next week's delivery.

When I get to Mrs. Janssen's house, I leave my bicycle leaning against it, more exposed than I would usually, pushing past her as soon as she answers the door.

"Is something wrong?" She doesn't have her cane, and she grasps the armrest to balance herself against the sofa.

"I need to get in the hiding place again."

"Why? What have you found?"

In the kitchen, I open the pantry, shoving canned goods aside. Mrs. Janssen limps behind me. "Do you think there's something we missed?" She watches me as I unlatch the secret door, pushing into the small room. "Hanneke, what did we miss?"

We didn't miss anything. We looked at every square inch of that barren, sterile room, Mrs. Janssen with her bad eyes and me with my good ones. We saw everything in the room. We just didn't see everything the right way.

I'm worried for a second that Mrs. Janssen will have thrown away what I'm looking for. But it's still there, the old issue of *Het Parool* that Mirjam was reading on the day she disappeared, already growing a little yellow around the edges.

Quickly, I unfold the paper I've brought with me from home. Just as I thought, it's the same one—a back issue from last month. Even though I know both newspapers will be identical on every page, I take Mirjam's copy back into the kitchen where it's light, and flip to the same section I'd inadvertently circled while I was making the shoe liners.

"What are you doing?"

"Shhh, I'm trying to think." I hold up a finger to silence her. Mrs. Janssen had always been so specific about the time-line of Mirjam's disappearance: Shortly before Mirjam disappeared, Mrs. Janssen brought her this edition of *Het Parool*. Before, I'd thought of the two events—the newspaper delivery and the disappearance—as completely unrelated to each other. But what if they were a chain reaction, in which one caused the other? What if Mirjam saw something in the paper that caused her to run?

On the first day, when Mrs. Janssen told me about Mirjam's disappearance, she told me that Mirjam loved to read every line of *Het Parool*, even the classified advertisements.

My eyes find the item I'd circled back home in my own newspaper copy: a simple three-line notice in the middle of the page.

> Elizabeth misses her Margaret,
> but is glad to be vacationing
> in Kijkduin.

It can't be a coincidence. This whole time, I thought I should get in touch with Amalia because she might have a guess about where her friend might have run to. I never suspected that Mirjam would try to run to her. Did Mirjam get on a train bound for Kijkduin?

"Hanneke, tell me," Mrs. Janssen says. I'd almost forgotten that I was still sitting in her kitchen. "You've been staring into space. Tell me! What is going on?"

"I think I know. I think I know what happened."

The first time I met Elsbeth:

She was seven, I was six. I was crying because it was my first day of school and I didn't know anyone except a boy who lived in the apartment below me and liked to pull my hair.

She said, "What's your name?"

I said, "Hanneke."

She said, "My name is Elsbeth."

She had a pretty ribbon in her hair, and she took it off and tied it to my braid instead. "You should keep this. It looks better with blond hair anyway," she said. "And you don't have to cry about that boy. Boys are silly. The first thing you need is a best friend."

SEVENTEEN

Stupid. I am stupid. I let my memories of Bas dictate what I thought happened to Mirjam. I'm the one who assumed that if Mirjam ran from a hiding space, it would be because she wanted to be with Tobias. Why didn't I realize that she could have been running to someone she loved just as much, in a different way?

The wind bites at my neck, down my blouse to my collarbone. I must not have buttoned my coat; it's flapping wildly behind me as I pedal. I try to gather it around my throat with one hand, but only succeed in veering into the path of an old man. He darts to the side of the road and curses after me.

What happened? Amalia's parents were going to send her to live with her aunt. That much, Mina had told me. But then what? At some point, once she was already with her aunt, she placed a greeting for her friend in the paper. Did Amalia know Mirjam was hiding at the furniture store? Were they in some sort of communication? Did they plan it out ahead of time, a secret message in the classified section of an underground newspaper? Was that the signal for Mirjam to run—or did she just see this greeting from her old friend, become overwhelmed by emotion, and decide to leave at the last minute?

Either way, why wouldn't she tell Mrs. Janssen? She must have known how terrifying her disappearance would be.

I pedal madly through the streets. Now that I have a lead, the gears in my brain begin to spin. I'll need to find Christoffel, to find out whether his father made it to Kijkduin and returned with a response from Amalia. If Christoffel's father didn't get to the hotel, I'll need to get there myself and search every room. Either way, I should go to the train station and see if I can find the regular conductor for that route. A fifteen-year-old girl in a bright blue coat traveling alone might have stood out. But how would she have gotten on the train? The station agent wouldn't have been allowed to sell a ticket to someone whose papers were marked *Jood*. I need to ask Mr. Kreuk if I can have a few days off. I need to find out if there's an underground transport, a way that Mirjam might have gotten to Kijkduin without riding on the train. I need to go back home first, to change clothes and come up with a story to tell Mama. I steer my bicycle in that direction and am so lost in my plans that, a block from my house, I almost run over Ollie, who is standing in the middle of the street and waving his arms to get me to stop.

Something's wrong.

Obviously something's wrong; he's standing in the middle of the road, waving like a lunatic.

But he's not waving like a lunatic. Ollie is waving his hands listlessly, like he almost wishes I wouldn't see him and wouldn't stop. When I screech to a halt in front of him, they drop to his sides.

"What are you doing here?" I demand. "I was just thinking about you. I have new information and need your help."

He kneads his hand into his side; he's been running and now he has a cramp. "I just looked for you at your house; your mother said you rode off in this direction. I need to talk to you."

"Good. You've found me."

"It's serious."

"I know it's serious. I found something at Mrs. Janssen's house. Actually, I found it at my house, but I didn't realize what it meant until—" Something is propelling me to keep talking, because if I'm talking, then Ollie won't be able to tell me what it is that's making his mouth twist like a scar.

"I have some bad news," he says. "I think we should find a place to sit."

"I don't want to find a place to sit. I discovered something today. We don't have time to sit." I force a laugh, like he's being funny. "Ollie, catch your breath, and let's go."

"No, Hanneke. Something happened."

"Something did happen. I know where Mirjam is. Let's go."

He doesn't follow me. He doesn't try to convince me again, either. He just stands there, letting me get all these protests out of my system, letting me feel how heavy the air around us has grown. "I can take you back to your parents, if you want. Or we can go to my house."

"What is it, Ollie? Is it—" Even now, I pause, because until I say the words, they're not true. "Is it Judith? Did something happen on the way to her hiding place?"

"Judith is still at my house. It's not Judith."

"Is it Willem?" I'll rip their names off like a bandage, starting with the ones that would hurt the most. *Let it be Leo*, I think. Let it be the person I know least well of all. There's something wrong with me for thinking like this, for wishing bad luck to Leo, but I know everything in life has to have a trade.

"Hanneke. Listen to me. I went to the theater to try to talk to Judith's uncle. And it's happened, Hanneke. Last night Mirjam was brought to the Hollandsche Schouwburg."

EIGHTEEN

hat?" I push Ollie away from me, repelling everything he just said. "You're wrong."

Of course he is wrong. Mirjam is not in the Schouwburg. My arms flail out at him, wanting to make him take it back.

"Hanneke, there was a big roundup late last night." He catches my wrists in his and holds them against his chest. "They were looking for people whose names were on their list, but when they couldn't fill their quotas, they started taking anyone they found who had Jewish papers. Dozens of people were brought in who weren't scheduled to be deported yet. One of the names on the list is M. Roodveldt. Mirjam is at the theater and she's scheduled to be transported in two days."

"But I know where she's going now," I insist. "She went to Den

Haag. They couldn't have caught her, because she wouldn't still be in Amsterdam. She wouldn't—"

"Maybe she got out of the city, but she was captured and brought back in. Or maybe her temporary hiding place was raided before she got out. A lot of things could have happened. All we know is that someone with her name is there."

Roundup. Raided. Roodveldt. His words float above me, but none of them make sense. Ollie's heart beats beneath my hands. "We'll need to figure out what to do next, then," I say finally. "To start, we have to go to the theater. You'll distract the guards. We have to go and get her out right now."

"Hanneke. Listen to yourself."

"You're right. First we'll get Judith's uncle to help us. He'll—"

Ollie presses down on my hands. "No."

"Let go. You don't have to come with me, but you have to let me go."

"No," he says. "Hanneke, do you want people to be killed? You cannot risk the network that we have spent a year building, just to go back and ask questions about one girl. We don't have anyone left on the inside now. Judith and Mina are out. Judith's uncle won't help us. He's terrified for his own life; the Council doesn't have any of the sway we thought it did. If you storm in now without knowing anything, you're putting the whole operation at risk."

"But—"

"No."

He's right. Even through my anger and frustration, I understand he's right. It's a logical argument that I might make myself if this were about any person other than the one I've been trying so hard to find. Why wasn't I at the Schouwburg last night? I was congratulating myself for tracking down Tobias's father, and I should have gone to the Schouwburg instead.

"Everything I've done is a waste. All of this—visiting dentists, talking to school friends—I should have just planted myself outside the theater the second you told me about it. Maybe I would have seen her go in and been able to help her."

Ollie takes his hands from mine and cups my face, holding my eyes steady. "You didn't know what the right thing to do was. Amsterdam is a big city, and Mirjam could have been anywhere."

"But, Ollie, what if it's *not* her in the theater?"

"Hanneke, I wish it wasn't her, but it is."

"No, *listen*. M. Roodveldt? Maybe it's a different name. Margot or Mozes, or . . . lots of names start with *M*, Ollie. Is there anybody in the theater who saw her or talked to her, who can say for sure?"

"I can't find out without asking questions that will give us away. We've decided we need to pause and regroup, now that they're deporting the Council's families."

Think, I instruct myself. *Think rationally*. If I can't get into the theater, how else can I find information? "Maybe if I found someone who lives across the street, or works nearby. Maybe they would have seen her go in."

Ollie's mouth opens, a quick movement he tries to cover up.

"What?"

"Nothing," he says, but it's not nothing.

"Ollie, what is it? Is there someone who might have seen something?"

"I can't tell you," he protests. "It's against the rules."

"Damn the rules, just tell me. Who saw something? Please, Ollie."

"Hanneke, we have the rules we do for a reason. We need to think of the greater good."

But I hear an opening in what he's saying, and I take it. "I know your 'greater good,' Ollie, but if the good that you're working so hard for is one that won't work to rescue a fifteen-year-old girl, then is it worth it anyway? What kind of society are you trying to save?"

Finally he exhales, angrily. I've upset him with my begging. "We are not going to help you get Mirjam out of the theater," he says. "We can't. But I will do one thing—*one thing*—to help you verify that it really is her in there, so that you don't spend the rest of the war not knowing. And I'm only doing it because you running around asking office workers if they saw her...that puts all of us at risk."

My shoulders go limp with relief. "Thank you, Ollie. Thank you."

"Only this. Don't ask for anything else."

He looks around to make sure nobody is watching, then takes a piece of paper from his pocket and scrawls something on it. An address, I can tell from upside down. "Memorize it, destroy it," he instructs. "It's where Mina is staying. She might be able to help."

"Why would Mina—"

Ollie looks down at his watch. "I have to go, right now. I can't risk being late getting Judith to her hiding place. I'll come and meet you when I can. It might be late."

"But—"

"Later, Hanneke." He looks regretful almost immediately; he's already doubting the help he's given me. I try to smile, to show him I'm grateful, that he made the right decision, but I can't hold it for long.

After he's left, I wheel my bicycle into an alley so I can memorize the address the way Ollie wanted me to. As soon as I read the numbers on the page, I know Ollie has made a mistake. What he's given me can't possibly be the right address. I've been to it before. I go there every week.

NINETEEN

The bell rings, but nobody comes to answer it. It seems that no one is home, but when I press my ear against the door, there's a faint scuffing sound, like chairs pushed back from a table. Finally the door chain rattles as someone locks it. One blue eye appears in the gap between the door and the jamb.

"Mrs. de Vries," I say.

"Hanneke." She arches an eyebrow. "I haven't ordered anything. I wasn't expecting you."

"I'm not here for a delivery. I'm here for something else. Can you let me in to talk?"

"I don't think so. It's not a good time."

She peers beyond me into the empty hallway, as if willing me to go away. I can't even begin to imagine what I look like: mismatched clothes, my hair loose and tangled, a run in my stockings.

"It's all right, Mrs. de Vries," I say, leaning in close. "I know."

"You know? What do *you* know?"

Again, I wonder if Ollie got the address wrong. Mrs. de Vries is as haughty as ever, an icicle of a human being. I lower my voice to barely a whisper. "I'm a friend of Mina's."

Her eyes flicker. She reaches her hand to her throat but covers the gesture by adjusting the brooch at her collar. "You should go, Hanneke. I don't need anything from you today."

"Please let me in."

"Really, this is quite out of the ordinary," she hisses. "I'm going to speak with Mr. Kreuk about this the next time I see him."

"We can telephone him now if you want. But I'm going to stand in this hallway until you let me in. I'll say hello to all your neighbors."

Finally, she closes the door to unlatch the chain, and when she opens it again, I step through before she can change her mind. Inside, the twins sit on the floor, playing with toy cars. Everything looks normal, exactly as this apartment has looked every time I've come to visit. No suspicious sounds. Nothing out of place.

Mrs. de Vries stares at me, taking out a cigarette as I stand in her foyer. She doesn't offer to take my coat. Neither of us knows what to say to the other.

"I came to see Mina," I say finally. "Where is she? It's important."

"Is something wrong? Do the police suspect my apartment?"

"It's a personal matter."

Mrs. de Vries exhales a trail of smoke before turning her back to me. For a minute I think she's ordering me out of her apartment, but I realize she means for me to follow her. I've never been invited back this way, down a long hallway with multiple doors on either side. The de Vries family is even wealthier than I'd realized; the furnishings in the rooms we pass are ornate and expensive-looking, with paintings on the walls and a rich, textured wallpaper. She stops in the doorway of what I assume is the twins' playroom; two rocking horses sit in the corner, and child-size shelves are lined with books and toys.

"Hanneke? A little assistance?" Mrs. de Vries has walked to one of those shelves and is looking back at me with irritation, waiting for me to help her push it aside.

I brace my feet on the rug, sliding the shelf over. Behind it, cut into the wall, is a small cupboard door, big enough for a person to squeeze through, but only on hands and knees. Mrs. de Vries nods permission for me to open it, and when I do, I see two oxford shoes and a pair of ankle socks. Mina quickly drops to her knees and tucks her head out of the crawl space.

"Hanneke! I thought I heard your voice!"

Once she's free from the cupboard, Mina throws her arms around me. "I didn't think I'd get to see anybody. Judith said it was too dangerous. Did Ollie get her into her hiding space? What's happened since I've been here? It feels like a year even though it's only been a day."

Before I can figure out which question to answer first, another scraping sound comes from the crawl space. Mina hears it, too. "It's all right, you two," she says. "It's safe."

"You're not alone?" I blurt out.

Another pair of legs, wearing brown men's shoes, appears in

the space Mina has just crawled out of. They belong to an old man with a white beard, blinking into the light. He's followed by an older woman, fussy-looking, with impeccable hair and makeup.

"This is Mr. and Mrs. Cohen," Mina explains to me. They both nod cautiously in greeting. "This is my friend Hanneke Bakker."

"A pleasure to meet you," I murmur, while trying to figure out why the name sounds familiar.

"Is everything all right, Dorothea?" Mrs. Cohen asks Mrs. de Vries. "The inner walls in this building have always been so thin, we couldn't help but overhear."

I turn to Mrs. de Vries. "The Cohens are—"

"My neighbors. Yes. They've been staying with me for a few days."

Mr. Cohen extends his hand. He smells faintly of cigarettes and leather, a reassuring smell that reminds me of my grandfather.

"But when your other neighbor was here—" I cut myself off. When the woman with the fox fur stole was here, Mrs. de Vries acted as though she was pleased the Cohens had disappeared. But then, what else could she do?

The Cohens nod politely at me, and then Mrs. Cohen suggests to her husband that Mina and I might like some privacy. They leave; Mrs. de Vries stays, as if unwilling to allow any conversations in her house she is not privy to.

"Here, I'll show you our hiding place," Mina says, taking my hand and pulling me toward the cupboard entrance before I have a chance to say no. The entrance smells like paint, the only clue that this hiding space has been recently constructed. The craftsmanship is impeccable. From the outside, it looks like it was built at the same time as the rest of the apartment. There are even scuff marks on the baseboards. Mrs. Janssen's hidden pantry is amateurish by comparison.

"We only have to go in here when strangers come," Mina explains. "The rest of the time we can move around the apartment." She closes the cupboard door again, and the entrance all but disappears. "When I got here yesterday, they made me practice, again and again, seeing how quickly all of us could gather our things, get into the hiding place, make sure we hadn't left anything out that would give us away. You should see one of our drills."

"I'd like that, but not now," I mutter, distracted. When Mina shut the hiding place door, it created a breeze, causing the window curtain to flutter open and reveal a view of a large, familiar stone building.

"The Schouwburg," I whisper. "This apartment building is right across the street from the Schouwburg."

I've only ever seen out the front windows of the de Vrieses' apartment building. Because I'd never been invited farther into the family's living quarters, I never put together what the view would be from the rear. Now I know why Ollie gave me this address.

"Mina. Did you—" My mouth has gone dry. I swallow and start again. "Did you see the group arrive yesterday after the *razzia?*"

Mina nods. "It was just after I came here. There was so much yelling. I stood behind the curtain and watched it all, feeling so guilty that I was safe, and everyone down there wasn't."

"This is important. Did you see Mirjam? Did you see her be brought in with those people?"

"Mirjam was in that group?"

"I don't know. Someone with her last name was. So you didn't see her? Are you sure?"

"I'm sorry, I'm sorry." Her eyes fill with tears. "I didn't know to look for her."

Another door closing. Another hope slipping away.

"I did take pictures," she offers, using her sleeve to wipe her eyes.

"You took *pictures?*"

"I left behind clothes so I could fit my new camera in my suitcase. I wanted to still be doing something. Even if I'm stuck in here, I can still take pictures of everything happening out there."

"Can I see them? Your pictures?"

Her face falls. "They're not developed yet. I just took them a day ago."

"Let's get someone to develop them, then. I'm sure we can find someone to trust." Mentally, I scroll through my list of black market clients, thinking of the artistic ones who might have basement darkrooms. There was the owner of an art gallery once, but when I went to his house, he had pamphlets with Adolf Hitler's face lying on the coffee table.

Mina shakes her head. "We can't—they're Anscochrome."

"What do you mean?" I've never heard this word before.

"They're Anscochrome. It's a color film, the special brand I was waiting for at my birthday. Most photographers won't have dealt with it before; it's a German-American brand. Even if we wanted to risk getting it across the border to a sympathetic German photographer, it would take weeks to come back."

"But maybe a teacher at an art school, or someone who works at a newspaper...they could rush it, or—"

"It's not a matter of hurrying. It's that regular photographers might mess this film up."

"But..." I trail off, frustrated. I can think of ways to find almost anything. But I don't know how to find a photographer to develop a film I've never heard of.

"Give the camera to me," Mrs. de Vries says. It had been so long since she'd spoken I'd almost forgotten she was still in the room. There she is, in the corner, her arms folded elegantly. "Give it to me," she repeats, a note of irritation in her voice. "I'll take it to one of my husband's business contacts."

"His business contacts?" I repeat blankly.

"He publishes a magazine," she reminds me. "A fashion magazine, full of photographs."

"But Mina just said that this is special film."

"And he has special contacts." She raises one eyebrow. "He knows all sorts of people with access to technology in private darkrooms. I won't promise, but I'll try. Give it to me."

Mina looks at me again, and I nod at her to give the camera to Mrs. de Vries. "Please be careful," she begs. "It's so expensive, and those photographs are dangerous."

Mrs. de Vries stares at her. She knows about danger; she is hiding three Jewish people in her house.

"Can you go right now?" I ask her. "Can you go this afternoon? Ollie said the next transport is in just two days. I need to know if the girl I'm looking for is in the theater, as soon as possible. Can you please go now?" I don't know if it's because Mrs. de Vries knows that I know her secret, and she thinks she has to obey me, or if it's because she wants this over with quickly so I'll leave her apartment. Whatever the reason, she now walks briskly out of the room, heels clacking on parquet floors, and by the time I catch up to her, she's already pinning on a navy hat.

"I'll be back soon," she says. And then, because she's still Mrs. de Vries, she says, "Please refrain from touching too many things while I'm gone."

She slips on her coat, and then it's just Mina and me, and nothing left to do but wait.

TWENTY

Mina and I stay in the playroom, perched uncomfortably on child-size furniture, while Mr. Cohen entertains the children, kneeling on the floor and letting them drive their cars up his legs and arms. Mrs. Cohen helpfully washes dishes in the kitchen and makes us cup after cup of ersatz tea.

"You need to be another mountain," one of the twins informs me, rolling his car on my shoe. "So we can each have our own."

I jerk my foot away. "You could each *be* your own mountains."

Mr. Cohen smiles. "How about I tell a story instead? There will be lots of fast cars and fast horses and mountains in it." He's so patient with them; I wonder if he has grandchildren of his own.

"Hanneke, I'm worried about something," Mina says, moving her chair closer to mine.

"What is it?"

She glances over to Mr. Cohen and the twins and lowers her voice. "The *thing* that I showed you when we went for a walk. It's still *there*." She reads my bewildered expression and raises both hands to her face, mimicking a gesture I immediately recognize. Her other camera. It's in the carriage, and she didn't have time to retrieve it. "Do you think it's okay?" she asks.

Even if I didn't, I don't see what could be done about it, or what use there would be in me making her worry any more than she's already worrying. "I'm sure that if one of your coworkers finds it, she'll keep it for you," I reassure her. The guards seem to leave the *crèche* alone anyhow.

After a while, the children start to complain that they're hungry. Mina finds potatoes and parsnips in the pantry, and boils them along with leaves of kale. We all eat silently. The children start yawning, and Mr. Cohen goes to put them to bed.

"Hanneke, you're going to miss curfew," Mrs. Cohen warns me. "You should go."

It's too late to leave now. I want to be here the second there is any news. Have I done the right thing, pressuring Mrs. de Vries to go out the way that I did? Mrs. Cohen takes up a pile of socks from Mrs. de Vries's mending pile and quietly begins to darn them. Mr. Cohen reads a book. The evening drags on. The sky outside turns from bruise-colored to pitch-black.

My parents will have started to worry an hour ago, with Mama turning white around the edges and Papa making loud jokes to cover up his own concern. After worry will come anger: Mama at me for being so selfish and not keeping track of the time, and Papa because I've worried Mama and because he's mad at himself for not being able to go out and find me. I don't know what comes after the anger stage. I've never tested their patience enough to find out. Tonight I'll have to.

In the distance, a church clock strikes another hour. The four of us exchange worried glances, and guilt begins to gnaw the pit of my stomach. Why didn't we ask for the address of Mrs. de Vries's photographer friend, or at least a name? Why did I insist she had to go now, when tomorrow morning wouldn't have made much of a difference? I don't like Mrs. de Vries, but I don't want anything to happen to her.

"She wasn't doing anything illegal," Mina says. "It's not illegal to visit a friend."

"I just hope that if she was stopped, it was on the way to the photographer's and not on the way back home," Mrs. Cohen says. Her perfectly applied lipstick has begun to fade. "They might not question a roll of undeveloped film, but if—"

"Hush, Rebekkah," Mr. Cohen stops her. "Can't you see—"

He doesn't finish. The lock in the door begins to turn. The four of us freeze in our seats. Mrs. de Vries comes in, her cheeks flushed, but otherwise unharmed. Ollie follows her inside.

"I got back an hour ago," Mrs. de Vries explains. "But there were soldiers loitering on the corner. I didn't think it was safe to walk past them, so I hid in an alley like a street beggar until they left."

"I was already hiding in the alley across the street," Ollie explains as Mina runs to hug him. "I could even see Mrs. de Vries in the shadows in her own alley, but I didn't dare call out to her; it was completely absurd, like we were actors in a stage farce. I thought the soldiers would never leave."

"Did you take Judith? Is she all right?" Mina asks.

Ollie nods. The farm where he's taken her is crowded, he says, and it has six people hiding there already, sleeping in a barn. But it's safe, with only a few soldiers assigned to patrol that region.

Mrs. de Vries removes her hat, smoothing her hand over her hair. "The children are in bed?"

"Sleeping," Mrs. Cohen reassures her.

"Did you find him?" I ask. Now that she's safe, I feel less guilty for asking her to go. "Your photographer friend?"

Mrs. de Vries pulls a small packet from her coat pocket. The envelope looks the wrong shape to contain photographs from an entire roll of film. "Slides," she explains. "I understand that's how this film works?" She raises an eyebrow at Mina, who nods. "I don't have a projector. My husband's coworker said he would lend us his, but obviously I wasn't going to tow it through the streets tonight. You can at least look at the slides to see if you can find your friend."

She doesn't wait for a thank-you, instead murmuring that she needs a hot bath. The Cohens excuse themselves as well. It's so late it's almost light, and they're both swaying in place. After everyone else has gone to bed, Mina and Ollie and I crowd around a desk in Mr. de Vries's empty study and remove the slides from the envelope—translucent images, each just an inch wide. The squares are so small and the people are so many it's going to be nearly impossible to pick out one in the crowd.

"If we hold them up to a lightbulb, we'll be able to see the images a little better," Mina suggests. She makes sure the blackout curtains are fully closed before turning on the lamp at Mr. de

Vries's desk. Gently, using only the tips of her fingers, she begins to pick up the slides one by one.

"They're in color!" Ollie exclaims.

Mina nods proudly. "I already told Hanneke. My parents bought it off the black market. I can't even imagine how much it cost."

Nor can I. I've never been asked to find any, but it's got to be outrageously expensive.

"Is this the right order?" I ask.

"Yes, that's the order I took them, at least."

Together, the three of us lean over the slides. The pictures don't begin with Mirjam's roundup, as I'd expected them to. Instead, the first image is from the summertime, of a public park, with grass, and flowers, and in the foreground, a row of men with yellow stars on their jackets and their hands in the air, and on their faces, terror, clear even in miniature.

"That was the first time I used my new camera," Mina whispers. "That was the first *razzia* I saw, too. I passed it on the street. Someone told me later those men were executed."

"Are all the photos you take like this?" I ask her.

"I ration the color because it's so expensive," she says. "But the black-and-white photographs are like this, too—they show the same things."

Even though Mina already told me the film was in color, I couldn't imagine how stunning the images would be. They show the corners of the war we aren't supposed to talk about. A hungry child. Two soldiers jeering at a frightened Jewish man. A basement full of onderduikers, waving at the camera to show they're all right. The color makes everything so saturated, so current, just like real life. When I look at black-and-white photos, it feels like I'm looking at something historical. But it's not historical. It's happening right now. Mina's work makes sense to me now. Each image is her own small rebellion.

Finally, we reach the photographs from yesterday at the theater. They tell a miniature story: In the first, a tram has just arrived, a streetcar, repurposed for these transports. It's full of people wearing *Jodensters*, carrying suitcases or cloth grocery bags. A woman with a rose-colored hat holds the arm of a man in a fawn-colored fedora. Two stooped ladies who could be sisters are dressed in matching lilac. The colors are beautiful and make my eyes ache.

In the second frame, everyone from the tram stands near the rear entrance of the theater. A soldier has his arm outstretched, obviously organizing them into rows. In the foreground, I can make out a teenage boy in a chocolate-brown coat sticking his tongue out at the soldier, in an unseen act of defiance.

We spend several minutes examining each frame. The story continues to unfold: A disorganized crowd of people become neat lines; couples cling to each other's hands for support.

Peach and red. Green and black.

It's not until the fourth-to-last frame that I see what I'm looking for. The picture is of the same scene as the others: scared people carrying suitcases. There are the captured prisoners, three or four abreast, filing into the theater.

There, in the bottom corner, is Mirjam.

TWENTY-ONE

Once there was a mouse caught in our walls. It only seemed to make noise when I was in the room alone; Papa and Mama never heard it, and if I brought it up, they would look over my head and say, "Right. Your *mouse.*" I was nine, maybe, and eventually even I began to think the mouse wasn't real. It was a pretend playmate I must have invented for company. Then one day Elsbeth came over to play, the mouse appeared by her chair, and she screamed bloody murder. That was the moment when the mouse became real, really real. When someone else saw it. When I wasn't alone.

"That's her." I point to the slide.

"What?" Mina asks. "Where?"

"The corner. In the right."

She crowds in, shoving her shoulder against mine. "Are you sure? It's so blurry and small."

Nearly out of frame is a girl with curly hair wearing a coat the color of the sky. The face *is* blurry, not that seeing it would help me anyway, this girl I've only met in description. What's not blurry is the bright blue coat, and, if I squint hard enough, a row of minuscule double-breasted silver buttons marching down the front. There she is, the girl who ran from a safe hiding space, the girl who was slightly spoiled, who loved a boy and had a best friend, who did well in school only to please her parents. Maybe her face is blurry because she's doing exactly what I like to think I would be doing: looking for an escape route rather than following the rules.

"Do you think Mrs. de Vries has a magnifying glass?" Ollie suggests. "Is there any way to see it a little closer?"

Mina finds an old-fashioned one with a carved wooden handle in Mr. de Vries's desk drawer. I press my nose as close as I can, going over the photograph millimeter by millimeter for anything else that might be useful, but find nothing more.

"It's still so hard to see," Mina says.

"It's her," I say definitively. It's her because I feel a pang in my heart when I look at this photograph. All the other people being herded into the theater seem to be with others—families or neighbors. She's alone.

"She's right there, Ollie," I say. From the window of the room I'm sitting in, I could see the building where she's being held, less than one hundred meters away.

"It's her," Ollie says evenly. He's watching me, wondering what I'll do next. "It's what we thought it would be."

"We have to get her out."

He's shaking his head even before I finish the sentence. He expected this.

"Yes, Ollie," I continue. "Look at her. She must be so terrified."

"Hanneke, nothing has changed since I told you that we couldn't help you."

"It *has* changed. We have a safe place for her, right here, across the street. Mina and Judith know the theater. Why won't you help me, Ollie?"

"I don't understand you, Hanneke," he snaps. "We've all been hoping, for the past four days, that you would help us with the resistance, with things that can actually matter for not just one person, but *hundreds* of people. And now here you are, telling me I have to risk the lives of all my other friends to help *you*? You really are—"

"What am I?" I challenge him, furious but keeping my voice down. "Crazy? *Damaged?*"

"I felt bad for you, Hanneke. For the fact that you had to grieve for Bas on your own. I felt so sorry for you, and I also thought you would be useful to us in the resistance. But if I had realized how bullheaded you would be, I wouldn't have brought you to the first meeting at all."

"Bas would help me." It's cruel, to compare Ollie to his brother right now, but I can't help it. It's true. "He would. He would wonder why we're even still having this conversation when we know right where she is. He would say we should go and get her right now. Do you remember his party that one summer when my parents wouldn't let me come because I was sick? He sneaked up the drainpipe just to bring me cake afterward. Bas wouldn't be able to stand that someone had specifically asked for help with finding her, and we were ignoring it."

"And he would be dead."

I reel backward, staring at Ollie. "What did you just say?"

"Hanneke. Bas was a thousand good things. A million good things. But he was brash, and reckless, and he never thought before acting. That night of the party when he brought you the cake? *You* were happy, but he was punished. My parents were furious at how late he'd stayed out. And now? Now Bas would try to help save this girl, and the Nazis would catch him, and he would die."

"You don't know that," I say.

"Don't you think I want to help you? Don't you know how hard it is for me to think about what might happen to that girl, all alone? I want to be like Bas all the time because he was charming and fun. But he wasn't perfect. Someone has to be the careful one. Someone has to think, every moment of every day, of how dangerous a single slip could be."

His hair is squashed to one side of his face; he has purple bags under his eyes. He must be exhausted. I don't know how many miles he had to bicycle into the country to take Judith to her hiding place, and then he came straight here after. Seeing him makes me aware of how tired I am, as well. Whole worlds have happened since the last time either of us slept.

"Hanneke? Ollie?" It's Mina, still sitting at Mr. de Vries's desk, still holding the slides. She obviously hasn't even been following our conversation.

Her face is frozen in horror.

"Mina? What is it?" I ask. She points to the slides in her hand, toward the last series of images that we hadn't yet looked at. "Is Mirjam in those, too?" I go back to the desk, leaning over to see whatever she's pointing to. "Let me see."

"It's not that. It's ... they're closing down the *crèche*." She hands me the magnifying glass before continuing. "Look, in this one— there are the other helpers, taking all the children into the theater. They never go in a big group like that. They're going to close the nursery and transport the children with Mirjam." I squint my eyes and see a parade of small children, and two of the young women I'd seen working in the nursery with Mina.

"I'm so sorry," I say to Mina. "I know you knew them well." But she's shaking her head, pointing again at the slide.

"No. Look," she says. "*Look.*"

I look. And I finally understand what she's talking about. The older children from the *crèche* are walking into the theater. Two of the younger ones are in carriages. And one carriage in particular. The carriage holding the photographs of the brutal war and secret resistance, and everyone I have met and grown to care about in the past few days.

"They'll find the camera in a minute," Mina says. "The Nazis. When the carriage goes to the transit camp. And then they'll find all of us."

Ollie looks completely confused; he has never heard of the camera and has no idea what Mina is talking about. But I do. And

I know that a few minutes ago, when we saw Mirjam in the photographs and Ollie told me that nothing had changed—he was wrong. Everything has changed.

Sunday

"What are we going to do?" Sanne asks for the fifth time, and for the fifth time, nobody has an answer.

Ollie flew around the city on his bicycle to gather everyone here, first to his apartment, where Willem had already left for an early class, and then to Leo, who promised to fetch Sanne and come straight to Mrs. de Vries's. Now everyone is here but Willem and Judith, who knows more about the theater than anybody else and who can never come to another meeting again.

"I can't believe you would be so stupid," Leo snarls at Mina. "I had no idea you were taking pictures. We're trying to save actual lives, and you're flitting around with your camera? I told everyone you were too young."

"Don't yell at her," Ollie warns. "Don't yell at all." He nods meaningfully toward the study's closed door. Mrs. de Vries is furious that we're all here. She hasn't moved once from the front window, promising she'll make us all leave immediately if she hears a noise coming from the study.

"It's already done, Leo, okay?" Sanne says. "It's too late to change that she did it. Now we have to figure out: What are we going to do?"

"Let's think it through," Ollie says. "Maybe nobody will find the camera. Mina was using it to take pictures for months, and the other volunteers in the *crèche* didn't realize it. Is that a possibility?"

Mina bows her head miserably. "You know it's not. When the transports get to the transit camps, they search everyone's personal items—sometimes people try to sew jewelry or money inside their coats and suitcases. The guards will rip that carriage apart at the seams. And when they do..."

We all know what will happen when they do. Pictures of the resistance workers. Pictures of dozens of hidden exchanges, of children going into hiding, of innocent, innocent people.

"But how do you even know they'll take the carriage to the station?" Sanne asks. "When people are called for transport, they're usually allowed to bring just one suitcase apiece. Why would guards let a family bring along a carriage? Maybe it will just be left in the theater."

"How is that any better?" Leo snaps. "Do you think the camera won't be discovered there just as easily?"

"It's not any better," Sanne says defensively. "I'm just saying that we don't know for sure that the carriage is going to be searched, or when, or by whom. We don't even know for sure that all the children will be on this transport. I know transports usually happen in the order that prisoners arrive, but sometimes they don't. Is there any way we can get into the theater?"

Ollie shakes his head. "They know everyone who works there, and they're not bending any rules to let in new people now. Everything has changed since the Council members and their families are being called up."

"What if we asked Walter?" Leo suggests. I know that Walter is the man who oversees the theater, who helps falsify papers for the children in the *crèche*.

Ollie's voice is final. "No. This isn't a resistance mission. This was us messing up. Our own idiocy. We're not going to drag him into it until we try to fix it ourselves."

"They *are* going to take the carriage to the train station," Mina whispers. "I just know it. They never leave things behind in the theater; it's too crowded there and they're always looking to pack more people in. The carriage is going to the train station; you have to believe me."

Sanne winces, then takes a deep breath and starts again. "Okay. So you are saying we would have to get the camera back, but not when it's in the theater. We would have to get it when the transport leaves the theater, on the way to the station. And it would have to be a secret. And nobody could see us. Correct?"

"We'd be out after curfew," Leo says. "So we'd need special papers, at least."

"Or a disguise," Sanne says. "A Gestapo uniform would be best—high-ranking enough to walk through the city after curfew without being questioned."

"We can't get one," Ollie says shortly. "If we could, that plan might work. But we can't. I know other resistance groups have stolen German uniforms to use for their operations, but we don't know anybody who has one now, and we're not going to be able to arrange a second secret operation to get one. Certainly not in the two days we have before the transport. Think of something else."

"You're all being stupid," Mina says, shaking her head. "Of course there's a way to get in the theater. I'm supposed to be in there right now. I was supposed to report for transport. So that's what I'll do. I'll report for transport, and then once I'm inside, I'll find the camera and I'll destroy it."

"And then you'll be sent to a camp," Ollie says quietly.

"And?"

"Mina—" Sanne begins.

"What?" she says fiercely, her voice breaking. "It's my fault, no one else's! Leo just said so. And you always talk about how the mission is more important than any one of us. So I'll do it. I'll turn myself in this afternoon."

Sanne opens and closes her mouth again. Ollie buries his head in his hands, and Leo stares hard at the desk. Nobody says anything. Nobody has to. Mina's offer is horrible, and it's also the best option they have.

I clear my throat. "I can get one."

It's the first time I've spoken in this entire exchange. Everyone swivels toward me. There are so many things I have done wrong in this war. Starting with Bas, starting from the beginning. But all through it. The times I have known things were wrong and told myself the best thing to do was ignore it. "Mina doesn't have to turn herself in. I can help you get the camera," I continue. "But when I do, I want to also get Mirjam Roodveldt. I won't ask any of you to help me with that part. I'll take those risks myself; if I'm caught, I'll say that I'm acting on my own."

Nobody responds.

"You're saying you need a uniform to get the camera," I say finally. "I'm saying I know how to get a uniform."

The second-to-last time I saw Elsbeth:

She was eighteen, I was seventeen, Bas was dead. She'd met her soldier by then. Her mother didn't mind the relationship. Her parents supported the German occupation, though they weren't obvious about it. It was a private, obsequious support.

It was six months after the invasion. My marks had plummeted, while the rest of the school tried to stagger on like everything was normal. Elsbeth was the only friend I still saw. She came over dutifully, every day, even while I stared at the wall and said nothing. She played with my hair, or told me the latest gossip, or brought random gifts that served no purpose other than to produce a shadow of a smile: A windup toy. A funny card. A lipstick in the ugliest shade of coral, which she smeared all over her mouth, puckering her lips and prancing around my room, telling me to kiss her.

One afternoon Elsbeth came over and sat on my floor, flipping through magazines she'd brought over, her latest effort to cheer me up. She was quieter than usual. I stared at my feet and Elsbeth smiled like a sphinx, like something had happened and she wanted me to guess what it was. Finally she couldn't hold it in any longer. "Rolf loves me," she said. "He told me yesterday, and I said it back."

"No, you don't," I said automatically. "You don't love him. You flirt with everyone."

She pursed her lips, and I could tell she was gathering patience before responding. "I've flirted with enough boys to know the difference. I love Rolf. He wants to marry me. After the war, I'll move back with him to Germany."

"You can't," I told her, but even as I said it, I wasn't sure what I was telling her she couldn't do. Marry a German? Leave the country? Have somebody when I had nobody? Her words had bludgeoned me, bludgeoned even the parts of me I thought were already dead. How could she want to marry one of them? "You can't, Elsbeth. You want me to be happy for you, but I can't be. I can't forgive you for loving the side that killed Bas."

"Rolf didn't kill Bas. Rolf doesn't even want to *be* in this country. He wants the war to be over so he can go home," she said. "He doesn't agree with what Germany is doing—he was sent here. You're just upset right now."

"Of *course* I'm upset right now," I exploded. "Can you even hear yourself? Are you listening to what you're saying? You want to marry a Nazi, after what they did to Bas."

"I'm sorry, Hanneke, that I can't sit with you and be depressed forever," she spat. "I'm sorry that my life is going to move on."

"I'm sorry, too. I'm sorry because it should be your boyfriend who is dead, not mine. I hope he dies soon."

She looked at me for almost a full minute before she spoke again. "Maybe I better go for now," she said finally. "I'm supposed to meet Rolf anyway."

"Go," I said. "And don't ever come back."

TWENTY-TWO

The streets are still quiet when I leave Mrs. de Vries's. A few schoolchildren, a few milkmen and street sweepers, but otherwise, our early-morning meeting is over before I would normally even leave for work. I'm somewhere between euphoric and half dead; floating spots drift in front of my eyes whenever I look too long at one thing.

Maybe my parents aren't awake yet. Maybe they went to bed last night and left the door unlocked for me. They've done it before. Not often. But at least twice they've gone to bed early without making sure that I came in before curfew. I peel my shoes off on the stoop of my building, tiptoeing up the inside stairs.

Three steps from the door, it flies open.

"Where have you been?" My mother crushes me to her chest. "Where have you *been?*"

"I'm sorry," I say automatically. "I'm sorry; I was with some people, and I didn't realize how late it had gotten. When it was past curfew, I just had to stay."

"Which people?" Behind my mother, in his chair, my father's face is flat and icy. He almost never gets angry, but when he does, it's so much more terrible than my mother. "Which friend would let you make your parents worry?"

"Someone from work," I elaborate. "I was helping Mr. Kreuk. It was for a funeral. He needed me to go talk to the family. That's why I ran out of here so quickly yesterday; I almost forgot. They were grieving, and I didn't feel like I could leave, and then curfew passed and I was stuck."

"Mr. Kreuk?" she says.

"He apologizes, too."

"I'm going to see him right now. I'm going to see him right now and tell him—"

"Of course," I interject. "Of course you should go visit Mr. Kreuk. I only hope he doesn't feel he needs to hire another person, if he can't count on me to work nights in cases of emergency." I'm praying that she won't go see Mr. Kreuk. She won't want to do anything to jeopardize my job.

"Do you have any idea what you put us through?" my father asks. "Do you have any idea what last night was like for us?"

"I do. I can imagine. But I'm fine. I'm fine."

Mama releases me from her hug, turning toward my father. Her hands dart in front of her face, swiping. Is she crying? When she turns back to face me, there are no tears, but her face is red and blotchy.

"I'm sorry," I start to say again, but she silences me with a shake of her head.

"Go and change your clothes, then come back for breakfast."

"Go and ... what?"

"Your clothes. I'm going to cook breakfast. You are going to eat breakfast. You are never going to stay out all night without telling us, ever again. But right now, you are going to change your clothes and comb your hair, and we will not speak of this morning."

I don't know why she's offering me this reprieve—maybe it's just that she's as exhausted as I am, maybe she doesn't want to fight today—but I'll take it.

In the bedroom, I drag a comb through my hair and pull on a plaid dress that Mama loves but I hate. It's an olive branch gesture, and she'll recognize it that way. My bed is still unmade from yesterday morning, and I desperately wish I could crawl into it. Instead, I splash cold water on my face in the bathroom and pinch life back into my cheeks. I want to see Ollie and the rest of the group, so we can keep making plans. But we'd been awake so long, we decided it was better to rest, change clothes, and freshen up. Ollie said he would find me later.

When I come out of my bedroom, Mama's rushing around the kitchen, pulling food out of the cupboards, not just the porridge that we usually have for breakfast, but the rest of our eggs and a side of ham I didn't even realize Mama was saving. Instead of the careful, responsible rationing she usually does, Mama is making breakfast like there is no war, like everything is normal.

"Bread?" she asks when she hears me come in, her upper body buried in the pantry. "If I sliced bread, would you eat it?"

I glance at Papa, trying to figure out how I'm supposed to respond, but he won't meet my gaze. "If you want to, slice it. I'll eat anything you make."

We sit down at the table to more food than we normally have in a week. I can tell Papa doesn't believe my lie. His eyes are on me with every bite I take, while I talk about any silly thing I can think of—the weather, the loose button on my skirt, the good price I saw on turnips—and secretly wonder how long I'll have to wait for Ollie to arrive. Will he try to get in contact with Judith first, to see if she has any ideas? Did he even specifically say he would come to me, or was I supposed to find him? I'm so tired I'm not even thinking clearly. Should I go to Leo's and wait?

It's Sunday, not a day I normally work, so I don't have any excuse to leave the house. Mama is watching me like a hawk anyway. Instead of escaping, I help with the chores that didn't get finished yesterday. We wash the windows, sweep the floors, and finish polishing the silver. When we run out of polish, I hopefully suggest that I could go borrow some from a neighbor, but Mama triumphantly produces another jar. When I suggest that I could go buy a newspaper for us all to read, Papa is the one who stops me, saying he has an idea of something he'd much rather listen to than news stories.

"Why don't you play something, Gerda," my father encourages my mother.

"Oh, a neighbor could be napping, and I need to peel the beets for lunch," she protests.

"No, play something, Mama. I'll peel the beets."

At first I suggest it because I think music will put her in a good mood. But when she sits down at the piano, I'm longing to hear her play, too, like she used to. Before the war, I'd be able to hear the music from halfway down the block, first a melody played by my mother and then a student's plodding, clunky version a few seconds later.

She doesn't play at once, just lets her hands rest on the keys. When she finally starts, it's a beginner's tune, one she even managed to teach me before admitting I had no musical skill. It's basic and simple, not the kind of music you would play to show off. The paring knife hangs in my hand. This song reminds me of being young and carefree. She plays it again and again, each time adding a new variation that makes the tune more complex, until the original simple melody is barely audible beneath the trills and chords on top of it. It's still there, though, when I listen closely.

After an hour, Mama is lost in the music and Papa dozes in his chair. I think my transgression is mostly forgiven. In another hour, I'll try to leave. I'll tell them I've made plans with Ollie. They like him. Just when I've settled on that plan, I hear a noise, under the sounds of Mama's playing. Mama hears it, too, and stops, her fingers poised a few centimeters off the keys.

"Hanneke!" The call comes from downstairs, and since the voice is half whispering, it's hard to make out who it belongs to.

I throw the window open with beet-stained fingers, leaning my chest out to see who's standing on our stoop. "Ollie? Are you there?"

"No, it's me." A tall figure standing next to a bicycle steps back and removes his hat.

"Willem? What are you doing here?"

"I'm sorry," he shout-whispers, trying not to disturb the neighbors. "Ollie gave me your address but not your apartment number. I didn't know which buzzer to ring."

"I'll be right down."

As soon as I close the window, Mama stands, the piano bench scraping across the floor. "Who is that?"

"A friend. He didn't know our apartment number." I start to pull on my coat. "I told him I'd be right down."

"No, you won't be right down. Not with a boy I've never met."

"It's Willem—he's Ollie's roommate." The bowl of beets still sits on the floor where I finished peeling them. "Do you want me to put these on the stove?"

"*No*." Mama slams the lid down on the piano, creating a sickening wooden crack. "I forbid it. You were out all last night."

"I'm not going to be out all night this time," I explain patiently. "I just want to go talk to Willem for a while."

Her chin quivers and her eyes have a wild look to them. "I forbid you to leave this house again. You are still my child, Hannie."

"Oh, Mama, I'm not your child." It's the sort of thing that I would usually scream in anger, only now when I say it, I just feel tired and sad. "I bring the money into the house. I buy the groceries, run all the errands. Mama, *I'm* the one who takes care of *you*."

Mama's face crumples, and all the goodwill we amassed during the breakfast and the piano playing disappears. "The daughter I know never would have spoken to me this way."

It's nothing she hasn't said to me a dozen times, but this time it stings. I'm exhausted by these comparisons to the girl I was before the war. By replaying all the ways I was better and the things I will never get back.

"That daughter doesn't exist anymore," I say to Mama, and my voice is resigned. "She is gone, and she's never coming back."

TWENTY-THREE

A re you all right?"

Willem takes my arm as soon as I get outside. I wonder if he heard the fighting coming through the open window, or if he's just reading my face.

"I'm fine."

"This is how you look when you're fine?" he asks lightly.

"No, this is how I look when I don't want to talk about it."

If I said that to Bas, he would have put his hands out in fake kitty claws, hissing and pretending to paw at the air until I laughed. If I said that to Ollie, he would say something equally sarcastic back to me, giving as good as he got. When I say it to Willem, he just nods, looking concerned.

"I'm sorry," I say. I don't want to think about the stricken look on Mama's face when I walked out the door. "Did Ollie send you?"

Ollie was going to come and see me himself, Willem explains, but he asked Willem to let him sleep for twenty minutes first. "I'm letting him sleep for a few hours instead," he says. "He'll be furious when he wakes up, but he was barely coherent. If I'd let him ride to your house, we'd be fishing him out of a canal this afternoon. He works too much. So it's just me, and with your help, you and me."

"You and me for what?"

"Sanne and Leo are bringing food to some of the children in hiding. When Ollie wakes up, he'll go to Judith's spot and find out anything she might know about the soldiers who usually lead the transport. You volunteered to get the uniform. And I'm hoping you'll help me do my job as well."

"What's your job?"

"My job is to figure out the escape route."

I don't know Willem nearly as well as Ollie, but he has a reassuring kindness that immediately feels familiar. While we walk through my neighborhood, he keeps his head bent toward mine as though we're having an intimate conversation, but what he's really doing is explaining the Schouwburg.

Some of it I already know. The theater is only a stopping place—Jews are brought there for a few days or weeks. After the theater, the next destination is a transit camp elsewhere in the Netherlands. Prisoners don't stay at those for long, either, Willem explains. They're just way stations before the prisoners are taken out of the country, to other camps with foreign-sounding names, to places where healthy young men may die of mysterious illnesses.

But before any of that happens, Jews are packed onto trains at a station on the outskirts of the city. And to get to the railway station, soldiers sometimes put the prisoners on trams or trucks. But often, they simply force the prisoners to walk.

It's not far, about two kilometers. They don't block off the streets or make any special preparations for the transport. Sometimes they do it at night, while the rest of the city pretends to sleep behind its blackout curtains. Sometimes they do it in broad daylight.

So that's our chance. Sometime in the space between the Hollandsche Schouwburg and the train station, we need to get the camera from the carriage—which will presumably have a child in it. And I need to spot Mirjam, distract the guards, and run with her to safety without anyone noticing. That's all.

"But the soldiers?"

"That's Ollie and Judith," Willem says. "That's their job today. You and me—our job today is just geography. We can do this. Everything is going to be okay."

I want to believe him. He sounds sure, and I cling to that certainty. Not because I think he's right, but because it feels good to have someone tell me everything will be fine.

Beside me, Willem looks at his watch and starts walking faster. "We need to hurry." He takes my hand to pull me along. "The deportations to Westerbork are usually in the order the people arrived in. The prisoners from the roundup with Mirjam and the carriage should be deported in a night transport tomorrow. I wish we could practice by watching another one happening in the evening, but there isn't one—we'll have to follow one this afternoon to figure out what route they take."

"What if there aren't any holes in the route?" I ask.

"There's at least one."

"Which is?"

"They probably don't think anyone is stupid enough to impersonate Nazis and stop a transport. So they won't be expecting it."

We stop at the end of the Schouwburg's block, close enough to see the theater's entrance without looking like we're actively watching. Willem leans over his bicycle; he's disabled his chain and is now pretending to fix it, working it back over the sprocket. It gives us a reason to loiter in the area. While he pretends to work, I watch the theater's heavy door.

It's a little before four o'clock. Precisely on the hour, it opens. I nudge my foot against Willem's, and he easily slips the chain back into place, sighing like he's sorry his broken bicycle held us up for so long. The soldiers appear first, two of them, one younger and one who reminds me of my father's older brother, the one who still lives in Belgium and used to send money on my birthday.

The prisoners follow, carrying suitcases, disheveled and tired like they haven't slept in days. The crowd is big, maybe seventy people, and the soldiers march them down the middle of the street. It's a lovely winter day in Amsterdam, and though there are other people on the street, couples like me and Willem, nobody acts like the forced parade of people is out of the ordinary. Our sense of ordinary has become horrifying.

There's no Mirjam, but there are girls her age or younger, surrounded by young couples and middle-aged men. One walks past, wearing a green tweed coat and felt hat. He keeps his eyes straight forward, but something in them is familiar, something about them makes me think of chalk dust. It's my third-grade teacher. The one who used to bring a box of hard candies on Wednesdays and pass them out to us, one by one, as we left. I can't remember his name. I didn't know he was Jewish.

The soldier who looks like my uncle yells something. It's in fast German; I can't understand the words, but I can understand the meaning as he gestures to the end of the block. In front of me, an older woman trips in the crowd. The man next to her—her husband, from the familiar, tender way he touches her—tries to help her up, and the soldier lifts his gun and gestures for the man to keep going. He moves again to help his wife; the soldier spins his gun around, using the butt of it to shove the man forward. He staggers onward, and now it's his wife who helps him. I try not to look.

"I wish their route didn't have so many open spaces," Willem says, walking his bicycle at a slow pace. Still we're pretending to have a casual conversation. Still, we're pretending not to notice the violence around us. "It isn't as good for us."

No, this route is not good for us. It's the shortest distance to the railway station, which makes sense. But it also means we're taking wide streets through open spaces, and long blocks that are uninterrupted by alleyways. There aren't many places along this route that would make for good cover, and we need good cover. A uniform will only get us partway.

"As we walk along, think about what you see." Willem's eyes dart furtively to the left and then the right, sweeping along the horizon. "What route would let you get away with the least chance of someone seeing you?"

"We'll be passing the Oosterpark," I suggest. It's a big, mani-cured municipal park, and it would be easy for several people to disappear into the Oosterpark's darkness.

Willem thinks. "But we don't have any contacts near the park. No one in our group lives there. Once you got there, where would you go?" He's right. Besides, the Oosterpark doesn't come until after we will have crossed two canals. It's not a good idea for an escape route to rely on bridges; they're too easily closed or blocked.

"It needs to be before Plantage Muidergracht," I think out loud. "Close enough to get back to Mrs. de Vries's. We should try to get Mirjam and the carriage as soon as possible after they leave the Schouwburg."

"I think you're right. If we get as far as the bridge, we won't have a chance."

Focus on escape routes, I tell myself. *Focus on how close you are to saving Mirjam. Focus on that one life.* I have to focus on Mirjam because I don't want to think about my third-grade teacher, who I won't be saving, or Mr. Bierman, who I won't be saving, or any of Mirjam's classmates or the entire group of people walking so close to us right now. I won't be helping any of these people.

"What about here?" Willem stops walking, pointing up to a building like he's merely interested in showing off the architecture.

We've come to an intersection where three streets cross each other, veining off at odd angles so that the sightline cuts off after less than twenty-five meters. If Mirjam and I ran from here, we'd be out of sight in five seconds, and two soldiers—assuming there were only two soldiers, assuming a lot of things—wouldn't have enough bodies to explore which direction we ran to.

Scanning the buildings lining the street, my eyes land on a butcher shop. A large awning hangs over the entrance, orange, the color of our exiled monarchy. Somehow this seems like a good omen.

"That butcher shop." I nod toward it. "Under the awning." The shop itself is tucked back farther from the street than the shops next to it, so it already has more natural cover. Under the awning is a large plaster cow, life-size, more than big enough for one or two people to hide behind.

Willem gives a loud sigh, squatting to the ground in mock annoyance with his bicycle chain, while really taking the time to observe the butcher shop. "Good," he says. "Between the cow and the way the doorway is built, you would have to know someone was standing there to see them."

Does he really think it's good? Do I? Or do I just want it to work? I can't tell. This intersection Willem and I have chosen— this overhanging awning and this plaster cow—it's more than one kilometer from the Muiderpoort station. That seems like a long distance. Is it enough space to save one life?

The transport has moved ahead of us now. Solemn, silent rows of people being taken to God knows what, and we stare after them, helpless. Then it's just me and Willem.

"Are you going to be okay?" he asks. "With your part? With the uniform?"

"I'll be fine."

"If you need me to try to put you in contact with anyone...I don't know that I know any of the right people, but I could—"

"It's all right, Willem."

He nods and hesitates before speaking again. "Hanneke, I hope you don't take this the wrong way," he begins. "It's just that getting a uniform is usually the kind of thing we would plan weeks for. I like you. I think you're a strong person. But Ollie...he is my best friend, and I can't let anything happen to him. To any of them. You weren't that eager to help us. I want you to tell me it's okay for us to put our trust in you."

I've spent two years wanting nobody to trust me, wanting not to be depended on. But now I have seen a transport, and I have seen a deportation center, and I have seen the hopeful handwriting of a frightened girl, and I have seen brave people forced to hide, and mean people become secretly brave, so when I open my mouth, I say to Willem: "You can. I'll do my best, Willem."

My throat starts to swell, and I look away, and when I finally look back, Willem is still holding my eyes, appropriately polite and achingly concerned. "I hope everything is okay with you, Hanneke," he says. "If there's something you want to talk about, I don't need to tell the others."

I bite down hard on my cheek because Willem's question is so genuine and because, after everything that's happened in the past twenty-four hours, I already feel so raw.

"It's nothing. I'm fine. I just—I don't sleep well," I say finally. "I don't sleep well, and I don't cry, since Bas died."

A half explanation. Still more than I've said out loud to anyone.

Willem places his hand on my arm again. "This won't bring Bas back, Hanneke. I know you know that already. But just in case your mind is trying to get you to believe otherwise. You could rescue Mirjam and still not be able to sleep at night."

TWENTY-FOUR

The doorbell has changed. It used to be a grinding, buzzing noise, and now it's a clear-toned bell. At first I think I must have misremembered it, but how could I misremember a sound I'd heard one hundred, two hundred, five hundred times in my life?

Elsbeth must have had a new one installed when her parents moved in with her grandmother, and she and Rolf took over her childhood home. It's strange to think of her this way, as a wife making domestic decisions about the way her household is run. I wonder if she tore down the wallpaper in the sitting room, too. She'd probably have the money to do that, and she always thought it was ugly.

No one answers the door, so I ring the new bell again, pressing my face close to the glass. Same sitting room. Same wallpaper.

I knew it would make me nervous, to come here. I knew it would be uncomfortable. I didn't anticipate the heaviness of the dread spreading through my stomach, though. I didn't know I would have to root my feet in place so intentionally, just to make sure I didn't run away.

Nothing—no noises from the inside, no flickers of light from a reading lamp. Nobody is home. It's better this way, I tell myself. Safer. Easier. I'd planned for a million contingencies: Her at home, him at home, both of them at home, and this is the one I knew would be the best scenario for me. It's why I came now, because Elsbeth's family always had a big Sunday dinner at her grandmother's house, and I bet this tradition has continued even through the war. So why does a part of me feel so disappointed to not see her face?

Another thing that hasn't changed about this house: the spare key on top of the doorframe, slightly rusty, cold in my hand.

Everything smells the same: the whole house, like cloves and laundry powder, the way it always did, the odor particular to the Vos family, the one I know well enough to have it be comforting. But this time I'm not a guest, I remind myself. This time I'm working.

Before I can second-guess myself, I slip all the way inside. The master bedroom is upstairs, at the end of the hall. I almost never went inside it, though Elsbeth would occasionally sneak in and return with her mother's rouge for us to practice applying. As soon as I step into it, I know it's wrong, though. This room doesn't feel occupied; the bed is piled with a half-finished sewing project.

My heart sinks. If Elsbeth and Rolf haven't moved into the

master bedroom, then that means I have to go into a room I was hoping to avoid. Back toward the stairwell. The first door on the right.

I open the door and am overrun by ghosts. Elsbeth's bedroom is where I spent so many afternoons: practicing dances, pretending to do homework, ranking our favorite film stars. Talking about how we would grow up and have babies at the same time, and eventually become old women together, walking around the square and holding each other's arms for support. *Stop. Stop.*

Her dressing gown hangs on the door. It still has a hole in the sleeve, from the time we smoked secret cigarettes on the balcony.

To steel myself against emotion, I'm clinging to the practicalities of breaking the law. Elsbeth used to share this room with her older sister. Nellie's wardrobe was on the left and Elsbeth's was on the right. When she installed her new husband in her childhood home, I bet she gave him Nellie's old space to use for his clothing. That seems like something Elsbeth would do, telling him to shove things aside, make room for himself anywhere. He would discover one of Nellie's forgotten brassieres, and Elsbeth would laugh at his embarrassment.

I slide open the left closet. I'm right. Inside, neatly pressed men's clothes, slacks and shirts, hang in a row. These are the clothes that Elsbeth's husband wears. Her husband. Rolf. For her new life, which I am not a part of.

No uniform, though. The uniform isn't in here; I check twice. He must have at least two—one to wear and one to wash—but there's nothing in here. Nothing draped over chairs, nothing lying across the quickly made bed. Where could it be?

Back in the hallway, I open the linen closet. Inside is a wicker basket, full of crumpled towels and bedsheets, waiting to be washed. I paw deeper, looking for flashes of gray and black, the color of death, the color of the Gestapo. Toward the bottom, I spot something dark-colored, so I pull it out.

How could I have forgotten? Elsbeth's grandmother gave gifts in twos. The Tonsil didn't fit, and Elsbeth gave it to me, giggling at my face when I opened the hideous dress. But Elsbeth had to keep its mate, another dress in dismal grayish purple.

It smells like her, like talcum powder and perfume, and I have a dozen memories of Elsbeth in this dress. Making faces when her mother suggested she wear it to a party. Wearing it anyway, but trying to "accidentally" spill punch on it. Gossiping at the party about what a good kisser Henk was, sagely telling me that a first kiss was never as good as a second one.

I kissed Ollie, I want to tell her. I kissed Ollie, and Bas is still dead, and how are you doing, and was it stupid for our friendship to end because you loved a boy, or is that just what happens?

I stuff the dress back into the laundry basket and grab at the black collar peeking out from the bottom. Rolf's shirt. And just as I'm grabbing the matching pants below it, the front door opens.

Without even thinking, I dive fully into the linen closet, squeezing myself next to the laundry hamper, Rolf's rumpled uniform clutched in my fists. I ease the squeaking closet door shut, all but a sliver—I'm too afraid of the clicking sound to close it all the way. My heart is pounding so loudly in my ears I'm sure anyone could hear it, and I tell it to slow down, but it won't obey.

"I can't believe you forgot the cake. Dinner is not worth having without cake."

Yet another thing that hasn't changed: Elsbeth's voice, teasing and bouncy and hitting me like a punch in the gut. My mouth opens in a whimper. I stuff Rolf's evil uniform against my lips.

"Apparently life is not worth living without cake, if you're my wife," he teases her.

"So I like the sweeter things in life." She laughs.

"Is there anything else you need while we're here?" Rolf asks.

"I might as well grab a sweater, since Granny's house is an icebox."

They're so normal together. I wasn't expecting that. They don't sound like war. They sound like jokes and kisses, like the friends I should still have. I hear her footsteps on the stairs, the squeak on the fourth tread. Her bedroom is the door before the linen cupboard; she'll have no reason to walk past. Next door, I hear her opening her wardrobe, riffling through hangers, humming something tuneless. Elsbeth never could sing.

"Have you seen my yellow sweater?" she calls downstairs to the kitchen.

"Didn't you put it in the hamper?"

Saliva pools in my mouth. I see Elsbeth's slim ankles approach, closer, and my nose is tickled by her talcum powder. She puts her hand on the knob. What will I do when she finds me? I run through the escape scenarios I do with every Nazi, except that in this case they're insane. I could hit her. I could hug her. I could greet her like the past two years never happened. But they did happen, and now I don't just hate and love and miss Elsbeth; I also have to fear her.

"Elsbeth, it's in here," Rolf calls. "Your sweater was on the chair."

She moves away again, heels tripping on the floor. My heart pounds out of my chest, both nerves and anger and grief. And then she's gone again, my old best friend.

When I get home that night, Mama and Papa are already in bed. It's too early for them to be asleep, but they don't bother to come out. For years I've begged them for this—to just go to bed without waiting up for me—but now I picture them in their nightclothes, listening to me hang my coat, and it makes me feel unsettled. Something shifted between us, after the last fight when I left with Willem. I'm still their daughter, but I'm no longer their child.

There's a letter propped against a book on my bedside table. I don't recognize the handwriting on the envelope, and when I open it, a small, star-shaped note falls out. Christoffel must have dropped it off while I was out, after his father returned from Den Haag. A response from Amalia. Just what I thought I wanted a couple of days ago, and now it doesn't matter at all.

Dear Hanneke, I read as I unfold the crisp notebook paper. *I don't know where she is. I wish I did. I miss my friend, too.*

I picture Mirjam joyfully reuniting with her friend, carrying a stack of magazines, carrying weeks' worth of thoughts and feelings to share, having the reunion that Elsbeth and I will never get to have.

When I fall asleep I have an old nightmare again, the one I used to have all the time after Bas died. He comes to me in his uniform with the letter I'd torn up. In the dream, he's pieced it back together and is angry that I never read it. "It means you've forgotten me," he says. "It doesn't," I try to tell him. "It doesn't mean that at all. I think of you every day."

"Look," I say to him. "I'll read it right now. I'll read it this very minute if it's important to you." But for every word I try to read, Bas turns a little paler and a little more gray. By the time I'm half-way through, he's a corpse standing in front of me, and I can't finish the letter, because I'm crying. When I wake up my eyes are dry—my eyes are always dry—but my sheets are twisted around my body and drenched with sweat.

The next night, just before curfew, Ollie knocks on my door. When my mother answers, he explains: His mother isn't well. He and his father need to take her to the hospital. Pia is afraid to stay home alone; might I come and spend the night with her?

My mother doesn't agree or disagree; she doesn't even look at me. She turns her head and says, "Do what you want to, Hanneke."

"I should go, then, for Ollie's mother," I say.

Except, of course, Ollie's mother is fine and Pia is probably home right now obliviously doing her schoolwork. Mirjam's transport is scheduled to begin in two hours.

TWENTY-FIVE

Monday

We have to stand very close and stay very quiet, underneath the awning of the butcher shop. It's a good spot, though. The awning and the ridiculous cow cover us as much as I hoped they would: Two pairs of soldiers have walked past without noticing we're there. I just hope the sky stays clear. If it starts to rain or snow, one of them might duck under for cover.

I can't see Willem, but I know he's not far away, a few blocks down, hiding with a change of clothes for Ollie.

Because Ollie, Olivier, Laurence Olivier, when Bas was feeling silly, is now wearing the gray Gestapo uniform of Elsbeth's husband's. It's too big around the shoulders. If anyone looked too closely at Ollie, they would realize he was all wrong, and if anyone who knew Ollie walked past and questioned his uniform, that would be even worse.

So this is the plan: for Ollie and me to wait under the awning until the transport comes. For him to stop the soldier leading it, saying he has orders to search one baby carriage for contraband. He'll get the camera. He'll meet up with Willem to change out of the uniform so that suspicious neighbors don't see him wearing it. Ollie must be nervous, but he doesn't show it. He stares ahead, into the night, at the people who hurry past on their way home. We have time. Half an hour, at least—we've gotten into position just before curfew—and we've been killing time by barking reminders and observations to each other.

"You'll only have a minute to get her," Ollie says abruptly. "I'll be querying them about the carriage, showing the false orders Willem created. I'll draw it out as long as I can, but you'll have barely any time, and they absolutely cannot see you."

"I know, Ollie."

"And then you'll run to the street around the corner, where I'll meet you and—"

"Ollie."

We both fall silent again. I know everything he can warn me about because we've been through every variation of the plan that we can think of, and because I've already been warned, several times: If I can't find Mirjam or get her to come with me in the period of time that it takes him to get the camera from the baby carriage, then she is not going to be rescued.

Then I will have failed her.

"What are you thinking about?" he asks me.

"Nothing," I say. "What are you thinking about?"

He turns away slightly, and in the shadows of the night, it's enough to mask his expression. "I'm thinking about Bas."

"You are?"

"Aren't you, too?"

I am, too. I am, always. Bas ice-skating with my mother. Bas bringing me cake. Bas driving me crazy. Bas alive. Bas dead.

"Tonight I'm thinking about..." He stops and swallows. "I'm thinking about, what was going through Bas's mind in the invasion, when he realized he was probably going to die?"

"Was he just thinking about how scared he was?" I say, and it's easy for me to finish Ollie's thought because I've had it so many times myself. "How scared he was and how much he wished he could be at home?"

"Was he in pain?" Ollie asks.

"Angry?" I say.

"Or was he just alone?"

"It was my fault," I whisper. The words fall, breaking in front of me for both of us to see. "It's my fault that Bas is dead."

His face in the shadows is impossible to read. "What did you say?" he asks.

"Bas. It's my fault that Bas is dead."

The most terrible thing, and now I've said it out loud, and the enormity of that makes me gasp. When you say a terrible thing, it should be like a weight lifted off your chest, but giving voice to this thought has only made the weight heavier.

"What are you talking about? What happened to Bas wasn't your fault. You were miles away. You didn't pull a trigger. You didn't release a bomb."

"I know I didn't pull a trigger." It's the same thing my parents told me after he died. That I wasn't there. That I didn't shoot him, or bomb him, or drown him, or do whatever it was, precisely, that caused Bas to no longer exist. "But I sent him. I told him to join."

"Hanneke, you knew Bas. You knew him as well as I did. Do you honestly think he didn't want to go? Do you honestly think he would have enlisted if, deep down, he didn't really want to?"

He's trying to make me feel better, but I only feel worse. I'm about to tell Ollie the secret that I never wanted to tell.

"He *told* me he didn't want to," I say. "During his party. I left, and he chased after me, and he told me he didn't want to go, and I said he had to. I said it was his duty to. And he gave me a letter to read in case he died, but I didn't. I took it home and threw it away because I was so sure he would come back, and I was so wrong, because he didn't come back. Do you understand, Ollie? *I made him go.*"

My throat is sore, like the words themselves caused physical pain coming out of my mouth. Now I've said it all. I can't look at Ollie, because I'm so filled with shame. He's standing very still, but I can hear him swallowing back lumps in his throat. When he speaks again, his voice is thick.

"My last conversation with Bas was after the party, too. It was late. Everyone had left. He came into my room, and I asked why he wasn't in bed, since he had to get up so early for training."

"You talked to him *after* I talked to him?" I don't know why this never occurred to me. Obviously Bas's family would have talked to him—he lived with them. In my mind, though, I was the last person. I talked to him and then he died. That's what I picture, and what keeps me awake at nights.

"Several hours after. The sun was about to come up."

I don't dare breathe. "What did you talk about?"

"I asked him how he was feeling. I asked him if he was scared. I said I wouldn't judge him if he was, that I would be, too, in his position. He admitted he was scared—but he said that if he weren't, it wouldn't truly count as bravery, would it? And he called me a delicate flower for not volunteering. And I asked what kind of flower. And he said definitely not a tulip, because no one with two lips was going to want to kiss such a wimp."

And now Ollie is smiling, at this memory of bold, silly Bas, and, amazingly, I'm smiling, too, even as we're both so sad.

"And he gave me a letter, also."

I freeze. Ollie reaches into his trousers pocket. The letter he pulls out is on notebook paper, the kind schoolchildren use for grammar exercises, the kind that Elsbeth and I, and Amalia and Mirjam, and young people everywhere use to share secrets. He holds it out. "Go ahead."

It's been folded many times over, carried in so many pockets, that the creases are soft and tattered. In the dark I have to hold it centimeters from my nose, laboring over every letter.

Laurence,

I'm sorry for being such a twit. You were a good big brother. Tell Mama she got to keep the good son, even though she won't believe it at first (who would blame her?). There's a little bit of money under my mattress, and you can have it. But I told Pia the same thing, so you'll have to see which one

of you is quicker. Tell Hanneke I love her. And to move on.
Not too fast. Maybe after two or three months.

—B.

Now I really am laughing, covering my mouth with my hand, because it's such an unsatisfactory letter, which in turn makes it so much like Bas: solemn one minute and ridiculous the next. Self-deprecating and sweet. "Why didn't you ever show me this before?"

"Because I assumed you had your own letter. And because you never came to visit, after the memorial. I thought you didn't want anything to do with my family."

"I thought you all hated me."

"I didn't."

"Ollie," I say. "Do you think he meant what he said to you, about how he was scared but glad he was going?"

"Do you think he meant what he said to *you*, about not wanting to go at all?"

I don't know. For two and a half years, I thought I knew. "I'm not sure."

"Maybe Bas wasn't sure, either," Ollie says. "Maybe he wanted to go one minute and wanted to stay another."

Tell her to move on, Bas said. Another thing I haven't been able to give him.

Ollie puts his arms around me. His cheek presses against my forehead. His breath is in my hair, and on my neck, and before I can really think about what I'm doing, I tilt my face up so that I'm looking directly into his eyes. He smiles at me, and I move my lips toward his. It's not even that I want Ollie. It's more that I finally feel, for the first time in more than two years, liberated from some of the guilt I've forced upon myself. My lips brush against his and—

"Hanneke, what are you doing?" Ollie lurches back, holding his palms up to stop me from coming closer.

My hand flies up to my mouth. "I'm sorry, Ollie. I—I misinterpreted the situation."

He shakes his head quickly; I can almost see him blushing even in the dark. "It's just, I don't think of you like that, Hanneke."

"No. Of course you don't. You were just being nice. I'm your brother's girlfriend."

"It's not that." He looks pained. "I love someone else."

I'm hideously ashamed. Ollie, who has been kind to me a dozen times in the past week—I just betrayed that kindness by trying to kiss him, *and* he's in love with someone else. Why didn't he tell me earlier? "Judith?" I guess. "You love Judith?"

"Judith? No." Ollie shakes his head. "I don't love Judith."

"Then who?"

He sighs. "How can I explain? It's like this: You helped the resistance because of one person, Hanneke. I joined because of one person, too.... Because Jews aren't the only ones who suffer because of the Nazis. I don't love Judith. I love Willem."

"You love ... *Willem?*" My brain trips over the concept. "You love Willem?"

"No one else knows."

I try to gather my thoughts. I know the Nazis have rounded up homosexuals and political prisoners. But I've never known anyone who was *that way.* "Are you sure?" I blurt out. "You kissed me, just a few days ago, in front of the Green Police."

"I did kiss you. And after I did it, you told me then that I was a good actor. I am. Better than you, probably. You pretend for the Germans, during the war. I pretend for everyone, every day. I haven't told anyone else. I'm an onderduiker, too. The world is my underground."

"But I don't understand. How did you know? How did you know that you—with Willem?"

"How did you know you loved Bas?"

"Because I did," I say.

"I know because I do. I've known for a long time."

"Are you in danger?" I ask, because I'm too stunned to think of the other dozen questions I'm sure I have.

"Will you tell anyone else?"

"Of course not."

"Then no. As long as nobody knows." His body stiffens. "The transport. It's here."

TWENTY-SIX

The sound of rows and rows of footsteps. It's loud, especially when you're tying your life to it. The thought of Ollie here with me comforts and then frightens me. So many people are putting themselves at risk. Willem in the shadows. Mrs. de Vries with Mina, waiting to take in Mirjam until we can get her to Mrs. Janssen's. Mrs. Janssen, praying back at her house.

"Blue coat," I whisper, as if I need the reminder. "I need to look for the blue coat."

What if she's not wearing it? What if she thinks the night is too warm, or she gave it away, or someone stole it? And the carriage—what if the carriage isn't even on this transport? What if it was left behind, in the theater? Ollie can't wear a Gestapo uniform indefinitely, to stop every transport. All the contingencies we couldn't anticipate are running through my head as I think of how slender the plan is that we've rested all our hopes on.

Two guards bookend the prisoners, the same as the transport yesterday: The older man with the craggy, deep-lined features who looks like my uncle is in front, and the young one follows the prisoners. Line after line of them. My heart sinks. I don't see her; it's hard to see anyone who isn't in the column closest to me. Beyond that, everyone is packed together, and their faces are visible only by the light of the full moon.

But in one of the rear rows, big and obvious and making noises as it rolls over the cobblestones: a baby carriage. And in the row behind it, another one.

Two. Which one is Mina's? I could tell if I were closer; I've seen it before. But Ollie never has. What will he do? Should I try to whisper a description to him? Before I can do that, he's gone, the heels of his boots clicking sharply across stones.

"Wait," he calls out in his perfect German accent. The young soldier hears him and looks around, confused, for the source of this disruption. "Wait," Ollie says again, crisply waving the papers Willem organized with his fake order on it. "There is a problem with this transport."

"Halt!" the older soldier calls out. His prisoners come to an uncertain stop in the middle of the street as the soldier sweeps a flashlight in Ollie's direction. "We didn't hear of a problem," he calls to Ollie.

"I don't think the Gestapo is in the business of telling theater guards about our intelligence operations," he snaps. "This order comes straight from Schreieder."

At the mention of the top Gestapo official, the soldiers exchange a quick look with each other and hurry toward Ollie. "Don't *touch* them," Ollie snaps as one reaches for his papers. "Do you think I want you smudging up my work orders?"

My eyes grasp at the prisoners corralled behind the soldiers, locking on each row, desperately scanning for sky-colored material. Now both soldiers are looking at Ollie's fake work order. Neither of them are looking toward me. I run.

I run straight into the Nazi transport.

I squeeze into the back, next to a woman who flinches when I press against her shoulder. "Mirjam Roodveldt," I mutter without moving my lips. "Blue coat?" She shakes her head as I push ahead to the next row. "Fifteen-year-old girl? Dark hair."

I edge up to the next line, repeating the name again. Most people ignore me. "Mirjam Roodveldt?" A few people shake their heads stiffly, begging me with their eyes to stop drawing attention to their vicinity.

"Mama, does this mean we get to go home now?" a young boy a few people over calls out, tugging on his mother's coat. "If that man said there's a problem? Can we go?"

"Silence!" the older soldier calls, breaking his conversation with Ollie without looking up. "Quiet the child, or I'll quiet him."

He's just joking, the terrified woman mouths to her son, even as she covers his mouth with her hand.

"Mirjam?" I whisper, moving to the next row. The mother looks at me now. *Stop,* she mouths.

Over by Ollie, the soldiers are having a disagreement. One of them wants to listen to Ollie; the other says they should go back to the theater and get confirmation. *A flash of blue—brilliant cerulean blue.* I see it and then immediately lose it again in the dark. It was after the woman with the rose-colored hat. It was before the family with the stoic father carrying the sleepy girl.

"Mirjam?" I whisper. "Mirjam!" a little more loudly.

"Please be quiet," whispers the woman with the hat.

"You'll get us all killed," the man next to her begs, his voice trembling.

"*Silence*," the older soldier calls again. "Kurt," he instructs the younger soldier standing next to him. "Shoot the next one who you hear talking."

All the prisoners freeze in place, their breath cold and white against the night.

But I saw something. A movement, the last time I called her name. A few rows ahead of me, a girl turned her head just a fraction of an inch. Even in the dark, her coat is the color of the sky. Blood rushes in my ears as I ease up another row. One more line, and now I'm right behind her. My heart is pounding so fast, and this time not only in fear but in exhilaration for what I've almost done. I've found her. She's going to be safe.

To my left, another movement. The soldiers have settled their disagreement over Ollie's papers, and now the three of them are walking purposefully toward the first woman with the carriage. They gesture for her to remove the child, do it quickly. While their flashlights are pointed at her, Ollie looks up, searches for me frantically in the crowd. Go, he mouths when he catches my eye. *Hurry.*

I touch the back of Mirjam's coat, and she swivels to look at me.

"Mirjam." I'm barely moving my lips. "Come with me."

Mirjam recoils, shaking her head in fear. Meters away, Ollie tells the guards that this isn't the right carriage; he needs to see the other one. I can hear his shoes clipping on the stones, and I can tell he's trying to walk slowly enough to buy me a few extra seconds. *Thank you, Ollie.*

"Mirjam, it's okay. I know who you are."

No, she mouths.

Over by Ollie, the woman pushing the second carriage takes her baby out of it. The baby starts to cry, a thin, piercing wail, but the sound provides enough cover that I can mutter instructions to Mirjam.

"We have to run. Follow me. People are waiting." I reach down and lace my fingers through Mirjam's. Her hand feels small and bird-fragile in mine. She's so young.

Ollie has the camera and the film, the camera that represents hundreds of lives. He's walking it past us, and in the moonlight his face is filled with terror, begging me silently to run, run now, leave Mirjam behind if she won't follow me. I can't. I've come too far. I'm holding her hand.

"Now," I hiss. I tug Mirjam's hand, pulling her to the side. Mirjam resists. "*Now,*" I plead.

The soldiers take their places again. "Hurry," one says. "Move."

And now everyone is marching again, and I'm marching with them. What have I done? Why didn't Mirjam listen to me? Ollie is receding, back farther in the shadows with the precious cargo he came for, and I'm getting closer to the bridge, with its wide-open, deadly spaces. If we get all the way to the train station, they might make me board. We have to try running.

Forty more steps until the bridge. Thirty-five. We're coming upon the final alley, the last place we could run before the bridge. I start pulling Mirjam toward it. Why won't Mirjam follow me? Something's wrong. Her hand twists in mine, struggles, breaks away.

She's running, but not in the direction I am. She's running directly onto the open bridge. *Oh God, oh God, what is she doing?* It's the worst direction she could have run in. Her blue coat flies behind her, flapping in the cold, running, running away from me.

"Stop!" I cry out at the same time a soldier yells, "Halt."

"*Halt,*" he calls out again, his boots clattering against the cobblestones. What should I do? Try to distract them? Run after her? Tell everyone else in this transport to run, too?

"Stop," I start to say again, halfway between the alley and the transport.

Suddenly, the wind is knocked out of me as a pair of strong arms wrap around my waist and drag me back toward the alley.

"Let me go!"

"Let you go?" Ollie growls in a loud, ferocious voice. "I don't think so. I saw you try to escape."

Mirjam is still running along the cobblestoned street, then onto the bridge with its thick iron rails. Her legs are spindly. Her shoes clatter against the wooden planks faintly, under the heavier sound of soldiers' boots. I claw at Ollie's hands around my waist, trying to pry them loose. The camera digs into my hip, and he holds me tighter.

"I am overruling these guards on this matter! You are obviously a part of this—of this *conspiracy plot*. I'm taking you in for questioning immediately!"

"Please," I say, and I've never heard my voice sound so desperate.

"*No*," he whispers, and this time it's real Ollie, talking to me, and not the Ollie pretending to be a soldier. "You can't."

"Please," I beg Ollie. "They're going to—"

Bang.

And they do. They shoot her. In the middle of the bridge, in the back of the neck so that blood bursts from her throat, slick and shining in the moonlight.

"No," I cry out, but my words are muffled by another gunshot.

Mirjam's knees buckle under her as her hands fly up to her neck, but I know she's dead even before she hits the ground. It's the way she doesn't bother to break her own fall, the way she crumples to the ground with her head and shoulders hitting the cobblestones.

The prisoners stare, gaping, at the body in the middle of the bridge, some of them letting out shocked screams, some of them clasping their hands in silent horror. The boy who called out to his mother earlier is crying, and she still has her hand over his mouth so the tears and the muffled sobs squeeze through her fingers.

The young guard, the one who shot her, comes back to his post. "A warning," he calls. His voice wavers; he wasn't expecting this to happen, and he doesn't know what to do now.

"Let's go," he calls out. "Quickly." He's not even going to move her. He's going to make the other prisoners walk right around her, leaving her in the middle of the bridge for the milkmen and street cleaners to find in the morning.

Ollie pulls me along, away from the bridge, one arm wrapped around my waist and the other holding the camera.

"Walk, Hanneke," he instructs me. "You have to walk."

I can't see where he's leading me, because I'm crying. Sobs wrack my body, the first tears I've cried since Bas died. They blind me and taste salty and unfamiliar on my lips.

I'm crying for Mirjam, the girl I was supposed to save but couldn't, and didn't even know. And for the mother who was shushing her son, and the man who begged me to stop talking. I'm crying for Mrs. Janssen, who has no one and who I told I would help and who trusted me and who I failed. I'm crying for Bas. I'm crying for Elsbeth and the German soldier she chose over her best friend, and for Ollie, who can't be with Willem, and for all the people in my whole country who saw the tanks roll in at the start of the occupation and have yet to see them roll out again.

TWENTY-SEVEN

Ollie leads me down back alleys and dark streets. I can't even tell if the path he's choosing is safe, if we're making our way toward Willem. I don't know if anyone else knows what happened, or if everyone is still waiting for us to return, thinking the plan has worked as it should. My feet move mechanically beside his. Finally he leads me down a short flight of stairs, and I realize we're in what must be his and Willem's apartment.

"Tea?" he says shortly.

It's the first phrase he's spoken. His hands shake as he opens cupboard doors and bangs them shut, forgetting where he keeps the cups. He looks toward the door, again and again. Willem is out there. Willem and Mirjam.

"Willem is still—" I start to say.

"I know," Ollie cuts me off, and from the way his eyes flash,

I can tell he doesn't want to talk about it. Finally, he stops going through the cupboards, leaning against the counter and gripping its edges so tightly his knuckles turn white. "You're okay?" he asks, his back still to me.

I don't answer. How am I supposed to answer? Ollie slams his hands against the counter; I jolt at the noise. "Dammit. *Dammit.*"

"What are you doing?" I ask as he starts to head back to the door.

"I have to make sure Willem is okay."

"Ollie, you don't know where he is."

He pulls on his coat, buttoning it up to cover the Gestapo uniform. "I'm not just going to *stay* here. I'm not going to leave him. I have to go find Willem."

"I'll come with you." I stand clumsily. "I can't leave Mirjam, either. I can't leave her body."

"No." His hand is already on the doorknob. "You can't go back. You were just spotted being escorted away by a member of the Gestapo."

"But I promised I would find her. She's out there all alone. I can bring her to Mr. Kreuk's. I have a key. I'll take her there." My voice is loose and out of control and doesn't even sound like me.

Ollie leans his forehead against the door, his back to me. His shoulders move up and down. "I'll get her," he says quietly. "Willem and I will."

"But why would you do that?" My eyes again fill with tears. "I was reckless and selfish. Why would you ever do this for me?"

He puts his hand beside his head on the door. "Because when

she fell on the bridge—we never got to see Bas after he died. We never got to see him at all."

There is no possible way for me to respond to such kindness. "Be careful," I say. "Be safe."

"Give me your key," he says, and then once he has it: "Wait here. Don't leave."

"I won't," I say.

I wait a long time.

Tuesday

I wake up, and I'm not on Ollie's sofa, which is the last place I remember sitting. Instead, I'm in a bed, and sun is streaming in through the windows, and Ollie sits across the room in an armchair. I jolt upright. I don't recall falling asleep, and I hate my body for letting it happen. I must have shut down, from worry, sadness, and exhaustion, while Ollie was stealing back into the night.

"Ollie," I whisper. My throat burns from all the crying last night.

"Good morning."

"What happened? Where's Willem?"

My panic clears when Willem appears in the doorway.

"I'm here; I'm safe."

Safe. No more deaths last night except for Mirjam. She's not safe and never will be. "Did you get—" I don't know how to finish that sentence. *Did you manage to get Mirjam off the bridge?*

"It's done," Ollie says. "It wasn't easy. But it's done."

"She's at Mr. Kreuk's?"

"Yes. And Mrs. de Vries knows what happened. And all the Nazis know, we think, is that two girls tried to run, and they shot one and caught the other."

I look around at the room I'm lying in, with two bureaus, one of which has a picture of Ollie's parents. "You gave me your bed."

"Willem carried you in," Ollie says. "We slept on the floor."

"I'm sorry. I'm sorry that you had to get Mirjam. I'm sorry for not running when I should have. I'm—" There's so much more I should apologize for: my thoughtlessness, the way I lost my mind and tried to drag everyone with me.

"We got the camera. At least," Willem says, too kindly.

"What are you going to do with it? Give it back to Mina or destroy the film?"

They look at each other. "We haven't decided," Ollie says. He hands me a mug that had been sitting on his armrest. "Drink." I lift the cup by rote, but when the liquid slides down my throat, it doesn't even register to me what it is. In the past twelve hours, I've felt everything I could possibly feel. Now I'm numb.

"I should go." I'm wearing my clothes from last night, though someone has removed my shoes. I'm wrinkled and soiled. There's a run in my stockings, my last pair. When I try to stand, my head spins.

Willem looks worriedly at Ollie. "She should have some breakfast. Shouldn't she, Ollie?"

"I have to go to Mrs. Janssen's. I have to tell her what happened."

Nothing in my body wants to make that visit, but prolonging it will only be worse. Sometimes hope can be poisonous. I need to put Mrs. Janssen out of her misery as soon as I can.

Willem brings me my shoes, telling me over and over again that I don't need to leave yet. Eventually he realizes he won't change my mind, and wraps some bread and an apple in a napkin for me to take along. I can't imagine eating right now, but I don't want to tell him that. I'll put the food in my bag as soon as I leave the apartment.

My bicycle is—I don't even know where my bicycle is. Still in the lobby of Mrs. de Vries's apartment, I assume, where I left it before Ollie and I took our positions at the butcher's. In a happier version of the story, I would have ridden it home this morning after leaving Mirjam there, safe and sound.

Without a bicycle, I have to walk to Mrs. Janssen's, which takes nearly an hour. I have a few coins in my pocket and I could catch a tram, but I think I deserve the pain. I worry along the way about how I'll tell her. Whether it's better to just come out and say it—"She's dead, Mrs. Janssen"—or whether I should start from the beginning, explaining what happened and where the plan failed.

It turns out that I don't have to say anything. Mrs. Janssen can tell, from my slumping shoulders or my rumpled clothes, or maybe just from the way I'm walking. She was waiting by the front window of her home, and when she sees me walk up the street alone, she drops her head to her chest.

"How did it happen?" she asks when she opens the door. It

feels wrong to deliver the news on the steps. But then, all of this feels wrong.

Each word hurts my throat as I force it out. "She ran. I tried to get her to follow me and she ran. They caught her. She's dead." I add the last sentence because *caught* could mean she was merely captured. I don't want to have to explain twice that Mirjam is never coming back to this house.

Mrs. Janssen leans heavily on her cane, and I feel like I'm watching another piece of her break. Numbly, I take her elbow and help her back inside her own house. We both sit on the ugly sofa in her living room. "What happened?" she asks. "Why did she run from you?" Her grief is quiet and dignified, and somehow this makes it worse. I think it would be easier if she had come completely undone, the way I did last night, when Ollie had to drag me home because I couldn't even think straight. But Mrs. Janssen is grieving in a practiced way, the way of someone who is used to losing things.

Why *did* Mirjam run from me? If she was willing to run to escape the Nazis, why wouldn't she run with me, the person who had just told her I was there to help her?

"I don't know," I admit. "But I was a stranger approaching her in the middle of the night, grabbing her hand, and telling her to follow me. Maybe she just got scared. The night was so confusing. We were all scared."

"Do you think she thought you were a plant, working for the soldiers? Or maybe that she wasn't sure which direction you were telling her to run in?"

"I don't know. I don't know."

"I should have come." Her face is stricken. "She didn't know you, but she knew me."

"You couldn't have helped," I say firmly. "Neither of us could have done anything." I don't know if that's true, though. Should I have mentioned Mrs. Janssen's name to Mirjam? Would that have helped? *Why didn't she follow me?* Finally I offer the only comforting thing I have, as small as it is.

"We have her body. My friends were able to rescue her body. It's at Mr. Kreuk's."

"Who is with her?"

"Nobody, right now. Mr. Kreuk usually comes in at eight thirty. When he gets in, I'll ask him to take care of her. I'll ask him to find a burial plot."

"I'll pay," she says immediately.

"I will pay," I say. I'll pay with the money Mrs. Janssen gave me to find her. It's the only thing I can do. We should be able to afford a headstone with that money. A simple one, but nice.

"You should go to the funeral home," Mrs. Janssen says.

"I can stay. I can keep you company."

"You should go, Hanneke," she says. "I don't want her to be alone."

I go to Mrs. de Vries's first, though. They already know what happened last night.

"Hanneke, I'm so sorry," Mrs. de Vries says when she opens

the door, sounding as sympathetic as I imagine she can. She must have seen me come in the building from outside, because none of the onderduikers are hiding. The Cohens sit on the sofa, holding hands. Mina runs from behind Mrs. de Vries and throws her arms around me.

"We saw the transport leave the Schouwburg last night." Her face is buried in my neck. "Then we didn't see anything. We kept waiting and waiting for you to get here, but we only knew for sure something was wrong hours later, when Willem came to us, looking for you."

The children are awake, still in their pajamas, standing dumbfounded behind their mother, watching Mina and me and obviously trying to figure out what's happening. Mrs. de Vries notices them and shoos them back toward their playroom, and the Cohens move to help her.

Mina and I stand, hugging each other in the entryway for a long time. In the back of the apartment, the twins laugh. I close my eyes and try to drown out the sound, which seems so inappropriate now. I want to crawl into bed for days. I want to give up.

Even Mina is crying. Brave, optimistic Mina who wanted to resist, even while she had to hide. And what good did it do? What good can any of us do against the monstrous machine that shoots young girls in the back as they run in fear?

I feel a soft tap on my shoulder. It's Mrs. Cohen holding what looks like a folded white tablecloth. She apologizes for disturbing me, and holds out the material for me to take. "For your friend," she explains. "I didn't know if you knew—people of our faith are often buried in traditional burial clothes. This is only a tablecloth;

in these times we cannot keep all our traditions. But I thought that perhaps you would like something to wrap your friend in before she is buried. Only if you want it. I don't mean to presume."

I dumbly take the tablecloth from her, the soft linen rippling through my fingers.

"We would also have a watcher stand with the body, so the deceased would not have to be alone. We can't be there for the burial, of course," Mrs. Cohen says. "But if you tell us what time it is scheduled for, my husband will make sure to begin the prayer of mourning at that moment."

"Thank you." I almost start crying again at this gesture. I barely know the Cohens; I'm not even sure how much they were told about what I've been doing or why. "Thank you," I repeat, because I don't know what else to say.

TWENTY-EIGHT

M r. Kreuk doesn't ask me any questions, about who Mirjam was or why I want to take care of her body, and for this I'm grateful. It's a repayment, I think, for all the questions I haven't asked him in the time we've known each other. At the office, he just pats me on the shoulder, and then neatly folds up his shirt-sleeves the way he always does before getting to work. A few hours later, he tells me that the body has been dressed, except for socks and shoes.

After leaving Mrs. de Vries's house, I'd gone home and sorted through my clothes to find something for Mirjam. Mama and Papa were gone at Papa's regular doctor's appointment. I chose a dress that they'd given me for my birthday a few years ago. It still fits—one of the rare nice things I own that does—but I folded it up anyway, and put my favorite patent leather shoes in a bag.

"Can I?" I whisper to Mr. Kreuk. "Can I be the one to do that?"

He looks startled. This is the first time I've ever asked to be in the same room with a body. Normally they're brought in through the back entrance, cleaned, dressed, and then placed in their caskets. I don't even go into that room.

"Are you sure?"

I nod. "It's important to me." Because I failed her. Because I found her too late. Because her blue coat is ruined, covered in blood.

He takes me into the small white room. I carry the shoes and socks and the linen tablecloth Mrs. Cohen gave me. I should have asked her to explain what I was supposed to do with it. Is it meant to be wrapped around Mirjam, or just placed over her? Was I even supposed to bring the other clothes, or is she supposed to wear only burial shrouds? Or does it even matter? Mrs. Janssen said the Roodveldts weren't observant.

Mr. Kreuk stands a few feet behind me as I look at the body that used to be Mirjam, lying on the cold table. I've been with a dead person only twice before, at my grandparents' funerals when I was eleven and twelve, and then there was dim lighting and music. Now there is just stillness, and Mirjam. She's so small.

Here she is, in person, the first real time I've seen her. Her face is heart-shaped, with her dark hair forming a widow's peak at her forehead, and her chin comes to a little point, with a small birthmark to the left of center. Her eyelashes are thick and long. Nobody told me that, when they described her, how velvety her eyelashes are. Her nose is blunted at the end, a bit too short for her face. Nobody told me that, either. Just below the collar of the satin dress, the edge of a white bandage covers up the exit wound of the bullet that killed her. I adjust the collar, cover it up.

"You've done—you've done a beautiful job. Thank you. She looks almost—" I'm supposed to say that she looks almost as she did in life, which is what people say to Mr. Kreuk when they want to thank him with the highest compliment. I can't say that, though, since I really have no idea what she looked like in life. "She looks peaceful."

"Is there anything else I can do for you? Or your friend?"

"I don't think so."

"The burial arrangements. Will you be needing a traditional plot or . . . or a special one?"

This might be his way of asking me if Mirjam needs to be buried in a Jewish cemetery. I know how difficult finding such a place would be for him.

"Just somewhere pretty. There won't be a funeral. Just a burial."

He hesitates, as if trying to decide whether to speak, and finally leaves without saying anything.

I can't bring myself to touch her yet. Instead I turn to where her blue coat sits folded neatly on a table. The collar and top buttons are drenched in dried blood, which spatters down the rest of the coat, rusty and brown. Mr. Kreuk has already checked the pockets and laid her personal effects on top of the coat. Her identification papers, shot through and now also rust-colored, and a letter, which must have been in her side pocket because the paper is clean and white.

> *If I could go back and never meet T to begin with, I would do that, right now. It was such a stupid thing to come between us. I'm going to make it up to you when I see you again.*

> *Love, Margaret*

Mirjam's last schoolgirl note about her last drama. Why did she write it? Was Amalia upset that Mirjam was spending too much time with Tobias? Had Amalia met Tobias and she disapproved of him? It's amazing how little any of that matters now.

As Mr. Kreuk promised, Mirjam is dressed except for her feet and lower legs, which lie bare below the calf-length dress. I pick up one white sock and begin to ease it over her toes and heel. Her feet are so cold. Her feet are so cold, and just hours ago they were running over the stoned streets, and suddenly there are tears falling down my face. All the games I used to play, to try to convince myself that Bas didn't die alone. But when it comes down to it, we all die alone.

The shoes I brought for her are my nicest ones. My party shoes for the parties I don't go to anymore, with satin bows at the toe. My feet are a little bigger than hers, so the shoes don't fit exactly, but she'll never know the difference. When I'm finished with the dressing, I pick up one of Mirjam's hands and fold it over the top of the other, smooth a few stray hairs away from her face, and adjust the hem of her dress, which rose high on her legs as I struggled with a sock. My tears start to flow at the oddest of things. The way her lips are chapped, like all our lips get chapped in the winter. Or her knees. Her perfect white knees, exposed and vulnerable until I brushed the dress back over them.

I tell Mr. Kreuk I'm sick and I need to go home. He knows I'm lying but doesn't say anything other than that he hopes I feel better soon, and that it would be helpful to know how many people will attend Mirjam's burial.

"Just me," I say. "As soon as possible."

He says he has a cemetery plot already and should be able to arrange for a grave to be dug by tomorrow morning. He gives me a time to come to the cemetery. I don't know how he's found a plot so quickly, unless it belonged to someone else, and that someone else no longer has a place to be buried.

Before I leave the office, Mr. Kreuk takes my hand and presses something into it. I look down. A large bar of Belgian chocolate, a name brand, better than any I've seen since the war started. He could sell it for twenty times its value on the black market, and that's how I know he cares. Giving away black market goods is any smuggler's greatest sacrifice.

I start for home. I should have thought to pick up my bicycle from Mrs. de Vries's when I was there, but I didn't. I've walked to every location I've been to this morning, miles and miles, and somehow barely noticed it. The cold seeping through my coat, and the brick punishing my feet: These feel like welcome pains, much easier to deal with than the empty ache in my heart. When I finally do get home, after forty minutes of trudging, my bicycle is waiting for me outside my building, and so is Ollie. His tired voice makes strained and banal conversation with my parents.

"I was just going to drop your bicycle off," he explains. "But your mother happened to see me out the window. I was just telling her how you let me borrow it to go to the hospital with my mother and father. Pia is so grateful you were able to come and stay with her."

"It was nice to see her again. And I'm glad your mother's illness was a false alarm."

It seems strange to me that I will get through all this and Mama and Papa will never know what happened. These lies I told them, about where I was and who was sick and which hospital Ollie's mother was at—they all feel foolish now. I sit down next to Ollie while my mother brings lunch. His hand finds mine under the table. It's warm and comforting, and when I squeeze it, he squeezes back.

"Mr. Kreuk has arranged everything for the burial," I whisper to Ollie when Mama is busy in the kitchen and Papa reads in the front room. "Thank you for picking up my bicycle."

"When is the burial? I'll come."

I tell him he doesn't need to, that he never knew Mirjam. It's a silly thing to say, when I didn't know her, either, though I felt like I did in ways that aren't worth explaining now. Ollie insists on coming and says he'll meet me at the cemetery tomorrow morning.

In the end, Ollie and Willem both come, and so does Mrs. Janssen. It's the first time I've seen her out of her house. She's walking heavily on her cane, and Christoffel has come with her in a taxi, helping her, offering his arm as she picks her way slowly over the bumpy grass and rocks.

Mr. Kreuk found a plain pine casket for Mirjam and brought it here in the hearse. It's the most basic option we sell, but still worth a week of my wages.

We stand around the empty grave while the casket is lowered into the ground. We don't have a minister or a rabbi. It's just the six of us and two gravediggers, who stand a few meters away under a cluster of trees, their hands resting on their shovels.

Mrs. Janssen mouths a prayer to herself, and I think Willem's lips move as well. Ollie and I don't say anything. We just stand while the casket is lowered into the ground, and after ten minutes of respectful silence, the gravediggers move up from behind us to begin filling the open hole with dirt.

TWENTY-NINE

Wednesday

When the burial is over, Mr. Kreuk pulls away in the hearse after telling me to take a few days off, to come back to work when I feel better. Mrs. Janssen leaves next, leaning on Christoffel for support as she folds herself back into the taxi. She asks me to come and visit her soon, and I promise I will, though right now doing so is difficult to imagine.

Ollie and Willem are both looking at me as we stand together in front of the cemetery's gates. "Should we ride you home?" Willem suggests. "Neither of us has class this afternoon."

"I don't really want to go home at all." My parents don't know today is anything other than a regular day. The idea of making up an excuse for why I'm home early and sitting with them in hidden mourning is unbearable. I should go back to work, but I don't want to do that, either. I've had enough death for today. "Could we do something else?"

"What did you have in mind?" Ollie asks.

"Anything. Anything besides go home or stay here. Something normal."

He looks blankly at Willem. None of us knows what a normal afternoon even looks like anymore, one in which we're not ferrying children from the Hollandsche Schouwburg, or trying to find places for onderduikers, or trading on the black market. If there were no war, and if we were normal young adults, what would we be doing today?

"How about..." Willem bites his lip. "How about we go for a bicycle ride?"

"A *bicycle* ride?" Ollie's mouth twitches. It's one of the coldest days of winter. We all ride our bicycles all the time anyway, just to get around, but it's hardly the weather for a pleasure ride. "I'm sorry," he apologizes to me. "I didn't mean to laugh."

The suggestion appeals to me, though, for the same reason that walking in the cold appealed earlier. There's a level of drudgery and unpleasantness involved. It won't be a purely joyful ride. It will be numbing, which seems pleasing.

"Yes." Willem is gathering steam now. "We'll go to Ransdorp. We'll ride through the countryside. We'll have a picnic."

Now he's deliberately being silly. Ransdorp is a village on the other side of the river, with farmhouses and a few little shops lining wide gravel streets. The idea of going to a quaint tourist destination now is especially absurd.

But we do it anyway, taking the ferry across the river, to the same point where I met Christoffel a few days ago and asked him to deliver a letter. We stop and find bread on the way, Willem and Ollie sticking loaves into their deep coat pockets while I tuck the bottom of my dress up enough that it won't get caught in my bicycle spokes.

It's cold, as cold as I expected it to be, but the sun makes it bearable, and when we get off the ferry, the pedaling keeps us warm. We must look strange: Ollie and Willem in dark suits and me in the only black dress that I own, cycling in a single line along the road next to a creek. I get a stitch in my side from the exertion. It feels good, so I pedal faster until I overtake the boys, first by a little and then by a lot.

"What are you pedaling away from?" Willem calls after me. His tone is light, but it doesn't feel like a joking question. I'm pedaling away from these past few days. From the sight of Mirjam on the bridge, and the sound of a gunshot in the still night, and the look on Mrs. Janssen's face, brittle and resigned, in her doorway. Gravel sprays off the back of my tires.

"Slow down!" Ollie calls behind me. He says something else I can't hear.

"What?"

"Slow down, there's—"

My bicycle slides over a patch of black ice, the wheels spinning out of control. I try the brakes, but there's no traction. I can't stop myself, and the bicycle goes careening into the ditch as I fly toward the frozen ground. My hands scrape along the dirt when I put them down to break my fall. They hurt, but my left knee is worse—I feel it crash against the handlebars when I fly over them, and then land on something sharp and painful.

"Hanneke!" Ollie calls.

The wind has been knocked out of me; I retch on the ground, trying to suck in enough air to answer. "I'm fine. I'm fine," I manage, holding up a dirty palm to let him know I can take care of myself. Slowly I ease myself onto all fours, but standing seems like too much, and finally I let Ollie help me sit back down on a patch of frozen grass. Tentatively, I pull up my skirt. My left knee is a bloody mess: one large rock jutting out of the center, with small gravel particles surrounding it.

Willem crouches to look at the wound. "We need to clean that out," he says. "I can't tell how bad it is." He runs to the creek, soaking his handkerchief and squeezing it out on top of my knee, rinsing away rivulets of dirt. The three of us examine the damage. The big rock isn't in as deeply as I feared, but when Willem pulls it out, a fresh stream of blood rolls down my shin.

"Did that hurt?" he asks.

"Yes," I say, and then, inappropriately, I giggle, because it seems so pedestrian after everything that's happened to have a scraped knee from a bicycle accident, and to have that be what hurts.

He gives me a funny look. "Are you all right?"

"Yes," I say, stifling another laugh.

"Well, press this down," he instructs me, handing me the handkerchief. "It doesn't look too deep. Except for that rock, the rest is just scratches. You'll probably have a little scar. If we tie up your leg with the handkerchief, do you think you'll still be able to pedal home?"

Once I'm bandaged up, I accept Willem's and Ollie's out-stretched hands, rising to my feet, and watch as Ollie drags my bicycle back up to the road. He hops onto it himself, riding in a few circles to make sure everything functions like it's supposed to. I look down at my now-expertly bandaged knee. Bending it sends shots of pain down to my ankle, but it's manageable pain.

"You're sure everything's okay?"

"Yes." But as I climb back on the bicycle, I realize I'm not sure. And it's not the pain. It's that something is bothering me, and I can't put my finger on it.

"We don't have to go fast," Ollie says. "If you want, one of us could ride ahead and try to find someone with a car to take you."

What is it that's bothering me? I pedal slowly, a rotating dull pain and sharp pain depending on which of my knees is bent. What's bothering me? It's right on the tip of my brain.

"Or you could ride on the back of one of ours, and we could come back later for your bicycle," Willem offers.

"I can ride."

My knee. My newly scraped, soon-to-be-scarred knee.

Mirjam's knees. The bare white legs I saw while putting on her shoes and socks.

"Hanneke?" Willem asks. "I asked if you wanted to go first or last? Hanneke?"

Judith remembered when Mirjam got her beautiful blue coat. It wasn't just a present, but a present she received because she'd torn her other coat beyond repair, mangling her knee, leaving a permanent scar.

Those knees in Mr. Kreuk's basement room had no scars; they were smooth and white and knobby.

Ollie cycles in front of me, weaving side to side and looking back to make sure I haven't fallen again. "Ollie," I ask. "Were you going to check in on Judith today?"

He slows to a stop. "Why?"

"If you do, could you ask her to tell you about the birthmark on Mirjam's chin? Ask her ... No, that's all. Just ask her to tell you about it."

Now he and Willem are looking at each other. "Hanneke, maybe you should wait here with Willem while I ride ahead and find a doctor," Ollie suggests.

I shake my head. Something is wrong, but it's not what Ollie thinks it is.

"I need to get back, right now. If you talk to her, come and find me. I'll be—" I think, trying to plot out where I'll be, and where it will be safe for him to find me. "Call me at Mrs. de Vries's; she still has a phone."

"What are you talking about? Hanneke, stop."

My legs burn, but I force them to pedal, harder, until I pass Ollie and head back down the gravel road toward the ferry. Ollie and Willem stand astride their bicycles, trying to decide whether to follow me. I can't waste the time to explain any more.

I know what I saw. I know everything I saw, when I dressed Mirjam on the table yesterday. I know her knees were smooth.

It's getting hard to breathe, but I don't think that it has

anything to do with how hard I'm pedaling, or with the cold air, or with my fall.

The ferry is in sight now. Passengers are trickling off. My knee stings, but I can't focus on the pain at all. Right now, in this world crumbling before my eyes, there's only one thing I can really focus on: the body I dressed yesterday. The body I cried over. I can only think of it like that now: the body. Because whomever I dressed— whoever that person was, it wasn't Mirjam Roodveldt.

THIRTY

How could the girl on the table not be Mirjam Roodveldt? Was there a different girl in a sky-blue coat leaving the Schouwburg, one I just didn't see? Was I trying to help the wrong girl escape?

By the time I get to Mrs. de Vries's, I've run out of new questions to ask, and the same old ones keep cycling through my brain. Mrs. de Vries doesn't answer, but I know Mina must be here. After three knocks, I finally call through the door softly that it's me and I'm alone.

"What's wrong?" Mina asks from behind the door as she opens it just wide enough for me to get through. "You know I shouldn't be answering the door—a neighbor could see me."

"Where's Mrs. de Vries?"

"At her mother's with the boys."

"And the Cohens?"

"Taking a nap, in the guest room. *What's wrong?*"

I keep my voice low, taking Mina's arm and guiding her back toward Mr. de Vries's study, where we sat together just a few nights ago. "I need to see your slides. The ones from last week. Please don't ask me what's wrong again," I beg, anticipating what she's going to say by the round, puckered O of her mouth.

"You...what?"

"From the Hollandsche Schouwburg. Did Mrs. de Vries's friend ever bring his projector?"

"He did," she says uncertainly. "Just yesterday. We haven't set it up yet."

"Let's do that now."

The projector is in its traveling case by Mr. de Vries's desk. While I turn off the light and close the door, Mina unloads it, black and heavy-looking, setting it on the desk so the lens faces an empty wall. When she plugs it in and presses a red switch, a white square of light appears.

"You want to see the one with Mirjam in it?" she asks. I nod, and she sorts through the slides to find the right image and position it in the slide holder. The white square of light disappears.

In the small slide, even with the magnifying glass, Mirjam was barely more than a smudge of sky blue toward the bottom of the frame. Now, on Mrs. de Vries's wall, she's several inches tall. I can see her more clearly, but it's still hard to make out details. She's still a blue coat, in profile, disappearing off the corner of the frame.

"Mina." I point to the girl in the corner of the frame. "Is this

Mirjam?" I am controlled, almost emotionless. I don't want to influence her answer with my tone.

Mina barely looks at it before turning back to me. "What are you talking about? Of course it's Mirjam. You said—"

"Forget everything I said. I want you to look at this picture and tell me if it's the girl you went to school with. Look closely."

Finally, Mina looks again, leaning on her elbows, studying the frame. The projector emits a low, warm hum. I stay where I am, trying to remain as still as possible. "Well?" I ask when I don't feel like I can wait any longer.

"Honestly, I'm not sure. That's her coat. At least, that's a coat exactly like the one Mirjam wore to school. But it's from far away, and her head is in the middle of turning. It's too blurry to tell. Why are you asking me this now?"

"Mina, look more closely. Is that girl Mirjam, or isn't it?"

"I can't *tell*, Hanneke." She's beginning to sound frustrated. "If someone showed me this picture and said, 'Are any of your former classmates in this picture?' I don't know whether I would point to any of them. But if someone said, 'Point to Mirjam Roodveldt in this picture,' then the girl in the blue coat is who I would point to. *Now* can you tell me what this is about?"

"I don't know. Something's not right, but I haven't figured it out yet. Can you make it any less blurry? By moving the projector closer to the wall or something?"

I examine the image from left to right like I am reading a book. There are the soldiers. There are the frightened people. There, a blur in the left, is a *crèche* worker. There, in the bottom right corner, is the girl who looks like Mirjam.

The ring of the telephone pierces the air, making me jump. It could be Ollie. I told him to contact me here. "Are you going to answer the telephone?" I ask Mina.

"I can't answer it. I'm not supposed to exist here, remember?"

I dash out of the room, toward the telephone extension near the front entrance, and manage to pick it up on the fourth ring. It *is* Ollie, calling from someplace with noise in the background.

"Hanneke, I've just talked to our friend in the country." He sounds formal and strangely controlled. "The mutual acquaintance from school that you were trying to remember? She didn't have a birthmark on her chin."

I keep my own voice as steady as his. "Interesting," I say. "Perhaps we're not thinking of the same person. Is she sure?"

"She's absolutely sure. The girl apparently had a small mole on her neck, and she had the scars on her knee, but she didn't have a birthmark." There's a long pause. "Would you like me to come over for dinner tonight?" he asks, which is really his way of asking *What's going on?*

"Thank you for the offer." I struggle for the same control he's maintaining. "But no. I'll be in contact soon."

I hang up the phone by depressing the button on the base, and immediately dial Mrs. Janssen's house, my finger shaking as I rotate the numbers on the dial, silently hoping that she still has a phone line. It rings.

What am I doing? A girl is dead. We buried her this morning. No matter who she was, it was sad and horrible and final. Maybe I should let it remain final. Maybe Mrs. Janssen has been through enough.

She answers on the fourth ring, groggy like I've woken her; I tell her how sorry I am to have called her and that I have a question I know will sound odd.

"Hanneke? Is that you?"

"Some friends and I have a bet about our acquaintance, Miss R," I say, waiting a beat to make sure she's following. "The bet was over whether she had a birthmark on her chin. Do you remember it?"

"Why are you asking me this?"

I close my eyes. "Please. Just answer. Did she have one?"

"I don't remember. No? I'm not sure. Yes? Can't you tell me what's happening?"

"I'm going to come over later," I tell her before hanging up. "I don't know when, but I will."

Mirjam Roodveldt didn't have a birthmark but did have scars on her knee. The girl on Mr. Kreuk's table had a birthmark, definitely, but no scars. The girl in Mrs. Janssen's pantry may or may not have had a birthmark; Mrs. Janssen doesn't remember seeing one, but admits she could have been wrong. Now the girl is in the ground and it's too late for me to get confirmation from any of the people who could identify her.

Was I right all along, that day I told Ollie that it might not be Mirjam at the theater? Do I still have a chance to save the real girl?

Back in the office, Mina sits where I left her. She doesn't ask me who was on the phone. She's obviously beyond the point of expecting answers. The slide is still projected on the wall. Everything looks the same as it did five minutes ago. Nothing makes any sense. There are the soldiers. There are the frightened people. The brown coats. The lavender hats.

On my third pass, I see it. Something that all at once seems so obvious I can't believe I didn't see it before. "Something is off with this picture," I whisper.

"What do you mean? The color might be off; the film was developed in a hurry."

"Not that." I move out of the way so Mina can see what I'm talking about. "Look at this closely. Really closely. Tell me if you notice anything about this girl's face."

Mina wrinkles her forehead. "I already told you; it's blurry, and it's hard to see her face. But I think she looks scared. As I would expect."

"Not the expression. The direction." I use the tip of my finger to draw explanatory lines in the air. "Here's the soldier, to the left. Do you see? Giving instructions to the prisoners. And just in front of him is his partner."

"And?"

"And every other person in the picture looks afraid of *the soldiers*. See the way this soldier is pointing? And how everyone else is looking in the direction he's pointing? It looks like he's telling everyone which way to go in the theater."

Realization begins to dawn on Mina's face. "What is Mirjam looking at?"

Mirjam's face is pointed in another direction. She's not paying attention to the soldiers at all. Whatever she's looking at is far in the distance, out of the frame of the shot. It's possible that it's just a fluke, that she'd been looking at the soldiers, and a noise or a movement distracted her. That's the most logical possibility and I know it. But I can't get rid of another feeling.

Mirjam doppelgänger, whoever you are. Is it possible that Nazis weren't the only thing you were afraid of?

THIRTY-ONE

Mrs. Janssen doesn't answer the door when I knock. I try again, as loud as I dare without drawing too much attention to myself. "Hello? Mrs. Janssen, it's me, Hanneke," I say softly.

"She went out," a voice calls, a middle-aged woman standing on the stoop across the street. Mrs. Veenstra, the woman whose son was missing in the country on the day Mirjam disappeared. Or not-Mirjam.

"Mrs. Janssen never goes out on her own."

"I know that, but she did, about ten minutes ago. I told her I could pick up anything she needed, but she said she needed to go herself."

"Did she say where?"

"No, but she looked upset. I figured she'd had bad news about one of her sons. Do you want to wait in my house until she comes back?"

"I'll just wait—" I'm about to say that I'll just wait on her steps when I realize I never tried the doorknob. I surreptitiously twist it now, and the door pops open. Next door, Fritzi starts barking. "I'll just wait inside. She's expecting me anyway."

Mrs. Veenstra looks uncertain. "I wanted to make sure I came today," I babble pleasantly, trying to think of an excuse that will convince her I belong in this house. "You know, with Jan's birthday. It's probably why she's so upset. I bet she's at church." I have no idea when Jan's birthday is, but I doubt Mrs. Veenstra will remember any better than I do, and I hope she can't sense how uncomfortable I am. A week ago, I was at this house, reminding myself how to behave on a social call. Now I'm reminding myself how to tell lies and excuses again. "Would you like me to pass on your thoughts as well?" I ask.

Finally she goes back into her own house, leaving me alone. Inside, Mrs. Janssen's is quiet. A clock ticks. A half-drunk cup of ersatz tea sits on the kitchen table, next to a half-eaten slice of bread. Those are the only signs of human activity. I walk quickly through the rest of the house to be sure: the lonely bedrooms belonging to Mrs. Janssen's sons; Mrs. Janssen's own bedroom, smelling of rose perfume and something musty; Mr. Janssen's home office, unused since his death. She's nowhere.

My knee throbs. I still have Willem's handkerchief tied around it, and drops of red have seeped through the white cotton. I rinse off the handkerchief in the kitchen sink and reapply it. I wonder if Mrs. Janssen has any aspirin powder and where she would keep it. Mama keeps ours in the pantry. The door to Mrs. Janssen's is already ajar, and the secret latch is open, revealing the hiding place from behind the jars of pickles and radishes. Inside, the quilt on top of the opklapbed is wrinkled, with a faint depression in the middle. Mrs. Janssen must have come in here last night.

No amount of searching for aspirin powder or performing other menial tasks is going to be enough to distract me.

The timeline doesn't reveal anything, no matter how many times I go over it. Four weeks ago, a girl appeared at the front door of this house, who may or may not have been Mirjam Roodveldt. One week ago, the same girl disappeared, and Mrs. Janssen hired me to find her. Two days ago, a girl was found in a raid and taken to the Hollandsche Schouwburg. I tried to help her escape. She was shot and killed. Was that girl the same one who knocked on Mrs. Janssen's door? Or was it a different girl, one who had acquired Mirjam's clothes and papers during the five days that Mirjam went missing?

Does any of this even matter anyway? There's a girl who is dead.

"Hello?" Through several walls, I hear the front door creak open and someone call out. "Hello, Mrs. Janssen?"

I rush out of the pantry, hurling the door closed behind me. A young blond woman I've never seen before stands in the parlor, dressed in the clothes of a shopgirl or store clerk.

"Can I help you?"

"Oh!" She theatrically puts her hand to her chest. "Where's Mrs. Janssen?"

"Who are you? What are you doing here?" I say, deciding the

best way to avoid answering her question is to ask a ruder one of my own.

"I'm Tessa Koster. I work—I worked—for Mr. Janssen in the furniture shop. The door was ajar. Are you...Mrs. Janssen's companion?" she guesses.

"Yes. Mrs. Janssen's not here. Can I help you with something?"

"Oh, no. I came by to drop some things off for Mrs. Janssen, but I'll come back later when she's home."

Tessa Koster smiles, flustered, and as she heads for the door again, I piece it together. The furniture shop employee. The one who was leaving on her honeymoon the day after the raid. "Photographs," I say. "You brought photographs for Mrs. Janssen, from Mr. Janssen's back room."

She looks unnerved that I know this; for all she knows, I'm a spy sent to trap her. "Is Mrs. Janssen coming back soon? I really should talk to her."

But I'm already shaking my head, looking as sympathetic as I can, because I want her to leave those photographs with me. "I don't know when she'll be back. I suppose you could come back tomorrow? You're brave, walking around with those photographs, though. It sounded like they were sort of"—I bring my voice down to a whisper and continue—"*illicit.*"

"I'll—I'll be fine."

"Did you ever meet the family who was in hiding?" I ask, letting her see I know more than she guessed I did. "The daughter? Mirjam."

"No, I didn't. You knew about that?" She looks back toward the door.

"Are you sure you never saw them? They were there for several months. You must have suspected something." Mrs. Koster averts her eyes, staring down at the new wedding band on her finger, and I have a new, ugly suspicion.

"Mrs. Koster. Were you the one who told the police that Mr. Janssen was hiding people in his back room? Did you report him to the Nazis?"

"Listen." Her eyes dart to the side. "I don't approve of what Mr. Janssen was doing, but I didn't tell on him. I didn't even know about it. I came into work, and the raid had already happened. These were in the back room; they had blood on them, so I took them home to clean them up, and then Mrs. Janssen wrote me a letter saying she wanted them. That's really all the involvement I want to have. Can I leave them with you? And then I don't have to come back again."

She digs in her handbag, blond curls falling in her face, and eventually produces a paper envelope. "Here. Take them."

I pretend to consider it. "Are you sure? You're not going to wait?"

She thrusts the paper in my hand. "Take them."

Once I see her out the door, I take the packet of photographs back into the kitchen. I'm not rushing this time. I'm infinitely precise. I'm infinitely patient as I sit down at the table, lay the envelope squarely in front of me, moving with an emotion it takes me a while to identify. Dread.

Most of the blood has been wiped from the photographs; only a few traces remain, making the corners of the pictures stick together when I peel them apart. I lay them one by one in front of me, a row stretching across the table, this gluey narrative of a family and life and death.

Here are Mr. and Mrs. Roodveldt, I presume, cradling a baby in a white dress, behind a table with a cake on it. A birthday. Here's one from a few years earlier: Mrs. Roodveldt's bridal portrait, her eyes lowered, a lace veil covering her hair and a small bouquet of lilacs in her hands.

The photographs skip back and forth in years, and the family marches across the kitchen table unstuck from time, beaming at me from their happiest moments. Parties. Holidays. A new apartment, a new baby, a different one from the first time.

And here is one with two teenage girls with their arms around each other. The girl on the left has dark curly hair, a faint birthmark on her chin, and long, lush eyelashes. Her eyes—which I've only really seen closed, on Mr. Kreuk's table—are large and expressive.

The girl on the right is slightly taller, also with dark hair, her mouth open in laughter. She's wearing a paper birthday crown. I've never seen her before.

With shaking hands, I turn the picture over: *Amalia and Mirjam at Mirjam's 14th birthday.*

There are so many things I wish I could forget. The hard parts. The nasty injuries, beneath the scarred skin, the things I'd like to disappear by ignoring.

The last time I saw Elsbeth, before I sneaked into her house:

It was a few months after the day in my bedroom when I told her I wished Rolf were dead instead of Bas.

She came to my house again. She had two wedding invitations, one for me and one for my parents. She awkwardly accepted tea from my mother and answered questions about her dress and the flowers at the church. When my mother left us alone "so we could catch up," Elsbeth turned to me.

"My mother said I should invite you," she said finally. "She said weddings mend fences. But I'm guessing you won't want to come." I couldn't figure out the emotion in her eyes: Hope? Anger? Was she wishing that I would come, or was she making it clear that she wanted my answer to be no?

"No," I said. "I don't expect I'll come."

"All right, then," she said. "I guess this really probably is good-bye."

It was so dignified. That was what made it so sad. To end a twelve-year friendship like this, while she sat in my kitchen with a wedding invitation in her hand. It was nearly unforgivable, and I've spent the past year wondering whether it was more or less unforgivable than the person Elsbeth wanted to marry, and which one of us should apologize to whom.

There are so many ways to kill things, it turns out. The Germans killed Bas with mortar. Elsbeth and I killed our friendship with words.

THIRTY-TWO

My heart has come loose from my chest.

Amalia. *Amalia.*

Amalia was the girl who Ollie brought to Mr. Kreuk's in the quiet of night. Amalia is the girl who is dead in the ground. The girl I have been looking for this whole time. The photograph of the birthday party is sticky in my hand; without meaning to I've left fingerprints all over it, touching the faces of these dead and disappeared girls.

In the other room, I hear the front door open again, letting in a whistle of air. Mrs. Janssen? But I don't hear the soft bump of her cane. It must be Tessa Koster again.

"I'm back here," I call out. My voice is a croak.

"Mrs. Janssen?" a confused voice asks. "It's Christoffel."

"Oh, Christoffel, it's Hanneke." Reflexively, I sweep the

photographs off the table, folding them back into the envelope they came in. I've just stuck the packet under the tea set when Christoffel enters the kitchen. He's still wearing the formal clothes he wore to escort Mrs. Janssen to the funeral earlier today.

"Where's Mrs. Janssen?" He uses his sleeve to wipe perspiration off his forehead. "When I stopped by a little bit ago, she said she needed me to take her somewhere. I told her I had to do another quick errand and I'd be right back."

"Mrs. Janssen…" I trail off. I'm having a difficult time finishing my sentences. Was *Amalia* imprisoned in the Hollandsche Schouwburg? Amalia, Mirjam's best friend? Amalia, who was supposed to be in Kijkduin? Vaguely, I realize Christoffel is still waiting for me to finish my sentence. "Mrs. Janssen was gone when I got here, too. Did she tell you where she wanted you to take her?"

He wrinkles his eyebrows. "She said she needed to go see you. But you're here. It sounded urgent; she was upset when I told her I couldn't go right away."

"Right. Right. I guess she and I got a little mixed up about who was coming to see whom." Dammit. I should have told Mrs. Janssen on the phone to stay put, no matter what. But I don't know how she would have gone to see me; Mrs. Janssen doesn't know where I live. I don't even think she knows my last name. If Christoffel wasn't here, I could go through the house to see if she left me a note somewhere, explaining more.

"It sounded like she was really worried about something," Christoffel says. "I'll wait here until she gets back."

"I'm sure you have better things to do, Christoffel. Why don't

I give you some money for your trouble, and you can get back to your life?"

But, irritatingly dutiful, he takes the other seat at the table, fiddling with one of the teacups. Minutes tick by. When Mrs. Janssen couldn't find me, what would she do next? Something rash? Would she try to go find Mr. Kreuk? Or Ollie? How much have I told her about him, and the resistance?

"Do you really think it's all right if I leave? I do have another place I'm supposed to be," he admits finally.

"Of course you should leave. I'll tell her you stopped by." Even the scraping of my chair sounds eager as I usher him out of his seat.

"Did I leave my hat?" he starts to ask, looking around his seat.

"Here," I say, exasperated, thrusting the gray cap at him that he'd set on the table.

We're almost out of the room when a squeak emits from the pantry, an un-oiled, plaintive sound. *Verdorie.* I remembered to shut the outer pantry door when Tessa Koster came in, but I don't think I locked the secret shelf inside. It must be swinging, loose, behind the closed door. "Old houses make the strangest sounds," I say.

We're at the front door now. All I have to do is shove him through it, and then I can figure out where Mrs. Janssen is. I'll start with Mr. Kreuk. That's who introduced us to begin with. Mr. Kreuk handled the memorial service for her husband.

"Next time I come I'll bring some oil," says Christoffel as I open the door for him. "That shelf always squeaks when the latch is open."

And.

He doesn't even realize what he's said. He doesn't realize it at all. It was just a sentence to him. A string of words, a helpful comment. He's putting on his cap. The door is open.

Slowly, like I'm watching my own actions in a dream, I close the door again, and it shuts with a whisper of a click.

"Hanneke?"

The shelf always squeaks when the latch is open. I replay the sentence again in my mind, searching for a way that it could mean something different from what I know it means. *Shelf.* He didn't say "pantry door." He specifically said "shelf." He would have to know that the shelf swung open with a latch. *Always.* As in, multiple times. As in, he knows the workings of that hidden, rusty shelf.

"Hanneke, I thought you said I should leave." He's looking at me, confused.

"You know about the hiding space." My voice comes out in an uneven whisper. "Christoffel?" He starts to shake his head, but it's too late. A light has flickered in his eyes. "What do you know about it, Christoffel?" I ask softly.

"I don't know anything. Please let's not talk about this. Please just let me go."

He reaches for the doorknob again, but I move in front of it. "I can't let you go. You know that."

"Hanneke, please leave this." His voice is so quiet I can barely make it out.

Outside I hear someone selling an evening newspaper, and the gritty, swishing sound of a broom over cobblestones. Life is going on and on, and I'm in here with a soft-faced boy who is drained of all color. "Christoffel, it's just the two of us in here. No matter what you tell me, good or bad, I can't ever call the police or talk to anybody but Mrs. Janssen about it. But please, please, just tell me: How did you know there was a space behind the pantry?"

Outside the sweeper has landed on something metal, maybe a coin. Christoffel stares at his thumb, at a vicious hangnail rubbed red from repeated worrying. He's an inch or two taller than me, but it's gangly height, the height of a recent growth spurt.

"I didn't know about—about *her*," he says. "Not at first. I swear, I didn't know at first. Usually when I'm here, Mrs. Janssen is in the room with me, and we're talking or making noise that would cover up sounds from the pantry."

"But not all the time?"

"One time I was delivering some things. Mrs. Janssen couldn't find her pocketbook. She went upstairs to look for it, and she was gone for a long time, and down here it was quiet. And I heard something. A squeak."

"Did you go to see what it was?" That would be so like helpful Christoffel, to hear a rusty hinge and decide to investigate it, repair it.

"I didn't have to. I heard the squeak, and then she came out of the cupboard."

Another person who saw her. Another person who knew she existed. Christoffel's face has a touch of wonder to it, as he remembers that moment. How strange it must have been for him, to be standing in the kitchen and have a girl emerge from the pantry. "She recognized my voice," Christoffel continues. "She said she'd just been waiting for an opportunity when Mrs. Janssen wasn't around."

She recognized. It's like my brain can't take in everything Christoffel is saying at once, so it latches on to loose phrases, here or there. *Recognize* is an interesting word. It would have made more sense for Christoffel to say "heard." We recognize the things that are already familiar to us.

"You knew her," I say, and as I'm formulating the words, I decide who "her" really was. "You knew Amalia."

"How did you know her name?"

"How did *you?*"

"We went to school together. The three of us, we grew up together. Me, Amalia, and—" Christoffel leaves a space where the name should go, one that I can't resist filling.

"And Mirjam."

"And Mirjam," he whispers. Then Christoffel does something I didn't expect at all and hadn't been prepared for. He sinks to the floor, sliding down along the wall. He balls his fists in front of his eyes, and he begins to cry. Not just silent tears: fat, noisy tears like a little boy.

I drop to my knees next to him. This is pain I recognize. "Christoffel, did you—did you love Mirjam?"

His throat is hoarse; he's barely whispering. "She didn't seem to notice me that way; she treated me like a brother. I assumed she didn't like me. Last year she told me it wasn't that she *didn't* like me, it was that Amalia did. She said Amalia liked me first, and Mirjam didn't want to betray her. I knew deep down, all along, I guess. Amalia started getting nervous around me. She got this laugh—a giggle, sort of. But I never thought of her as more than a friend."

"You're T. Not Tobias. You." Christoffel looks up at me, confused. "I found a letter," I explain. "It mentioned a boy whose name she abbreviated as T. It was a boy she liked."

Those stupid English princesses. The letter wasn't from Mirjam to Amalia, something she never got a chance to send. The letter was from Amalia to Mirjam, something Mirjam was rereading in class.

"My nickname," Christoffel says. "It's dumb. I don't even remember when I got it. I guess that I must have been T."

Earlier, I thought Christoffel's friends at the ferry were all calling him Mr. Great. That's what *Tof* means: "Great." "Cool." But they weren't calling him that—they were calling him Tof, his nickname, from the middle of Christoffel.

"How many times did you see Amalia in the pantry?"

"Just twice. The second time I came, she waited until Mrs. Janssen was gone again, and then she said there had been a notice in the newspaper and that she needed my help to escape."

Het Parool. The three-line notice in the classifieds: *Elizabeth misses her Margaret, but is glad to be vacationing in Kijkduin.*

The first day I came here, Mrs. Janssen told me she brought Mirjam a newspaper, and then told her to stay quiet because the delivery boy was coming. Mrs. Janssen never mentioned to me that she had left Christoffel alone in the kitchen. She wouldn't have thought she needed to. Why would Mirjam announce her presence to the boy who came to deliver groceries?

"You helped her escape?"

"I did."

"But I don't understand. She must have told you that Mrs. Janssen thought she was Mirjam. Why would she leave without telling Mrs. Janssen that she was going? And how was Amalia carrying Mirjam's papers on the night of the raid?"

He kneads the palm of his hand into his eye, clumsily wiping away tears. I don't have a handkerchief, and I don't know if I would offer him one if I did. Am I comforting him? Interrogating him? This boy in front of me has the answer to every question I've been chasing for a week. He helped launch a series of events that caused pain and anguish, and I still don't understand why.

"She—she told me that the night the Roodveldts' hiding space was ransacked, she ran into Mirjam on the street," he says. "Mirjam was running for her life and she thought she would be caught soon. Amalia made her switch coats and identification papers. Amalia said that if Mirjam had non-Jewish papers, she would be able to escape, and Amalia could just go to the authorities later and be issued new ones. But the soldiers were too close. She didn't have time to run home, and she worried that with Mirjam's clothes and papers, she would be shot on sight. So she came to Mrs. Janssen's. Mirjam told her the address."

"But when she got here, why didn't she tell Mrs. Janssen who she really was? Why didn't she ask Mrs. Janssen to help her get new papers?"

He shrugs morosely. "I don't know. She just said she didn't want Mrs. Janssen to know."

Because she wanted to make sure Mirjam was safe before she

told anyone the truth? Because she didn't want anyone to know the real Mirjam Roodveldt was still out there, escaped, living under a different name? Because there are some parts of this story that are never going to make sense, no matter how many questions I ask?

"Where did she go?" I ask. "After you got her out of the house?"

"She stayed with me for a while. Papa travels so often he didn't suspect someone was in the basement."

In his basement. Until just a few days ago, the girl I was looking for was living at the home of a boy I'd seen multiple times.

"What made her leave?" I ask. I can understand why Amalia never went to the authorities and said her own papers were lost or stolen: Since she was under eighteen, the authorities might have demanded her parents' signatures, and they were already out of the city. I can understand why she might have wanted to stay with Christoffel instead of Mrs. Janssen—an old friend rather than a stranger who didn't even know who she really was. What I can't understand is why, after she'd gone through all that trouble, she would then leave his house. "Why did she keep running from the places she was safest, Christoffel? I just need some of these pieces to make sense." He's still crying, tears flowing faster as I demand answers. "*Why* did Amalia leave your house that night?"

"*I told her to,*" he finally yelps. "She told me a secret and I made her leave. I never meant for her to die. I swear I never meant it. I was so mad at her. I told her the Nazis would treat her better than I would if I ever saw her again. I chased her to the street. She was running away from me; I saw her run face-on into a soldier. When

she was caught in the roundup, she was running away from *me*."
His voice is high and keening.

"What was the secret? What was it that made you refuse to let
her stay in your house?"

"I can't. I can't." He's become hysterical; if I had a paper bag,
I would make him breathe into it. Instead, I pat the back of his
sweater, damp with sweat and heaving as he gulps in air. He's
just a few years younger than me, but he's a small boy right now.
"I don't want to talk about that," he gasps out in between deep
breaths. "Please don't make me."

"Okay. Okay. Okay," I repeat, because pushing him right now
is only going to send him further over the edge.

Just one thing more. Not even a thing that matters, in the
large scheme of things, but something I have to have settled, for
my own peace.

"You said Amalia asked you to help her escape on the day she
saw the notice in the newspaper. But you *couldn't* have helped her
right then. Mrs. Janssen saw her later in the evening. Did you find
a way to sneak back in the house while Mrs. Janssen was across
the street at her neighbor's? Were you the one who figured out
how to close the back door from the outside?"

"No. She hid in the house while Mrs. Janssen was at the neighbor's. I came back the next day."

His timeline must be off. The next day, I was here. The next
day, I was sitting in the kitchen listening to Mrs. Janssen tell me
Mirjam had already disappeared. "You're misremembering. I was
here that day. I saw you come in. You were picking up some furniture to sell for Mrs. Janssen."

"I did do that. I did pick up the furniture."

Christoffel is silent. I am silent.

He's allowing me this, this one kindness, the ability to put the final pieces together myself. If I don't want to, I can tell Mrs. Janssen that it was Amalia in the pantry and now she's dead, and it will be true, and how she escaped won't matter. Or I can put the pieces together and everything will hurt more.

I have to put them together. Because without even meaning to, I'm remembering the way Mina cheerfully handed me a baby's bag filled with firewood and I carried it on my shoulder for more than a kilometer without realizing that I was transporting an important part of their ruse. I'm remembering the fact that the carriage was really a camera. I'm remembering the fact that Ollie didn't love me or Judith; he loved Willem. I'm remembering the fact that nothing in this war is what it seems, and I have spent too much of it not seeing what's in front of my own face.

Amalia was folded up in the opklapbed. Christoffel rolled it out of the house on his pushcart. While I was trying to figure out whether I should help Mrs. Janssen find her missing onderduiker, she wasn't missing at all. She was just a few feet away.

"She was waiting in the opklapbed for you to sneak her away. That was the plan all along."

I am weary. He is weary. We both want this to be over, finally, completely. "She waited for hours," he said. "She let herself sit in the office while Mrs. Janssen slept, but once she heard Mrs. Janssen wake up, she climbed back in. I told her I would come as early as I could in the morning."

"And then you left. With her. While I sat here. Did you know I had been hired to find her?"

"A friend asked me for help," he says finally. "That's what I was thinking about."

I try to figure out how to respond. Should I tell him about Mrs. Janssen's desperation when she first learned the girl in the pantry was gone? Should I tell him about what it looked like when Amalia's knees buckled and she crashed to the ground?

In the silence, he's crying again.

"Shhhhh," I say to him. "Shhhhh," because it's what people said to me when I cried about Bas and because, at this moment, there aren't any other words.

THIRTY-THREE

Saturday

When things come to an end in a way you don't expect, in a way you never could have imagined, do they really come to an end? Does it mean you should keep searching, for better answers, for ones that don't keep you up at night? Or does it mean it's time to make peace?

It takes me two days to find a space on a train to Kijkduin.

The train goes to Den Haag first, a city that seems like it's swarming with even more German soldiers than Amsterdam. I transfer to Kijkduin, a suburb on the sea, and as the train gets closer, the air becomes briny. Today I'm the only person to get off at this station, holding my small suitcase, looking like a mad vacationer who has elected to come to the sea in the middle of winter. My hair is whipped by the wind coming off the water, and my eyes burn in the salty cold. The town had been a resort destination, new and planned, for only a decade or so before the invasion. Now the beach has a fort near it, taken over by Germans and used for training.

I pass only a few people on my way into town, locals who live here year-round. The second, a young boy, tells me I'm a long walk yet to my destination and offers to give me a lift. I climb on his bicycle carrier while he pedals us into the small downtown.

"Here you are." The bicyclist coasts to a stop, and he nods to a cluster of buildings across the street. The middle one is pale green.

I thank him and smooth down my skirt. Amalia's aunt's guesthouse has a painted porch and a cheerful sign hanging out front, assuring guests that they're open for the winter. I know what's behind this door, or I think I do, at least, but I still feel like an interloper. I didn't send any word before I came. I'd dealt enough in speculation and fog this week; I wanted proof I could see. The black marketer in me, I guess, seeking reassurance and finding value in the tangible world.

When I knock on the door, a middle-aged woman answers eagerly. Off-season business can't be easy to come by, especially not since the Germans have blocked so much of the coastline with barriers against the invading Allies.

"Are you interested in a room?" The woman I assume is Amalia's aunt is already extending her hand to take my suitcase. "Come in. There's a fire going in the parlor, and I'll fix you something to eat."

I follow her inside and think of what I should say and how much I should tell her. I didn't come with any script today, either.

What I'd come to do, after all I'd experienced, seemed too real for games.

In the end, this is what I told Mrs. Janssen, when she came home that day at her house: I told her that the girl she sent me to look for was dead, but the girl she wanted me to find might not be. I told her that I could never bring back the girl who she had grown to love over several weeks of hiding, but that I might be able to find the girl whose family was all gone, just like Mrs. Janssen's son and husband were gone. I showed her the picture, and I told her that I knew it didn't make sense. I told her I would try to find a way for it to make sense, but it maybe never could. I told her I was sorry.

Christoffel refused to tell her anything. He left before Mrs. Janssen returned. He said he couldn't handle the guilt. I wanted to tell him a lot of things: How he'd caused destruction. How he'd been unthinking. How he needed to give me Amalia's secret. But when he said he was crumbling under the guilt, I couldn't bring myself to say any of that. Because I understood what that felt like. Because I'd spent more than two years and all of a war feeling that myself, certain that my actions had caused the death of someone important to me.

"A room, then?" The woman is still waiting for me to respond.

"I'm interested in—" I'm still not sure what to say. Should I ask for Amalia straightaway? Or should I wait until I have a room, and I've come down for dinner around a cozy fire? But it turns out I don't have to worry about it, because all at once, there she is.

A girl a few years younger than me, petite, fine-featured,

comes down the stairs carrying an armful of linens. On her right shin, visible even in the dimness of the indoor light, a thin pink scar jags down from her knee.

"Amalia," the older woman instructs. "It looks like we're going to have a guest tonight. Can you show her up to room three?" She turns to me and winks. "It's the largest we have, with the most comfortable bed."

She's changed a little from her birthday picture. She's older in the face, and her body has curves that the girl in the picture didn't. I let her take my suitcase, this dream girl come to life in front of me, and follow her up to the second floor. Upstairs, room three is decorated in pale blues and seashells, and the window is opened a few inches so the sea air can come in, even in the cold.

"We serve dinner at six," she says, the first time she's spoken to me. Her voice is lower-pitched than I expected. "It's not fancy, but there's usually fresh fish."

"I know." This is what escapes from my mouth. Not a grand speech, but the simple declaration I've waited days to deliver.

She smiles. "Have you been here before, then?"

I shake my head, and her name breaks from my mouth. "Mirjam. Mirjam, I know."

Color drains from Mirjam's face. She looks over her shoulder, seeing if anyone heard the secret name. The door behind her is closed. The streets outside are empty. "Who are you?"

"I wrote you a letter. I folded it into a star."

"I never got a letter."

Of course, Christoffel would have passed it to the real Amalia, not the girl pretending to be her in an inn by the ocean. "I've been looking for you," I say, and then I realize that if she never got the letter, she doesn't know any of what happened, and I am going to have to be the one to tell her, from the beginning.

It takes me a long time to explain everything: Christoffel, Amalia, the Nazis, the bridge. I keep repeating the things she doesn't seem to understand, because she assumed Amalia would be coming to visit her soon. She assumed Amalia was safe. She listens to me with a frozen, stunned expression and her lower teeth biting her upper lip, a habit I never imagined for Mirjam. I spent a week trying to learn about this girl, but I really don't know her at all. Everything I heard was an amalgamation of her and Amalia. I knew people's memories of each of them, and I stitched them together to form a person, but it's a different person than the one standing in front of me.

Mirjam sinks down in a chair next to the doorway. "Are you sure?" she asks when I've finished. "Could you have made a mistake?"

It's the same thing I asked Ollie, when he told me someone named Roodveldt had arrived in the theater, wanting deeply for there to have been a mistake.

"I'm sure. She died because she was acting like she was you," I say. I didn't mean for it to sound harsh. I said it because I'm still trying, so desperately, to understand how it happened.

Her eyes fill with tears. "Have you ever had a best friend?"

I nod. My throat is tight. "Once. Not anymore."

"Then you know. You know what it's like to love someone like you love yourself and then lose them."

I don't know whether to leave her with her grief or to push on, but I've come this far and I can't help wanting to go further. "What happened on that night, Mirjam? The night you changed places?"

She drops her head. She doesn't want to tell me, or she doesn't want to remember, and for a while I think she's not going to answer me at all.

"We only had a few minutes. I was running from the furniture store. I didn't know where I was going, and then Amalia was *there*, with me, in the street. She was already crying; her hair was undone and her blouse was untucked, and when she saw me, she grabbed me so hard I could barely breathe. It was before curfew, and the streets were so busy with people rushing home that nobody paid attention to us. I told her what happened—that my family was dead—and she didn't even have to think before she took off her coat. She said that I would become her, that there were identification papers in the pocket, and money. She was supposed to be on a train that night anyway. To come here. The ticket was already booked. Her aunt hadn't seen her since she was a child. So she told me to go to her aunt's house, and then she promised that she would never reveal where I was or what had happened until I told her it was safe."

"And that was it?"

"Almost." She looks at me again, but her eyes are harder now, somehow, closed off and protective.

It's the *almost* that keeps stopping me, that has stopped me all week. I've had so many occasions of thinking I almost understood something only to realize I didn't understand anything at all.

"Mirjam, Amalia had a secret. She told it to Christoffel. It's why he made her leave his house. It made him so angry that

Amalia was afraid of him. Do you know what it was? What Amalia could have told him that would have upset Christoffel so much that he sent her away from a place where she was safe?"

She pinches her lips and looks away. "I don't know anything."

"Please, I'm just trying to understand what happened. You have no idea how badly people wanted to find you. Mrs. Janssen would have given anything to know what happened."

She wants to tell me. I can tell that she wants this to be done with as much as I do, so that we can all start over.

"Mirjam. You said Amalia was already crying when she ran into you. Why would she already be crying? Why was she out that night to begin with?"

Tell me. Tell me and let us be done with this.

Slowly, deliberately, Mirjam reaches into a pocket on her dress. She pulls out something shaped like a star. "In Amalia's coat pocket, when we traded. In the pocket was the money to come here. And also this."

I take it from her and unfold the flaps. Mirjam rises from her chair and goes to stand by the window, looking out into the sea.

Dearest Elizabeth,

Forgive me. Forgive me. Forgive me even though I have done something you shouldn't forgive me for.

I'm writing this on the tram, and if I get to you in time, I won't have to give this to you at all. This is just in case. A just-in-case letter.

T and I have become close while you're away. He listens when I talk. He laughs at my jokes. It's like he really sees me, for the first time, and I know you wouldn't mind, because you never loved him like I did, because you always said that you wished he felt about me the way he felt about you. And I thought he was starting to love me back. But he wasn't. He wasn't, because this afternoon he looked at me and said, "You should wear your hair like Mirjam's. Hers is so pretty. When the war is over, maybe she'll show you." And I could see in his face that he was never going to love me, not ever.

I'm telling you this because I want you to understand that I was heartbroken. Even though it's not an excuse, I want you to understand that I was heartbroken when I got home and my uncle was visiting and he asked me why I was looking so blue. I want you to understand that I wasn't thinking when I told him that I was blue because the boy I loved would rather pine after a girl who had to hide in a furniture shop until the war was over than be with me. My uncle laughed. He told me the boy was dumb. He asked me to tell him more about this girl. I did. I told him all about you. I forgot he'd joined the NSB.

Or did I? Dearest Elizabeth, I've been thinking about this from the moment I realized what he'd done, from the moment I ran for the tram. Did I really forget that he joined the NSB? Or did part of me remember and know exactly

what I was doing? I'm going to try to stop this. I'm going to
fix it if I can. Forgive me. Forgive me. Forgive me.

"She turned you in," I say. "She was the reason the Nazis raided your hiding space."

Mirjam turns to face me. "Didn't you see? She regretted it almost as soon as she realized what had happened. That was why she was out that night in the street. She was running to warn us all that she'd told. She was hoping there would still be time for us to run."

"But it *was* too late."

Mirjam's eyes are webbed with tears. I can't even imagine what it must have been like that night. Two best friends meeting on the street to say so many things at once: *I betrayed you, I love you, I want to save you, I'm sorry.* All around Europe, people are dying by the hundreds of thousands. And here, in my city, the Nazis slaughtered a family because of events that started with love and jealousy and a slip of the tongue.

"You'll want to hate her." Mirjam stares down at her folded hands. "I did. More than I ever hated anybody. But she didn't know. I have to believe that now. When she told her uncle, I think she did it without realizing what could happen. She didn't mean to." She looks up at me with enormous eyes. "Do you believe me when I say that?"

"I believe that if you believe that," I say.

I don't know why Mirjam should care, if I think well of Amalia or not. She doesn't even know me.

Except that, it occurs to me, I would care if it were me or my friends. All of us—Bas, Elsbeth, Ollie, me—I would care that someone understood we were flawed and scarred and doing the best we could in this war. We were wrapped up in things that were so much bigger than ourselves. We didn't know. We didn't mean it. It wasn't our fault.

Mirjam goes to the bed and sits, and I sit beside her, and neither of us says anything. We just stare out the window as waves batter the barricaded shore.

THIRTY-FOUR

In the end, I don't stay the night at Amalia's aunt's hotel. Mirjam doesn't know me well enough for me to be a comfort to her, and after a while I realize I don't know what to say. I tell her I'll go back to Amsterdam, where she would have a home with Mrs. Janssen if she wanted it, but in truth it's probably better for her to stay here until the war is over, tucked away in a guestless hotel with safe papers.

I walk back toward the railway station and pester the station agent until he gets me a spot on the next train back to Amsterdam. The woman in the seat next to me whispers that the Battle of Stalingrad is over and the Nazis lost—their first official surrender of the war.

"Thank God," I say, which I soon realize is taking a chance: If she's a collaborator, my response should have been neutral or despair. But she's not, because she reaches down and furtively squeezes my hand, a shared gratefulness. And then we're done talking, because neither of us knows who could be listening, and we keep to ourselves as the train heads home. I feel tired. More so than I would have expected, after so much resolution. Maybe we can't barter our feelings away, trading good deeds for bad ones and expecting to become whole.

When I get home, Mama and Papa will ask where I've been. I'll go and have dinner with Ollie and Willem and Sanne and Leo. I'll visit Mina when I can. My heart will still ache sometimes. Maybe more often than not. I think it's possible to be healed without feeling whole.

I found a girl who wasn't the girl I was looking for. I let go of a friend I'll still miss every day. I'll go back to work. I'll get better. I'll get better slowly. I'll find all the secret, hidden things.

The first time I realized I loved Bas:

He was sixteen, I was fifteen. It wasn't the afternoon in his house when we listened to the radio. That was when he realized he loved me. I actually realized it the week before. It was in the school yard. Someone was saying how they liked to read the last pages of books first, to make sure everyone turned out okay. Bas said that was the dumbest thing he'd ever heard. Bas ordered that the book in question be passed to him, and when it was, he flipped to the back page, took out a pencil and started writing on it. I thought he would write *Everyone turned out okay*, but when he passed the book back, he'd actually written, *Everyone was mauled by a bear, it was very sad, let's go get ice cream.*

Then he grabbed my hand, pulled me up from where I'd been sitting, and said, "Maybe the bear didn't maul you. He just scratched you a little bit." Then I made a face, and then he kissed me, and then we walked to get ice cream, in a relationship at its beautiful beginning, in a world that was closer to the end than we ever knew.

A NOTE ON
HISTORICAL ACCURACY

Though the stories and characters in this book are all fictional, the locations and historical events mentioned were real places and occurrences in Holland during World War II. The Netherlands was invaded in May 1940. More than two thousand Dutch servicemen were killed in the Battle of the Netherlands, and German occupiers began to put into place a series of increasingly severe restrictions on the Jewish population.

Some one hundred thousand Dutch Jews died in the Holocaust— nearly three-quarters of the Jewish population, a much higher percentage than in nearby countries. There's a lot of speculation as to why this happened: The Netherlands was a flat, developed country without many forests or natural places to hide. The countries that bordered it were also occupied, limiting escape routes. Resistance work was slow to be organized—the Netherlands had been neutral in World War I and so citizens didn't have the infrastructure or knowledge for creating underground networks. The Dutch collaboration rate was comparatively high, and even those who disapproved of the occupation were lulled into a false sense of security by the gradual way that Nazi restrictions were enacted: The country was a frog in slowly boiling water.

The Jewish Council, composed of leaders in the community, originally believed that their role as liaison between Nazis and the Jewish population would improve the treatment of Jews in the Netherlands. Instead, many today believe that the Council's acts inadvertently made it easier for Jews to be tracked, persecuted, and deported to their deaths.

There were, however, extraordinary acts of heroism within the country. Ollie and Judith and their friends represent an amalgamation of several different types of resistance activities, but they are most closely based on the Amsterdam Student Group, an organization of university students who specialized in rescuing children, and on the mostly Jewish workers who were assigned to work in the Hollandsche Schouwburg. The Schouwburg was a place of terror, but also one of Amsterdam's bravest rescue operations. An estimated six hundred Jewish children were sneaked out of the nursery across the street: sometimes hiding in laundry baskets, sometimes passed over the courtyard wall to neighboring buildings, and sometimes escorted out in plain sight by workers who conveniently "miscounted" the number of children they were supposed to be looking after. The acts of my characters were inspired by reading about, or listening to the oral histories of, many people who were affiliated with the theater. To name a few: Piet Meerburg, the cofounder of the Amsterdam Student Group; Henriette Pimentel, who ran the nursery and was killed in Auschwitz in 1943; and Walter Süskind, who falsified children's records while running the Schouwburg and was killed in 1945.

The resistance work of photographers was real: A loosely joined network of professional photographers became officially known as the Underground Camera in 1944. They risked their personal safety to take secret photographs of soldiers and civilians, and their images remain some of the most illuminating records of Dutch life during Nazi occupation. Female photographers were particularly adept: They hid their cameras in purses and handbags. Lydia van Nobelen-Riezouw, though not a member of Underground Camera, did live in an apartment abutting the Schouwburg's rear courtyard, and she did take photographs of the Jewish prisoners when she recognized a childhood friend among them. Mina's storyline draws from this experience.

Het Parool was a real newspaper; in fact, it still exists today. The publishers risked their lives to print every issue: Thirteen of its workers were executed in February 1943, just a few days after the events of this novel conclude.

I'm a journalist by trade, and I've always believed that people's real stories are more moving, more interesting, and more heartbreaking than anything I could invent in fiction. My initial interest in this project began with a vacation to Amsterdam and visits to several Holocaust-related sites there. I subsequently did a lot of research and have a lot of people to credit for helping me discover the real stories of Amsterdam in 1943.

Over repeated visits, the librarians at the US Holocaust Memorial Museum in Washington, DC, helped me find stacks of books and DVDs on topics ranging from ration coupons to what kind of coded language resistance workers would have used when talking to each other on the telephone.

Greg Miller at Film Rescue International had several patient exchanges with me about the tricky process for developing color images in the 1940s. Paul Moody, who directed the Dutch documentary *The Underground Camera*, was similarly patient in corresponding with me about the role of photographers during the war; he recommended the book *De illegale camera (1940–1945)*, a collection of war photographs containing many of the images that I described and credited to Mina. Military historian Allert Goossens dug through his research files to help me come up with a plausible scenario allowing Bas to have joined the navy at seventeen years old, which was below the draft age. In Holland, Michigan, the staff at Nelis' Dutch Village fed me lots of Dutch food, including banketstaaf, which makes an appearance as one of Hanneke's favorite treats. Pat Boydens, a native Dutch speaker who now lives in Virginia, read the manuscript for linguistic truthfulness, helping me determine, for example, which types of curse words would be most likely used by a teenage girl. Laurien Vastenhout was a meticulous fact-checker, combing the manuscript for historical accuracy, and the staff at Sebes & Van Gelderen Literary Agency also provided invaluable historical feedback related to character names and Dutch culture.

There were some occasions in the book when I did veer from history books. A few examples: I have the nursery in the Schouwburg closing in January when in fact it didn't close until several months later. *Het Parool* did not have a classified ads section, at least not in the winter of 1943, and it was not, as far as I know, used by individuals to pass secret messages. Those decisions, along with any other departures from history, were made solely by me for artistic purposes, and I hope that none of them are unforgivable.

Hanneke Bakker was not, after all, a real person. Nor were Bas and Ollie Van de Kamp, Mirjam Roodveldt, or any of the other characters mentioned by name. But as people continue to ask how an event as monumental and atrocious as the Holocaust ever could have happened, I wanted to tell a story of small betrayals in the middle of a big war. I wanted to illustrate the split-second decisions we make of moral courage and cowardice, and how we are all heroes and villains.

ACKNOWLEDGMENTS

Writing is a sort of lonely process, because at the end of the day only one pair of hands can fit on a laptop, and most of the time— at least midproject—I wish they were anyone's but mine. For this book, I am grateful for the people who symbolically shared the keyboard and made writing feel like a team sport.

My agent, Ginger Clark, read three paragraphs of an early plot description and immediately informed me that the book I was describing should be about teenagers, rather than the adults I'd been envisioning. She was right, as she is about most things.

My editor, Lisa Yoskowitz, was instrumental in suggesting so many plot and character developments that I hesitate to enumerate them here, lest I reveal myself to be a total idiot.

Robert Cox, my husband, offered scrupulous notes over multiple drafts, and pancakes at IHOP when they became necessary. I could not have asked for a smarter reader or a better partner.

It's daunting, and perhaps a little presumptuous, to try to tell a story about a culture and time that don't belong to you. But I knew from the beginning that I wanted this story to be set in Amsterdam, in World War II, and I wanted it to feel authentically Dutch. Getting the dates and geography right was one thing, but getting the Dutch sensibility right required an entirely different level of nuance. And so I am grateful to the tour guide in Amsterdam who first introduced me to the phrase "God made the world, but the Dutch made the Netherlands." I am grateful to the cyclists in the city who gently chided me when I misunderstood the rules of bicycle culture. I am grateful for Amsterdam's exhaustive, absorbing museum collections, and for the private citizens who bothered to create websites—in English!—on topics ranging from the proper pronunciation of Dutch names to the fate of each naval torpedo ship during the German invasion.

I am deeply grateful, on a literary and on a humanistic level, for the Dutch resistance workers who later wrote about their experiences, which provided such rich, textured accounts of a time and place. Reading the memoirs of Miep Gies, Corrie ten Boom, Hanneke Ippisch, and Diet Eman, among others, taught me a great deal about what it felt like to live through World War II in Amsterdam. And finally: So much of what the world knows about the war, the city, and the human experience is because of one particular book, written from an attic, in the middle of the occupation. I am most profoundly grateful to Anne.

DISCUSSION GUIDE

1. How does Hanneke react to Mrs. Janssen's story of Mirjam Roodveldt? Why do you think she reacted that way?

2. What is the significance of the scene with the Biermans that Hanneke and her parents witness during lunch?

3. Why does Hanneke believe that her old boyfriend, Bas, would not recognize her? How does that impact her thoughts about finding Mirjam?

4. Why has Hanneke decided to get involved with finding Mirjam? What would you do if you were in Hanneke's shoes?

5. Analyze Hanneke's interactions with German soldiers. How does she manipulate the interactions?

6. Summarize what the reader has learned about Bas and Hanneke by the end of chapter six. Why is the author pacing out the details of their relationship rather than revealing them all at once?

7. Imagine you are Hanneke and are invited to listen in at the meeting at Leo's apartment. What do you notice about the attendees? What do you think of their purpose?

8. How does Mina handle the German soldier with the empty baby carriage? What does that exchange reveal about Mina? What does Hanneke's reaction reveal about her?

9. What's special about Mina's photography? Do you think her work is worth the risk? What clues are hidden in the color slides?

10. How does Hanneke's choice to stay out all night change her relationship with her parents? How have all these young people changed because of the war?

11. What happens between Ollie and Hanneke as they wait for transport? How does it change their understanding of each other and their relationship? What does it make Hanneke realize about the war?

12. After the funeral, when the group goes on a bike ride, Hanneke has an epiphany. What was it? Why does she react the way she does?

13. Explain Christoffel's part in the whole story. Why does Hanneke have great empathy for him?

14. Throughout the book, Hanneke often reflects on her friend Elsbeth. How does this relationship mirror the friendship between Mirjam and Amalia?

15. Explain the significance of this quote: "Maybe we can't barter our feelings away, trading good deeds for bad ones and expecting to become whole."

16. How does the author keep tension throughout the story? Whose story fascinated you most and why?

17. Why, do you think, does the author chose to close the story with a memory of the narrator and her first love?

18. Read the author's note. How did the author's training as a journalist help her write this book?

Turn the page to start reading the next
tour de force historical mystery from
Monica Hesse

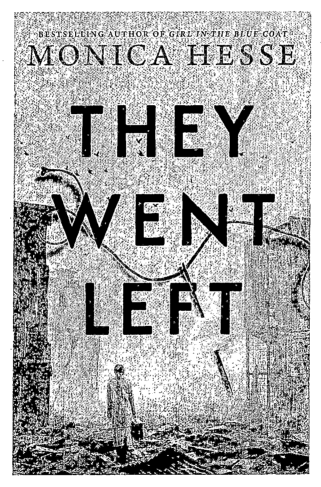

BESTSELLING AUTHOR OF *GIRL IN THE BLUE COAT*

MONICA HESSE

THEY
WENT
LEFT

Available April 2020

THE LAST TIME I SAW ABEK:

Barbed wire, rusty metal knots. I was being transferred. We all were, we lucky girls who could still sew and still stand, and as the guards marched us past the men's side of the camp, the men were lining up for roll call. Our eyes scrambled over them, greedy, searching the living skeletons for our fathers and cousins. We were good at whispering without making a sound by then; we were good at reading lips. Rosen? Rosen or Weiss? *we girls mouthed, passing family surnames through the fence like prayers.* Are there any Rosens from Kraków? From Łódź?

His cheeks were still round. His eyes were still clear; I noticed that. The older men must have been giving him their bread. In the beginning at least, we would sometimes do that for the youngest among us. I saw a healthy Abek and gave thanks for all the times I'd given bread to anyone's sister in my own barracks, a barter with the universe that someone else should be doing the same for my brother.

"Abek Lederman," I mouthed to the girl next to me. "Third row."

She took his name and whispered it through the fence, and on the other side, I saw the men part, reaching for his shoulders and pushing him closer.

I knew we would have no more than a few seconds. Barely enough time for me to grab his hand or pass him something. What did I have to pass? Why hadn't I saved half a potato, a piece of string?

Ahead of me, a woman stopped to take a rock from her shoe. Stupid. This guard would hit you for such an infraction, any of them would. As soon as the woman bent, the guard brought her mallet down on the woman's back, and she yelped in pain. But as she cried out, she also looked back at me, and I understood this delay was a gift; this delay would give me enough time to speak to my brother.

"Zofia!" he cried. "Where are they taking you?"

"I don't know," I mouthed. I could already feel tears pooling in my eyes but bit them back so as not to waste time. I reached for his hand through the fence, his little-boy fist that I could still cup my palm around.

"Abek to Zofia," I told him.

"A to Z," he said back.

"When I find you again, we will fill our alphabet. And we will be whole, and everything will be fine. I promise I will find you."

This is the version I have dreams of sometimes. Clear as day, sharp as a needle, so I can see every hair on his head. And when I dream this scene, Abek nods at my promise. Like he trusts me, like he believes me. For a moment, I feel at peace.

But then something changes. Then dream-Abek's face twists, and his words come out pained: "Something happened," this Abek says. "But we don't have to talk about it yet."

Lower Silesia, August 1945

L INES. I AM GOOD AT LINES. I AM GOOD AT LINES BECAUSE YOU don't have to think in them, just stand in them, and this line is easy because now only a few people are in front of me, and easy because I understand the reason I am in it, and it's a good reason, and I am good at lines.

At the front of it, an official-looking woman—from the Red Cross, I think—sits behind a table. It's a nice, indoor table, as though it was carried out to the street from someone's dining room. Except, instead of sitting on a rug, it sits on cobblestones, and instead of candlesticks, it's piled with neat stacks of papers and smells of furniture polish, or I imagine it would; it looks like that kind of table. A solitary cup also sits on it, next to the papers at the proper two o'clock of an imaginary place setting like a leftover from the table's former life. A cup of tea for the official worker.

"Next," she says, and we move forward because this is how lines work; they move forward.

I look back toward the door, but the other nothing-girls don't come out to say goodbye. I'm the first one of us to leave the hospital. In the early weeks after the war, there were always goodbyes from the healthier patients, always plans being made. You could look out the ward window almost any time and see a truck grinding past, stuffed with German soldiers on their way home, Polish soldiers on *their* way home. Russians, a few Canadians, everyone traveling in a different direction, and every direction was someone's home, as if the world were a board game and all the pieces had ended up scattered in the wrong corners of the box.

But none of the nothing-girls were well enough then. So we don't have a protocol yet for what to do when one of us leaves. We have no addresses to exchange. We have nothing. We weigh nothing, we feel nothing, we existed on nothing, for years.

Our minds are nothing. That's the biggest nothing, the reason we are still in the hospital. Our minds are soft. Confused.

"Zofia? I didn't know if you wanted to keep this."

I turn to the voice, the little blond nurse jogging out the door, mouth like a red bow. She hands me a letter, addressed in my own handwriting. *Return to sender.* The sender was me; the addressee was—I'm not even sure who the addressee was this time. For months, from the day I was well enough to pick up a pen, I have been writing letters to everyone whose address I'd ever known. *Have you seen him? Tell him to wait for me.* But their addresses weren't their addresses anymore, and the mail wasn't the mail anymore. And I wasn't me anymore, but it became clear I couldn't do what I needed to from a hospital bed. If I wanted to find him, I would have to pull myself out of it.

Even though my mind is still soft, that's why I'm standing outside and the other girls are still in the window.

Tell him the doctors won't let me leave by myself until I'm better, I wrote. *Tell him I won't be better until I leave and find him.*

"Here, I also made this for you," the blond nurse says, passing me a bundle of cloth, still warm. Food. The heat feels nice against my stomach. I start to unwrap the cloth so I can hand it back, but she says to keep it.

So now I own this checkered cloth. It is mine, and that will bring the number of possessions I own in this world to six. Later, I can fold it and use it as a kerchief for my hair, or I can cut it in half, in triangles, and have two handkerchiefs; that would bring my number of possessions to seven. I also have a dress, undergarments, a pair of shoes, a donated bill of money in a large denomination, and a document saying I was a prisoner in Gross-Rosen. It's supposed to connect me with relief organizations, help with food rations. The workers who gave it to me said it would be my most valuable possession.

"Next," the official woman says. She's my mother's age, with lines on her brow that have only begun to soften her face. The queue behind me has grown, as more soon-to-be-discharged patients come out. Another worker arrives to help.

The blond nurse, still watching me. "Did you forget anything else?" she asks. *Urbaniak*, I remember. *Her surname is Urbaniak.*

"My shoes. Where are my shoes?"

Why didn't I realize before? I've just looked down at my feet, and the brown leather boots I'm wearing are a stranger's.

"Those *are* your shoes. Your new shoes. Remember?" She's gentle, and then I do remember: These brown boots are mine now, because when I was brought to the hospital months ago, I was wearing the shoes the Nazis had assigned to me, ill-fitting and full of holes. My frostbitten feet were so swollen that a nurse couldn't pull them off; she had to slice them at the tongue. The nurses said I cried; I don't remember crying.

It turns out, if you have to lose toes to frostbite, the third and the fourth are possible to lose and still be able to walk and balance.

"Are you sure you don't want to stay longer, Zofia?"

"I remember about my shoes now; I just forgot for a minute."

"You had already asked me about them once today."

I force a smile. "Dima is leaving; he's going to his new post, and he has a car to drive me."

Dima-the-soldier is the one who brought me to the hospital, which was not a hospital then, just a building crammed with cots and bottles of iodine. Dima's Red Army jeep was crammed, too, with people. The Russians had liberated Gross-Rosen three days before, but it had finally become clear that none of us, including the Russian soldiers, knew what liberation was supposed to look like. Hundreds of us were still inside the gates, too weak to leave. Dima found me barely conscious in the women's barracks, he later told me in the broken Polish from his mother. It was lucky I'd passed out, because by the time he stroked life back into my face, all the good rations had been handed out already: waxy chocolate, tinned beef.

Our stomachs were too weak for rich foods. I watched people who'd lived for months on a potato a day eat the beef and never get up again. We were liberated and still dying by the dozens.

"*It's over now*," the soldiers said to us in February. It wasn't over, not officially, not for a few months, but what they meant was, the SS officers were not coming back to the camp.

"*It's really over now*," the nurses told us in May, spoon-feeding us sugar water and porridge. We could hear cheering and yelling in the corridor; Germany had surrendered.

What did they mean, it was over? What was over? I was miles from home, and I didn't own so much as my own shoes. How was any of this over?

"Next," says the official woman, and I take another step forward.

A puff of smoke, the growl of a motor. Dima pulls up in his jeep. He leaps out when he sees me waiting, and I'm struck again by how much he looks like a cinema poster, like the film version of a soldier: Square chin. Nice cheekbones. Kind eyes. Dima, who postmarked my letters for me. Who, when I begged him, asked his soldier friends about Birkenau and found out for me that it had been liberated a few weeks before Gross-Rosen. And who repeated the same thing for me again when I forgot, and then again when I forgot again. *Remember, Zofia? We discuss already.* My mind is a sieve, and Dima is how I am allowed to leave this place—because he is leaving with me.

"I would have come inside, Zofia." He places his hands on my shoulders. His hair is shorter above one ear. He must have cut it himself again in the mirror. "You get too tired. You know I worry about you."

"I have to stand in this line now."

"She has to be processed," Nurse Urbaniak explains. "The aid organizations are keeping records."

A tap on glass, like a bird. I look up. In the second-floor hospital window behind me, the nothing-girls have woken; they're touching the glass and waving. To Dima as much as to me; they love him. He waves back.

"Next," the Red Cross woman says. I wait for a minute before realizing it's finally my turn. Her uniform is a single-breasted blue suit. My dress is also pale blue. The nurse who gave it to me said it went with my hair and eyes. *Kind lies.* My hair then was patchy and scabbed over, short as a boy's. It's grown back almost to my chin, but a thin, timid brown instead of lustrous curls. My eyes are still the color of empty. "Miss?" says the matronly woman. "Miss?"

"Zofia Lederman." I wait for her to check me off on her papers.

"And you're going home?"

"Yes. To Sosnowiec."

"And who would you like me to put on your list?" I stare at her, and she reads my confusion. "We're asking if you have any names."

"Names?" I know what she's asking must make sense, but my brain is fogged again; it can't parse the words. I start to turn back to Nurse Urbaniak and Dima for help.

The worker places her hand on mine until I look back at her. Her voice has softened from its clipped, official tone. "Do you understand? We're logging where you're going, but also the family you're looking for. Is there anyone who could be looking for you?"

Names. I did this once already, months ago, with some charity workers as soon as I was conscious. Nothing ever came of it, and now his name hurts in my throat.

"Abek. My brother, Abek Lederman."

"Age?"

"He would be twelve now."

"Do you know anything about where he might be?"

"We were both sent to Birkenau, but I was transferred twice, to a textile factory called Neustadt and then to Gross-Rosen. The last time I saw him was more than three years ago."

I watch her make careful notes. "Who else?" she asks.

"Just Abek."

Just Abek. This is why I need to go home. Birkenau was liberated before Gross-Rosen. Abek could already be waiting.

"Are you sure that's all?" Her pen hesitates over the next blank line. She's trying to figure out how to be delicate with me. "We've found that it's better to cast as wide a net as possible. Not just immediate family, but cousins, distant relations. All will improve the chances of your finding someone."

"I don't need to add anyone else."

Distant relations. She doesn't mean it this way, but it reminds me of when my old teacher would bring candy to lessons. *Don't be choosy,* he'd warn, walking around with a bowl.

Don't be choosy. You'd be lucky to have any relatives at all; just pick something.

"Look at all these empty rows." The worker gestures to her paper, patient, as you'd talk to a baby. "There's plenty of room to add as many people as you'd like. If you're looking for only one person—one on this entire continent—it could be impossible."

One person. Impossible.

I look at her empty lines. There aren't enough of them, not even close. Not nearly enough space for me to tell the story of the people I'm missing. I squeeze my eyes shut, trying to keep my thoughts from leaking, because I know the nurses have been wrong all along: Sometimes it's not that I have trouble remembering things, it's that I have trouble forgetting.

Behind me, Dima shifts his weight, concerned. I can tell he wonders if he should help.

If there were enough empty lines on that sheet of paper, this is how I would start:

I would start by telling her that on the twelfth of August in 1942, all remaining Jews of Sosnowiec were told to go to the soccer stadium. The instructions said we were to be issued new identification. It seemed suspicious even then, but you have to understand—I would tell her, *You must understand*—the Germans had already occupied our city for three years. We were accustomed to arbitrary orders that sometimes became terrifying and sometimes benign. I would tell her how my family had been moved from our apartment to another across town, for no other reason than imaginary boundaries had been drawn on a map, and Jews could now live only inside them. How Baba Rose and I had already made stars to pin on our clothes, cut from a pattern in the newspaper.

Papa had already reported to the stadium once: The Germans made all men. They were taken, but they were returned, ashen and not wanting to speak of what they'd seen. *They returned.*

I would tell this Red Cross worker that our identification cards were how we survived: Without one, you couldn't buy food or walk in the street. So we had to go, and we wore our best clothes. The instructions told us to do this, which we took comfort in, because maybe they really were going to take our pictures for identification.

But then we got there, and there were no cameras. Just soldiers. And all they were doing was sorting us. By health. By age. Strong-looking into one group; weak or old or families with young children in another. One line to work in factories. Another line to camps.

It took hours. It took days. Thousands of us were on the field. All of us had to be sorted. All of us had to be queried about whether we had special skills or connections. The SS surrounded the perimeter. Behind my family, an old man I recognized from the pharmacy was praying, and two soldiers came over to jeer. One knocked the pharmacist's hat off; the other kneed him to the ground. My father ran over to help him up—I knew he would; he was always kind to old people— even while my mother and I begged him not to, and I thought, *What's the use.*

My mother and I took turns curling our arms around Abek and telling him fairy tales: *The Frog Princess. The Bear in the Forest Hut. The Whirlwind*, his favorite.

Abek was tall for his age, which made him look older. When we realized how the soldiers were sorting us, we told ourselves that would matter. *Abek,* Mama said. *You are twelve, not nine, all right? You're twelve, and you've been working in your father's factory for a year already.*

We made up these reassurances for all of us. We looked at Baba Rose, my sweet, patient grandmother, and we told ourselves she looked much younger than sixty-seven. We told ourselves nobody in Sosnowiec could sew half as well. Customers who bought suits and skirts from my family's business did so because of the embroidery done at Baba Rose's hand, and surely this counted as a special skill.

We told ourselves my mother's cough, the one that had made her weak and gasping over the past months, the one Abek was starting to get, too, was barely noticeable. We said nobody would even see Aunt Maja's limp.

Pinch your cheeks, Aunt Maja told me. *When they come to you, pinch your cheeks to make them full of life.*

Beautiful Aunt Maja's face was so pretty and her laugh was so gay, none of her suitors ever cared that she was born with a mangled hip that made her lurch instead of glide. She was much younger than Mama, just nine years older than me. She used to tell me to pinch my cheeks so I would be as pretty as she was. Now it was so we would both be safe.

Darkness fell; it started to rain. We opened our mouths to

catch the drops; we hadn't eaten or drank in days. The water on our now-sunburned skin felt nice for a minute, and then we were cold. Next to me, Abek tucked his hand in mine.

And Prince Dobrotek crept into the horse's ear, I said, telling *The Whirlwind* again. I was always good at telling stories. *And when he crawled out the other side, can you remember what he was wearing?*

A golden suit of armor, Abek said. *And then he rode the horse to the moving mountain.*

Pinch your cheeks! Aunt Maja called to me. *Zofia, pinch your cheeks and smile.*

I kept Abek's hand in mine and dragged him with me to the soldiers.

Fifteen, I told them. *I can sew and run a loom. My brother is twelve.*

Do you see why there isn't enough room on this woman's intake form for me to explain all this? It would take her hours to write it down. She would run out of ink. There are too many other Jews, millions of missing, whose information she also needs to collect.

Dima steps forward. "Zofia doesn't have more names; she's not well."

"I can do it," I protest, but I'm not even sure what I mean by *it.* I can keep standing in this line? I can be well again?

The official woman adds my records to her pile. Dima extends his hand, and I accept it. I fold myself into the passenger side of his jeep and allow him to arrange his coat over my lap while Nurse Urbaniak makes sure the bundle of food is secure on the floorboard.

What I should have told the official woman is this: I know I don't need to put anyone else on my list, because when the soldiers sorted my family, they sent us all to Birkenau. And when we got to Birkenau, there was another line dividing into two. In that line, the lucky people were sent to hard labor. The unlucky people—we could see the smoke. The smoke was the burning bodies of the unlucky people.

In that line, Abek and I were sent to the right.

On this continent, I need to find only one person. I need to go home, I need to survive, I need to keep my brain working for only one person.

Because everyone else: Papa, Mama, Baba Rose, beautiful Aunt Maja—all of them, all of them, as the population of Sosnowiec was devastated—they went left.

Turn the page to start reading another
masterwork of historical fiction from
Monica Hesse

HARUKO

Of all the things that happened there, in that place full of enemies and dust and spies and sadness; of all the things Margot said to me—the calculations that sounded like friendship, the casual shattering of my life—out of all those things, I am grateful for only one: that I never loved her. If I had loved her I couldn't bear any of it, and so I am grateful for this lack of love, this one remaining thing I can bear. Because even if it's a terrible thing to have, if I didn't have that, I'd have nothing.

MARGOT

If Haruko said that, she was lying. She did love me. I loved her too.

ONE

HARUKO

"I WISH WE WERE ALL HOME NOW," TOSHIKO WHISPERS, AS IF I'LL
have a different response than I had the last time she said the
same thing. She pokes my side to get my attention, which she
knows I hate. But I stay serene because it's part of our unspoken
pact, my sister and me, that we're polite because we're too afraid
to be anything else. And because we promised our mother.

"Your little sister is not your enemy," Mama told me the
last time Toshiko and I argued, which was the first time I
learned about Texas. "I know that," I said meaningfully, and
then I didn't say anything else because I didn't want to talk
about who the real enemy was.

Now my mother sits across from us, wedged beside our
stack of suitcases, keeping her back straight so her hat doesn't

get crushed against the seat of the Pullman car. Her eyes are closed. I can't tell whether she's sleeping or train-sick, a kind of sick I didn't know existed until we got on the train and people started making retching sounds into the paper bags provided by the guards patrolling the aisles. For more than a thousand miles now, that hat has been pinned to my mother's head. Everything else in the car is wilted: her dress, my dress, my sister's entire body, pressing against mine as I decide not to respond to her last statement. Instead I lean my forehead against the window. Brown grass. Brown dirt. Dirty horses, ridden by men with bandannas over their noses across land that is unbearably flat.

The last time I saw Denver, the sky was clear enough to see all the way to the tops of the mountains.

"Haruko." Toshiko pokes my side again, below the rib cage.

"Helen," I correct her.

She rolls her eyes. "Everyone here is Japanese. They can pronounce your real name."

I will myself to keep looking out the window instead of glaring at Toshiko. "My friends call me Helen."

"About five people ever called you Helen."

We're becoming testy at the edges, not just my sister and me but the whole train, exhausted by three days of politeness and stale sandwiches. My head is pulsing with the screaming rhythm of the train's motion. It aches in my jaw, in my teeth; my nostrils are filled with oil and smoke. I cover my nose and try to take fewer breaths.

"Helen." Poke, poke. "Can I look at the letter again?"

I want to tell her no, not because I'm trying to provoke her but because I hate the letter. My mother has heard Toshiko's question, though, and opened one watchful eye to make sure I do what I'm asked. She loves the letter; they both love the letter.

The letter has an official stamp and a return address explaining the people who sent it are from the Department of Justice of the United States of America. I take it out of my handbag and hand it to Toshiko, who unfolds it reverentially. What does she think will happen if she tears it? They won't let us in? The whole point of the letter is that they won't let us out.

Dear Mrs. Tanaka,

You are informed that your application for reunion at a family internment facility with your husband, Ichiro Tanaka, has been approved. Please be informed that the only individuals accommodated through this agreement are Mrs. Setsu Tanaka (age 44), Miss Haruko Tanaka (age 17), and Miss Toshiko Tanaka (age 12). Arrangements will be made for such a reunion at Crystal City, Texas.

Crystal City. We are going to a place called Crystal City. I'd put faith in the name at first, because it leads you to believe you are going somewhere beautiful. A place where there might be a reason to pack nice things. My best dress. My new handbag. My bottle of Tabu perfume.

The train has other families on it, and we've gotten to know some of them.

Mrs. Ginoza and her little daughter, from Los Angeles. Old Mrs. Yamaguchi from Santa Cruz. Families with stories that sound exactly like each other's except for a few details. My mother still politely listens to everyone else's even though she must know by now how they will end: *And then we got on this train.*

We were sitting down to dinner; the FBI men didn't let him finish the meal.

They said it was because we were hiding Japanese correspondence. But it was letters from my mother-in-law that we saved in a hope chest. How could that be hiding?

We knew an attorney, but he said there was nothing he could do; it's all legal. President Roosevelt issued a proclamation.

Even now, I can hear my mother retelling our own story to the bride across the aisle, the one whose husband was taken two days after their wedding.

"They came on a Saturday morning when Ichiro was still at work and they sat in my kitchen until he came home," Mama is saying. "They wouldn't let me telephone him, in case I used a code to tell him to stay away. We had to wait for hours; my husband was staying late to help a guest arrange a hiking tour. He was always staying late to take care of things. The men said he was using his job to pass information between guests traveling overseas."

She leaves so much out of this story. She leaves out the fact that the Albany, where my father was a night clerk, was the nicest hotel in the city. That some of the guests were Japanese, but most of them were white, and they liked my father, and sometimes brought us gifts from places they'd traveled. Paper fans from Paris, a snow globe from New York City. She leaves out the fact that the governor came in once, and that my brother sold his secretary an orange soda in the hotel's pharmacy, and I gave her the straw to drink it with. Governor Carr's secretary told me I had lovely American dimples, and Kenichi and I spent the next week elaborately reenacting this scene as we mopped the floors at the end of the day. "Am-*er*-ican dimples are fine, I suppose, if they're all you can get," Ken would say. "Though I prefer my dimples to come from *France*."

Somewhere in the telling of this, when we imitated the secretary we started giving her a posh accent that she didn't actually have. "Did I say American dimples? *Heavens*, I meant American *pimples*." Nobody else thought it was as funny. Nobody else ever thought our things were as funny as we did.

On the day the agents came to our apartment, I wasn't helping out in the soda fountain. Ken had left to become an American war hero by then. Papa and Mama didn't want me to work there alone.

What I was doing was putting on my volleyball uniform

because I was going to meet some of the other Nisei girls from the California Street church. My mother called me out of the bedroom to translate for her; I still had rollers in half my hair. It took a while for me to figure out how to explain what the men wanted. Some of the terms I didn't have translations for. *What is subterfuge?* I asked one of the agents, who thought I was being cheeky.

When my mother tells the story, what she leaves out is my whole life.

A little while after the letter from the government arrived, a separate one came from my father, addressed to my mother but written to all of us—in English, I was sure whoever monitored his mail had insisted it be in English, so I had to be the one to read it out loud. *There is a beauty salon,* he wrote. *A grocer's. They are building an American school and a swimming pool: one hundred yards in diameter with a diving platform! People can have jobs, for extra money, but everyone receives housing, and tokens for food and clothing, whether they have jobs or not. You will like it.*

The least my father could have done would have been to refuse harder, to tell my mother he forbade us from coming to Texas. Instead when she insisted we were coming, we got cheerful snippets that sounded like a vacationer's postcards, with exclamation points that my father would have called vulgar if I'd used them myself: *So many Japanese people! Movies shown for free in the community center! Haruko, tell your*

*mother that the hospital is looking for volunteers, and also that
some of the women have started a tofu factory, right in camp!*

This is how my father tried to make us excited about the barren desert of Texas. A tofu factory.

I did tell my mother about the hospital, and I watched her light up. My mother, who graduated from the Tokyo Women's Medical Professional School, who never officially became a doctor because instead she moved to America to marry the stranger-son of a family friend, and who never became fluent in English, and who instead made it her profession to worry about the length of my volleyball uniform.

Personally I would worry about a place that allowed a woman twenty years out of medical school to volunteer as a doctor, but my mother lit up and so I said nothing. Serene.

Toshiko jabs me with her elbow. The train has slowed and the brakes are creaking. "I think we're stopping," she whispers to me. "I think we're picking up more people."

"Maintenance break," I whisper back. "Window shades."

If it were an actual station, the guards would have told us to pull down the window shades. They do that at every stop, though they haven't said whether it's because they don't want us to be able to see where we are, or because they don't want people in the towns to see us.

But no, it turns out this time Toshiko and I are both wrong. The train car has stopped, fully stopped, without anyone making us pull down the window shades and without any new people standing outside waiting to board. The train is finally quiet, and the quiet is heaven. We all press our faces against the hot glass and nobody yells at us.

The short, pale guard walks the aisles, counting our heads, murmuring the numbers under his breath. When it's clear he has the number of people he's supposed to have, he tells us to line up. Keep orderly, no need to rush, leave the suitcases, someone will bring them.

I feel the shove of the heat as soon as the train door opens. It can be hot in Colorado sometimes, but this is hot like putting your face in front of an oven. It feels unnatural and stagnant and rolls thick into the train. I watch as every person ahead of me pauses at the door, swaying against the force of the heat, before they step down.

We're at a station. Or, really, more of a stop because there's no station building, just a sort of gazebo: rusty beams supporting a metal roof with a bench in the middle of the open space. A hanging sign: CRYSTAL CITY.

After we've all finally gotten off the train and been counted again, there's confusion. A bus was supposed to be here to take us to the camp, but apparently it's broken down in the heat and now we're stranded. The man who delivers this news, a Caucasian man in a suit with sweat at his temples, is apologetic about this "development." He keeps telling us that if we're willing to be a little patient and wait—

If we're willing to be a little patient and wait, I translate for my mother.

"Then another bus will come," the man says. He has thinning hair and a round face; he's tall and blocky looking. I can tell that he's a boss of some kind. He has a clipboard; other people who look like employees scurry over and whisper things while he makes notes.

Then another bus will come.

Here's what's around us: A post office with an American flag. A tiny weathered restaurant. A boardinghouse I wouldn't want to stay in. Low one-story houses, standing far apart from each other. In Denver we lived on the upper floor of a duplex. In Denver you were never more than a flight of stairs away from borrowing a needle or a tin of shoe polish.

While I've been orienting myself, other passengers have been talking. The more vocal ones, like Mrs. Ginoza, who persevered in asking for extra water for her daughter while my mother told Toshiko and me to swallow our own spit, have decided they don't want to wait for the bus. Somehow it's been decided we'll walk to camp: What's one more mile after the thousand we've already traveled?

The sweaty Caucasian man doesn't like the way it looks to have a bunch of tired women and children marching in their best traveling clothes, but we're already doing it. Mrs. Ginoza has spotted a sign so we follow her out of the tiny town, which has no glass buildings, nothing resembling crystal. Past some fields, which the man says are spinach. "Crystal City is the Spinach Capital of the World" is actually what he says, like he can regain control of the situation if he pretends it was his idea to be a walking tour guide. "We're very famous for our spinach here; we have a statue of Popeye the Sailor," he says, and I'm almost embarrassed for him. The sun is directly overhead and my dress is damp with sweat, first under my arms, and then as we walk farther, all of it, clinging to my legs and my waist.

And then, when my tongue is so swollen from thirst that there is no more spit to swallow, we're standing fifty yards from a gate. Behind it, a swarm of faces, the reason we're all here to begin with.

Our fathers and husbands crane their necks. They must have been told we were coming; a few hold up a welcome banner. Vaguely, through the sweat pouring down my face, I am aware of a brass band playing, and even more vaguely I see that it, too, must be part of our welcome ceremony.

At first I think my tired eyes are playing tricks on me, but it's true: A few of the men in the background have light hair and Caucasian features. German prisoners. Something else Papa told me about the camp. We'll share our space with Nazis.

"I don't see your father," Mama whispers anxiously.

I scan the crowd, landing on a fence post. A girl sits on it, frizzy blond hair, bony knees balancing a notebook in which she's recording something. She looks official like a camp employee but too young, close to my age. I should have realized that the German detainees would bring their own children. She scans the crowd, too, gawking at the new arrivals, and her eyes lock on mine for a brief moment before she bows her head and writes something else. I raise my eyebrows in annoyance. I have had too many people with notebooks check me off their lists. Too many noting when we've eaten, slept, used the bathroom.

"Haruko! Haru-chan!"

It's my father. *My father.* I haven't seen him in five months. My heart jumps before I remember that I'm not sure how I feel about seeing my father now, that the last time I saw him was strange.

He seems thinner, gray at his temples, standing near one of the other fence posts and waving a handkerchief over his head like a flag. I hear him before my mother and sister do. When he catches my eye, the handkerchief falters and I see something in his face that looks like uncertainty. "Helen," he tries again. It's not uncertainty, it's hopefulness, willing me to look in his direction. Toshiko was right. Only the other popular girls at school called me Helen. My family never did. He is trying so hard. I should be so happy. "Helen, I'm over here."

I nudge my mother. "There's Papa." My mother's eyes scramble until she finds him. Then she breaks into a smile and, with my wrist clamped in her hand, she rushes toward the entrance gates, toward the fence.

The chain-link fence surrounds the camp on all sides. Ten feet tall, topped with barbed wire, and the corners that I can see are occupied by guard towers and soldiers with guns.

My father didn't mention this in any of his letters. It must have slipped his mind. *Here in Crystal City, Haruko, we have outdoor movies, a tofu factory, and jagged, sharp fences guarded by men who will shoot you if you try to leave.*

It's funny the things you can leave out. It's funny the way you can paint a picture that is both completely true and the falsest thing in the world.

My father doesn't come out to greet us because he lives inside this fence. He brought us to this fence. And even though I know that I'm supposed to be excited to see him, I can't help but think that when my mother said, *Your sister is not the enemy,* what I wanted to ask was, *Is my father?*

Suddenly my left arm wrenches. While my mother is trying to move us forward, Toshiko is pulling my other wrist back, her mouth a wide O of panic.

"Stop it, Toshi, you're hurting my arm."

"I don't want to go in."

"Don't be silly, you've been talking about it for days."

"Now I don't want to," she shrieks. I can feel her about to cry.

"Toshiko, stop it. If you want to see Papa, you have to come this way."

My mother is still trying to press us forward. Through the crush of bodies, her hat tips forward; a sprig of blue petals bobbles like it might come loose. I turn back to my sister, who is still a mule in the mud. "I wish we were all home now," Toshiko says. "I wish we were picking up Papa, and then we were all going home."

She's crying, wet and sniffly, and as she tries to enlace her fingers with mine, I jerk my hand away. Without meaning to, I pull that same hand back and slap her across the face.

My fingers sting at the contact with Toshi's soft baby skin. Her mouth falls open and she reaches to where there are four white finger-shaped lines appearing on the side of her face. "Haruko—" she starts, because I've never hit her before, and because I did it hard.

I'm breathing heavily, we both are, and the regret I feel is mixed with a nauseating kind of relief, because slapping my sister feels like the first true thing I have done in months.

"This is home now," I tell her, as she gulps back new sobs. I pull out a handkerchief, waiting while she wipes her face. "No more wishing. This is home."

Robert Cox

MONICA HESSE

is the author of *Girl in the Blue, Coat,*
American Fire, The War Outside, and
They Went Left, as well as a journalist with the *Washington Post.* She lives
outside Washington, DC, with her husband and their dog. She invites you to
visit her website at monicahesse.com.

HISTORICAL FICTION FROM
BESTSELLING AUTHOR
MONICA HESSE

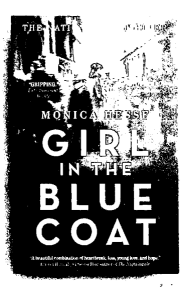

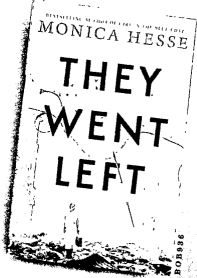